ROYAL BLUE

SOVEREIGNS OF SAVANNAH BOOK ONE

MEGAN LOWE

Royal Blue © 2019 by Megan Lowe

Royal Blue is a work of fiction. All names, characters, events and places found therein are either from the author's imagination or used fictitiously. Any similarity to persons alive or dead, actual events, or organizations is entirely coincidental and not intended by the author.

Cover Design: Bex Harper Designs

Editing: Hot Tree Editing

Proofreading: Trysh Thompson

Formatting: Pretty In Ink Designs

E-Book ASIN: B07VKZT653

Paperback: 978-0-6486536-0-8

 Created with Vellum

For all the girls who don't take any shit.

Sovereign:

Noun.

1. A supreme ruler, especially a monarch.

Adjective.

1. Possessing supreme or ultimate power.
2. Acting or done independently and without outside interference.
3. Possessing royal power or status.

PROLOGUE

I MAY NOT BE the obvious choice, but I am the only choice.

I may look nice and friendly and a million other synonyms, but I'm not.

Underestimate me at your peril.

I know my strengths. I have no weaknesses.

It might be small, it might only be for a fleeting moment in time, but this school is my domain.

When you walk through those doors, you are at my mercy.

I will not bend.

I will not break.

I will not bow to anyone.

My name is Cerulean Tremont, and I am one of the Sovereigns of Savannah.

Forest Park Academy is my queendom, and with my sisters by my side you *will* bend to our will.

Nothing and nobody can stop us.

Nothing and nobody can bring us down.

A tip? Don't fight it; it'll only make it worse.

HARLEY

SUPPRESSING A SIGH, I walk up the steps of yet another school in a long line of schools. Being the new guy isn't new to me. In fact, I've been the new guy so many times, I should probably change my name to that. *But,* I remind myself as I walk through the wide, imposing, solid oak doors, this time this move is all for me.

College scouts don't take notice of quarterbacks, no matter how impressive his stats are, if he's living in Switzerland. That's where we've just come from. Before that it was Botswana. Before that Morocco, which was preceded by Indonesia, Japan, Australia, and Germany.

If I want to play ball, which I do, then back home in the good ol' US of A is where I need to be. With that in mind, my dad, the highly esteemed Cary St. James, begrudgingly packed up his family and moved us here, to Savannah, Georgia.

Which brings me, and him as the new principal, to Forest Park Academy.

As far as schools go, it's on the nicer end. Of

course, I've been educated in reed huts with dirt floors, so it's all relative.

According to the brochure, Forest Park Academy is the oldest private school in Savannah and one of the oldest in Georgia. That also makes it one of the most elite. Which means for the next year I'm stuck with a bunch of entitled brats who only care about having the best clothes, cars, purses, *things*.

The only thing *I* care about? That there's someone in this godforsaken school who will get on the end of my passes and get his ass into the end zone.

"Hey, man" comes a voice from my right. As if God himself was listening to my thoughts, now waiting by my side is every QB's dream in a wide receiver.

"You're Harley St. James, right?" he asks.

I nod and stick out a hand. "Nice to meet you," I tell him. "Please tell me you're the guy who will make me look like the god I am out on the field."

He chuckles. "That I am. I'm TK."

TK, aka the guy who will make me look good, is a beast. He has to be at least six foot three, and I'm going with two hundred and twenty pounds. Lean, but solid. He's got his white hair styled in some hipster style and the lightest blue eyes I've ever seen. He kind of reminds me of a human polar bear, come to think of it.

"What's the deal with the rest of the team?" I ask as we walk down the marble-floored hallway toward my locker. A perk of having the principal as my father means most times coming in, I'm able to spend a bit of time wandering the halls before classes start, get a feel of the place.

A good athlete always knows what he's up against. I don't intend to be just a good athlete; I intend to be the best, and that means I need to know everything, *now*.

"They're pretty solid," TK says. "For a private school, we've got a decent amount of talent."

"Scholarships?" I ask as we reach my locker.

As luck would have it, TK's is only a few doors down from mine.

He gives me a look as he opens his.

"What?" I ask.

"Look, I know you've been all over the world, but you're back in America now."

"So?"

"So, in case you've forgotten, this is Georgia, the peach of America's South. Football isn't just a game here; it's a way of life. My parents were taking me to Bobcats games before I could even walk."

"Of course."

"You were born here, right?" he asks as he shoves his books in his locker.

"Yup, Maine."

"Ah, that explains it, then."

"Explains what?"

"Why you're so clueless. Don't worry, QB1, I got your back."

THE MORE POPULATED the hallway becomes, the more stares I get. I don't mind; it comes with the territory. The girls want to know who the mysterious new guy is. The guys want to know what threat I pose. I can tell them here and now that I am the biggest threat they have faced so far. I'm their mother-fucking QB1, here to bring a state championship to this hellhole of a school and be the god they so desperately need.

TK introduces me to a few guys on the team as we head to our first class. The crowd swells around us. I smile and wink at the girls and give the guys a look that leaves them with no doubt as to who's in charge.

We come to a section of the hallway that's less crowded, occupied by only a group of four girls, sisters from the look of them. Blonde goddesses.

The tallest one has a body Victoria's Secret models would kill for and the lightest hair of them all. She rocks the hell out of the Forest Park uniform. I'm pretty sure the black and gray skirt *isn't* supposed to be that short, or the white blouse *that* tight, but you won't hear me, or any guy I suspect, complaining.

The girl next to her is a little shorter, but a hell of a lot more curvy. She has a woman's body.

The shortest also looks to be the youngest. She has honey-blonde hair and is huddled into the lockers, like she's trying to hide.

All three of them are stunning, but it's the fourth and final that takes my attention. Tall, probably five foot six, five foot seven. She's skinnier than I usually go for, but she has an air about her, a supreme amount of confidence. It makes me smile.

I slap TK. "Who're they?"

He scoffs. "You don't wanna go there, man. The Hued Hussies have chewed up and spat out better men than you."

"The Hued Hussies?" I ask.

"Cerulean, Indigo, Magenta, and Vermilion Tremont. Obviously their parents were stuck for names so they did a grab bag in a pack of Crayolas. They call themselves the Sovereigns of Savannah, but I prefer the Hued Hussies, it has a better ring to it."

Just then the one in the middle, the confident one, looks up.

"Which one is she?"

TK laughs. "Don't even think about it. That's Cerulean, the leader. She may only be a junior, but don't let that fool you. That girl will eat you alive."

As I continue to stare, she shakes her head.

"She doesn't look that bad," I say, giving her a smile and a wink as we walk past.

TK shakes his head.

"What?" I ask.

"When it all blows up in your face, don't say I didn't warn you."

"I don't know—"

"Hey, I get it, they're hot, but I guaran-fucking-tee you, you will not make it out alive."

I slap him on the shoulder. "I appreciate the concern but you forget who you're talking to."

He scoffs again. "If you say so, man."

I nod. "I do."

CHAPTER TWO

"UGH," I say as Captain Dick and his band of merry men walk past. Sure, he looks like a football player: tall, I'm going with six foot one-ish, wide shoulders, strong hands, but so what? And okay, he *might* be good-looking, with stunning deep brown eyes and perfect dark brown hair, but he's a *football* player. No matter how attractive I find him, that's an automatic turnoff.

Indigo snickers as she shuts her locker. "Eyeing another victim, C?"

"Hardly."

"I heard he's the principal's son," Vermilion says.

"So?"

"I'm just saying," she says before ducking her head.

"Why should it matter if he's the principal's son?" Magenta asks.

"M...," Indigo scolds.

"What? You know how this works. If he needs to be put in his place, then he'll be put in his place."

Indigo sighs and shuts her locker. "I'm familiar

with how it works, I'm just saying that this one is cute."

"I hadn't noticed," I tell her as I examine my nails.

"For fuck's sake," Magenta swears.

"It's the eyes, right?" Indigo asks, slouching against the locker. Magenta turns and storms off.

An image of the deepest brown eyes I've ever seen comes into my head.

"It's the way he thinks he owns this school after being here all of two seconds," I say as I push off the lockers and stalk to class.

AS MUCH AS I love Indigo—she is my eldest sister after all—life isn't all hot guys and getting laid.

"Please tell me you're not going to do anything with that douche," Magenta says as I slip into a seat beside her. Even though we're in the same grade, Magenta is actually Indigo's twin. She repeated a year after becoming pregnant with my niece, Emily, last year.

"I'll do what I need to. No more, no less."

She huffs in response.

"What?" I ask, turning toward her.

"It's a slippery slope," she warns.

I cross my arms over my chest. "If he needs to be put in his place, he will be."

"*But those eyes*," she says, imitating Indigo.

I shrug. "He has two of them, what's your point?"

She gives me her no-nonsense stare.

"Can you stop staring at me like that?" I ask. "Please?"

"Like what?"

"Like you're our mom and you know we've done something we weren't supposed to."

"*Have* you done something you weren't supposed to?" She arches a perfectly manicured brow.

"He's been here all of two seconds, M," I remind her. "When would I have had the chance to do something?"

She shrugs but her shoulders drop fully. "Let's not pretend you're not the most resourceful out of all of us."

"I don't know," I say, leaning back in my seat. "I'm sure Indigo can be inventive when she needs to be."

Magenta shakes her head. "All I'm saying is be careful."

"I appreciate the concern but it's not needed. *Really*," I stress when she doesn't look convinced. "I know who I am, M, who *we* are, and nothing and nobody will take that away from us, I promise."

"I just don't want you to get carried away."

"Don't worry about me," I say as Mr. Perot, our homeroom teacher, walks in. "No one will *ever* get the best of me."

THE MORNING PASSES in a blur of monotony only disinterest can provide. My last class before lunch is Media Studies, chosen for the easy A I hope it will provide.

Don't get me wrong, I know school is important and I'm good at it, I'm just focused on other things. I have plans, and none of them center on Savannah, or hell, even Georgia. No, my plans center around the Carver Institute in D.C., where, unofficially of course, there's a spot waiting for me at the best business and policy school in the country. I may joke that I rule this school, and let's be real, I *do*, but one day I'm determined I *will* rule over something worthwhile.

Business, politics, both, I don't care, but I *will* be the sovereign of something worthwhile. With a degree from the Carver Institute and with their connections, world domination shouldn't take long at all.

I want to follow in the path laid down by our mother. She's the CFO for a multinational corporation headquartered in Switzerland. Because of this, she hasn't been home in, oh, ten years, give or take. It's okay though. We've been more than capable of taking care of ourselves, of raising ourselves. We're four strong, independent women, and we did that without the help of our mother. Yes, she has friends at Carver, but she didn't have a hand in getting me my spot. *I* did that all on my own. It was *my* effort, *my* grades, *my* potential. I *will* take over the world, and it will be because of me, not my mother.

One day I want little girls to look at the *Forbes* Most Powerful lists and see an ever-increasing number of women on there. I want them to know that being a woman isn't a handicap, it isn't a disadvantage, that we kick ass just as much, if not more, than men.

My mother gave up her family for her success. I'm not bitter or scarred by it; I recognize it for what it is, a sacrifice for the greater good.

Our dad does his best, and by best I mean largely leaving us to our own devices, but we prefer it that way. We all have our own agendas to push. We recognize this and act accordingly. Our lives are our own.

I may be the second youngest, but I'm the most determined, the most protective, the most stubborn. There's nothing I won't do for my sisters and our futures. So for Magenta to suggest I would risk it all on Captain Dick? It's laughable.

I slide into my seat and take out a notebook and pen and start making lists about all that needs to be done and what I want to achieve this year and into the future.

I'm so focused on my task I don't notice someone takes the seat next to mine. That is, until he leans over my shoulder to see what I'm doing.

"Funny," a husky voice says. "I would've thought you were more a hearts and flowers girl."

I rear back, shocked that A) I've been so focused on my lists I didn't realize someone had sat next to me, and B) that that person is Captain Dick himself.

Recovering quickly, I scoff. "Hearts and flowers? Me? I don't think so."

He nods. "Good to know."

"Oh, yeah?" I ask. "And why would that be?"

He leans towards me again, his scent—Viktor and Rolf, if I'm not mistaken—washing over me. "What? A guy isn't allowed to get to know a girl?"

"He isn't if that guy is you and the girl is me."

"And why would *that* be?" he asks, repeating my words.

"Because it will never happen."

"What won't?"

"Whatever you're dreaming up in that miniscule brain of yours," I tell him. "I'm not here to be your plaything or someone who will look good on your arm. And while I'm at it, I'll let you know that you might be some hotshot jock, but that won't get you anywhere with me. This is *my* school, *my* domain. If you think you can come in here and fuck shit up, I'm here to tell you different."

His brown eyes twinkle as he chuckles. "All right, no need to get your panties in a twist."

"No twist, just letting you know how things work around here."

"Consider me informed." He nods.

"Good," I say, turning to face the front and Ms. Victoria, who is about to begin her lecture.

"THIS SEMESTER we'll be examining the media and its role in gender stereotypes." I scoff. "Do you have something to say, Miss. Tremont?" Ms. Victoria asks.

"Yeah, I do," I reply, crossing my arms over my chest. Beside me, Captain Dick swings around to face me, an amused grin on his face. "The media's role in gender stereotypes is to perpetuate them. Their job is to sell a lifestyle, a lifestyle the powers that be deem appropriate or that will sell the most of their advertiser's product."

"Yes, well—" Ms. Victoria begins before Captain Dick interrupts.

"The media only prints what they see in society," he says. "They're reporters, a mirror. They deal in facts. Do you honestly think they'd sell magazines or get people to watch TV shows or movies if they were widely out of touch with their audience?"

"Of course. They sell us what they *want* us to see. They tell us what they want us to know. 'They deal in facts,'" I scoff. "Please. I can think of a dozen examples of major injustices caused by the media's misreporting of facts."

"Name them, then," Captain Dick challenges.

I open my mouth to do just that when Ms. Victoria steps in.

"All right, you two, that's enough."

"But—" I start.

"We will have more than enough time to discuss that and much more during the semester." Her stare dares me to argue.

"Sounds good, teach," Captain Dick says, breaking the tension in the room.

I turn my glare on him instead. In reply he gives me a toothy smile while Ms. Victoria goes back to her lecture.

BY THE TIME CLASS ENDS, I'm more than done, both with this class and Captain Dick. The bell rings and we all scramble to put away our books and get the fuck out of here.

"So, that was fun," Captain Dick says, slinging an arm around my shoulders as we walk out.

"What will be fun is cutting off your balls and feeding them to the poor horses who do the carriage rides around Midtown," I reply as I push his arm off me.

"So you've been thinking about my balls, huh?"

"I've been dreaming about a world without you in it," I counter.

"Come on, now, baby doll, isn't that a bit harsh? You know your life would be dull without me in it."

"First off, I'm not your baby, your doll, your honey, your babe, any of it. Second, don't think because we just spent fifty minutes in class together that you know me. I'm telling you here and now that you don't and never will, so you may as well give up now."

I turn away from him, but he grabs my arm, a tingle emanating from where we touch. "And you obviously don't know me if you think that little speech is enough to make me give up."

I wrench my arm out of his grasp. "Touch me again and see what happens," I dare.

He holds his hands up in surrender.

"Good, now if you'll excuse me." I push open the door to the girls' bathroom, quickly locking myself in the nearest stall. As quietly as I can, I rifle through my bag, searching for the tin that holds the pills that are keeping me together, that are the key to my future.

Popping the lid, I take one of the little white tablets and swallow it dry. Even though I know it won't have taken effect yet, a sense of peace washes through me.

HARLEY

CHAPTER THREE

MUCH TO MY DELIGHT, I discover I also share English and Math with Miss Cerulean Tremont. She may think she warned me off after Media Studies, but all she did was make the chase sweeter. Not that there is a chase, but there's definitely a desire to get to know the blue beauty better.

But for the moment, that has to be moved to the back burner.

Reaching up, I pluck a football from the air.

"You sure you're set at QB?" TK asks. "'Cause those skills right there could give me a run for my money."

I laugh. "I just like having a ball in my hand, that's all."

"How'd your first day go?"

I shrug. "It is what it is. It isn't as if I haven't done this a million times before."

"At least this is the last time, right?"

"Except for college and when I'm picked up by an NFL team, sure."

"Man, after this season, we're gonna make sure

everyone knows your name. You won't be walking in anywhere as a nobody anymore."

I slap his hand, nodding my agreement, and continue to warm up.

Today is the first day of the rest of my life.

PRACTICE IS BRUTAL, but this isn't Switzerland. This is Georgia. It's where I want to be; it's where I need to be in order for me to get where I want to go, and that's the top. Once my mother got an inkling of my talent and love for football she did her best to make sure wherever we were I was able to get some kind of coaching. Over the years I've had fifteen different coaches, all at varying degrees of skill. Army guys, ex pats, then eventually online coaches and a few summer camps Stateside my mother somehow managed to convince my father to let me attend. It was hard work but I'm here.

I shower and change before making my way to the parking lot. As a welcome home/eighteenth birthday present my parents bought me a brand-spanking-new, what I'm calling cranberry red Mustang. I haven't had much need of a car or to drive but it was one skill I insisted on learning, and now I can take advantage of that.

The heat of the day is now gone, leaving a relatively pleasant evening.

Looking to my left, TK is leaning against the wall, a girl, probably a freshman, caged between his arms.

"You know it's only the first day of the year, right? What's got you so stressed you have to come to me?" he asks.

I'm too far away to hear her response but it makes TK chuckle.

"And just what exactly are you going to do for me in return? I mean, it's no problem to get what you need, but one favor deserves another, don't you think?" He plays with the top button on her blouse. I don't know what's going on here, but it doesn't look good, and that girl looks far too young to be doing *anything* with TK.

"Hey, man," I say, clapping him on the shoulder as I pass. "Good practice today. You keep that up and the state championship is in the bag."

He turns and slings an arm around the obviously frightened girl's shoulders. "Thanks, QB, and state is a sure thing."

"No doubt." I nod. "Ah, just a heads-up. I don't want to break up the cozy time you've got going here, but Coach looked like he was about to head out, so you might want to pick this up another time. Wouldn't want him to think your focus is off, even at this early stage." After practice, Coach made sure to sit us down and drum into us the expectations of the Forest Park system, as well importance of maintaining our focus and not being "the stupid teenage boys that we are."

"Oh, shit," TK says, thankfully disengaging from the freshman, who shoots me a relieved look. "If he finds me with my pants down again he threatened to bench me."

"So yeah, why don't you two crazy kids go your separate ways before you screw up our season?" I joke.

"Thanks, man," he says as he holds out his hand

for the manly slap/hug thing that seems to be the norm. "Good lookin' out," he shouts over his shoulder as he heads to his... is that a McLaren?

The farther away TK gets, the more the tension in the air dissipates.

"How are you getting home?" I ask the freshman.

"I-I was going to t-take an U-Uber," she stammers.

"Where do you live?" I inquire, adjusting the heavy gym bag on my shoulder.

"H-huh?"

"Your house, where is it?"

"Oh, um, Ardsley Park."

I nod and start walking to my car. When I realize she's not following me, I stop.

"You coming?"

"Oh, I, um, didn't think.... It's okay, I can.... Um, okay," she says, scrambling to pick up her book bag and trailing after me.

"What's your name?" I ask as she slides into the passenger seat.

"Kingsley," she squeaks.

"Kingsley who?" If someone was to ask me why I have this girl in my car or why I stepped into whatever was going on between her and TK, I couldn't answer. All I know is that something didn't feel right and walking away from *that* didn't feel right.

"Kingsley Lee," she replies.

"Nice to meet you, Kingsley Lee," I say, holding out a hand. "I'm Harley St. James."

She snorts as she takes my hand. "I know who you are. *Everyone* does."

I sigh as I start the car and motion for her to put

her address in my GPS. "The advantages of being the principal's son."

She scoffs. "I'm *pretty* sure that's *not* the reason everyone knows your name."

"Oh, yeah?" I ask, taking my eyes off the road for a second. "Then what is?"

"Er, maybe the hope that you're going to be the savior of Forest Park football? Not to mention your—" She cuts herself off.

"Oh, come on," I plead. "You can't leave me hanging like that."

Her mouth is mashed in a tight line, and she shakes her head.

"You know I'm just going to fill the blanks myself if you don't finish that sentence."

She shakes her head again. "Forget about it. I'm just a stupid, naïve freshman and you're Harley St. James. Tomorrow at school this won't even be a memory for you, whereas it'll be, like, the highlight of my life."

I laugh. "The highlight of your life? You don't think that's a slight exaggeration?"

She sighs. "Not really. I've lived here my whole life and I know how it's all going to turn out, or how my parents have planned it to turn out." The more we talk, the more she opens up to me.

"Oh yeah? And how's that?"

"I'll graduate Forest Park and be accepted as a legacy to the University of Savannah, where I'll pledge a sorority and get in because I'm also a legacy. I'll do some frou-frou degree I don't care about because my sophomore year my parents will introduce me to a friend's son, Eric Frogmore the fourth or something ridiculous like that. We'll marry not long after graduation, whereupon I'll pop out Eric the fifth and Kingsley Jr. and begin my career as mom and homemaker."

"Man, that's bleak."

She shrugs. "It's my reality."

"And you don't mind?"

"Eh, my husband will probably cheat on me, but I want kids so I'll be the best mom ever. When we eventually divorce because he got his nineteen-year-old personal assistant pregnant, the kids will want to stay with me. His parents will always bring me up to his new wife at Thanksgiving and Christmas, so I guess it's okay."

I can't help but laugh. "You are one weird chick."

"Thank you."

"Look," I say as I pull up to her house. "I know I'm the new guy and I've been here all of a day, but stay away from TK. He seems like an all right guy, but what I saw and where it was going was not somewhere someone as awesome as yourself should be going, okay?"

She sighs. "Yeah, I know, I just.... That scenario I just spun you?"

I nod.

"Sometimes I think I can change it, write it myself. TK has... stuff I thought could help."

"Why can't you?"

"A good southern woman knows when to rock the boat. This isn't it."

I sit and consider what Kingsley has told me for a moment. "Why'd you tell me all that?" I ask. "You don't even know me, and you wouldn't even finish that sentence about how good-looking I am."

I laugh when she blushes.

"I told you I'd fill in the blanks."

"I don't know," she says as she plays with the end of her blonde/brunette-ish braid. "Maybe you're easy to talk to."

"Maybe."

"Or maybe I wanted you to know how it is for girls like me."

"Why?" I press.

"Because guys like you have the world at your feet. It's easy to forget about everyone else when that happens. But a damsel in distress who you save from making a colossal mistake then pours her heart out to you? *That* may stay with you."

She starts to get out of the car. "Or maybe I want you to feel sorry for me and if or when we pass in the hallway, you smile and say 'hey,' thus making me the most popular freshman at Forest Park Academy. Thanks for the ride."

She shuts the door and walks to her front door while my mind reels.

What is it with the girls at this school?

HARLEY

CHAPTER FOUR

DRIVING home to our house on Skidaway Island, my head is buzzing with all that Kingsley told me. Why *did* she tell me all that stuff? Is it even true?

Girls have never been a problem for me. I don't say that to beat my chest and brag about how much of a stud I am, it's merely the truth. But none of the girls I've been with have been anything like the two who put me in a spin today.

But all that fades away when I open the door and a familiar, albeit older, face is there to greet me.

"Mrs. Stark?" I ask.

She smiles and opens her arms. "Get over here and give me a hug."

As her arms envelop me, her signature lavender scent strong, a million memories hit me. Her cleaning a scrape on my knee, coming home to cookies and milk after kindergarten, her tucking me in when my parents were at some function, saying goodbye to her when we left for Germany and taking my cat, Cookie.

"Look at you, all grown up," she says, rubbing her hands up and down my back.

"And you haven't aged a day," I reply as we break apart.

"Always a charmer." She cups my face; her gray eyes shining with unshed tears.

I'm not sure how long exactly Mrs. Stark has worked for my family, but I know while we were here, she was an integral part of it.

"How come you're here? I thought you'd be back in Maine, enjoying retirement and eating all the lobster rolls you can?"

A sad look crosses her face. "I had every intention of doing that, but Joe passed away last year and the kids have all moved away and have families of their own. So when your mother called and said you were moving back, I decided 'what the heck?' and made the move too."

"I'm sorry to hear about Joe," I tell her. Joe was Mrs. Stark's husband, but God help you if you called him Mr. Stark. It was Joe or nothing. While Mrs. Stark worked inside, keeping our household running, Joe was our groundskeeper/handyman, whatever he needed to be. There wasn't a gadget he didn't have or something he couldn't fix.

She nods, a sad smile on her face.

"What about—" I'm cut off when a large black cat with white paws and a white patch on the end of his tail winds though my legs.

"Cookie!" I bend down to pick him up. Immediately he rubs his cheek against mine, a deep purr rumbling through his furry body.

"I can't believe you still have him." I'm told Cookie was a present for my first birthday and at the time the only words I could say were "Mom,"

"Dad," "Kark," "Joe," and "Cookie," hence the name.

Mrs. Stark comes over and scratches his head. "Of course I do, he's been a good friend over the years."

"I thought he'd be gone for sure."

Mrs. Stark shakes her head. "He's got arthritis and a thyroid problem, so he doesn't get around as easily as he used to, but he's still hanging in there."

I bury my face in his fur, inhaling his funky cat smell.

Being an only child in this house sometimes was lonely, and Cookie was my only friend.

I pull back and look him in his yellow eyes. "Hey, buddy, I missed you. Did you miss me?"

He swats at my mouth. I hug him tighter, and his purrs increase so I'm taking that as a yes.

I put him down and he winds through my legs again before sitting on my shoe.

"Looks like I'm not the only one glad to be back," Mrs. Stark says, patting me on the shoulder before heading to the kitchen.

IF I THOUGHT Mrs. Stark's presence would lighten things up, I was sorely mistaken. You'd think, seeing as though often we were the only English-speaking people in whatever town we were in—with the exception of Australia, but theirs is another dialect altogether—we'd be a close-knit family. You'd be wrong. My mom, the esteemed Dr. Heather St. James, is fine and does her best to be around, but as a doctor, that's not always possible.

No, it's my father and principal, Cary St. James, who's the real hard-ass, although that might insult to hard-asses. He's a bastard, plain and simple.

I give you exhibit A.

"How was practice today?" my father asks over a dinner of pot roast and mashed potatoes.

"Fine," I reply, once I've swallowed my mouthful. I learned the hard way to never talk at the same time as I'm eating.

He puts his knife and fork down and pats his mouth with his napkin. "Just fine?"

"It was good. More intense than what I'm used to, but yeah, good," I finish lamely.

"You are aware that the reason we left Switzerland, where your mother and I were both more than happy to remain, was due to your refusal to give up your American customs and play a common local sport?"

I look my father in the brown eyes he passed on to me. I also got his height but Mom's coloring otherwise. "I'm aware, sir, and I'm grateful for the sacrifice you and Mom have made for me and my future."

He nods. "We brought you back because we were told you could be the best. If that is to transpire, I expect your practices to be more than 'fine' or 'good.'"

"Cary," Mom warns as he goes back to the meal in front of him.

"This is what the boy wanted, Heather. If he doesn't take this seriously, then what was the point of all of this?"

I want to tell him the point is that I'm his son and this is what parents do for their children but I know it'll only set him off further.

"May I be excused?" I interject. "I've got home-work to do."

"Sure, sweetie," Mom replies, while I get a terse nod from my dad.

Up in my room, Cookie has made himself comfortable on my bed, just below my pillows.

"At least I've got you," I say to him, scratching under his chin and getting a round of purring in response.

THE NEXT DAY, when I see Kingsley in the hall, I give her a smile and a nod. She smiles back. I still have no idea why she told me what she did, but some-times I think you have so many things on your mind you have to get them out. Maybe I was the only person available at the time? Either way, I don't mind. She seems like a cool chick, and I need all the friends in my corner that I can get.

Just like yesterday, the crowd parts as I walk to class, revealing Cerulean and her sisters. Once again, the reception I get from her is less than hospitable. Arctic would be more accurate. On the other side of the coin, I *do* get a flirty smile and a wink from one of the others—Indigo, I think her name is.

With a quick glance at Cerulean, I smile back at Indigo, giving her a wave. TK shakes his head.

"What?" I ask.

"You're playing with fire."

I shrug. "I'm simply making friends," I reply.

He shakes his head again as we walk to homeroom.

. . .

"STAY AWAY FROM MY SISTER," Cerulean says as she throws her books down in Media Studies later that day.

I hold up my hands. "I'm not doing anything."

"Oh, I know what you're doing, and I'm telling you to stay away from my sisters—all of them. They don't need you to distract them or turn them into soppy, love-crazed messes."

"Love-crazed messes?" I ask.

"We don't need you, and we certainly don't *want* you."

"Are you sure about that?" I lean back in my seat, balancing on two legs, my hands behind my head.

She kicks the remaining two legs out from underneath me. Thankfully, because of my superior reflexes I avoid smacking my head on the desk behind me.

"I'm certain," she says before taking her seat and facing the front.

I pick up my chair and sit down, properly this time. Ms. Victoria walks in, but before she can begin her lecture, I lean over.

"You can warn me off all you want, baby doll," I tell her. "But none of that will matter when you're the one who comes to *me*."

She grits her teeth and her eyes narrow. Oh yeah, I've got her good and pissed off now.

CHAPTER FIVE

"YOU NEED to stay away and stop encouraging Harley St. James," I tell Indigo when I get to our table at the cafeteria.

"Aww, why? I was having fun," she whines.

"You're giving him ideas."

"That was the point."

"Well, I'm telling you to stop. He's a distraction and beneath us."

"Beneath us?" She snorts. "He's the all-hail quarterback who will take us to state. I'd hardly say he's beneath us."

"But he *is* a distraction," I insist. "He's a threat to everything we've worked so hard to build. I will *not* see all that fall down around us because you can't keep your legs shut."

"Hey!"

"What'd I miss?" Magenta asks as she takes a seat next to Indigo, stealing a carrot stick from Vermilion's tray.

"Cerulean is warning Indigo to stay away from the principal's son," Vermilion answers, not even bothering to look up from her book.

M turns to Indigo. "Really?"

Indigo shrugs. "He's cute and looks like fun. This place could use lightening up. Besides, it's my senior year, I want to enjoy this before I'm forced to go out into the real world."

"Oh, please," Magenta says. "Quit playing like you're not applying to every party school in the country."

"Cerulean isn't the only one with dreams and promise, M."

Magenta's shoulders lower, her eyes less squinty. "I know that, I didn't mean—"

"I know I may be the fun sister," Indigo says, cutting her off. "I know I might be the one who plays fast and loose, but it doesn't mean I don't take my future seriously. I've got dreams and plans too. So what if I like to have a little fun every once in a while? It's not a crime, Magenta."

"I never said it was, I just—"

"All right, all right," I interject before things get even more heated than they already are. "I—we—never said not to have fun. I just don't want you to get carried away and lose yourself to Captain Dick or any other idiot who may come along. We know you have dreams, and you've got the balls to go out and make them and *so* much more come true." Indigo sends me a grateful smile. Our mother leaving us may not have scarred us, but Magenta's relationship with Emily's dad, Beckett, sure did. She was smitten with him but he turned out to be nothing but a waste of air. After seeing what she went through we all decided we would never let a guy take over our lives or depend on them for anything.

I look around at all three of my siblings, my family, people I would absolutely do anything and everything for. "We're the Tremont sisters," I remind them. "The motherfucking Sovereigns of Savannah. This is our school, our town. Nothing and no one can take that from us. We will not bend to their ideals. We are four intelligent, shrewd, savvy, strong women who will bow to no one." They all, including Vermilion, who has finally looked up from her book, nod. "We know who we are, we know what we are, and we will get everything we want and more because this world is ours for the taking."

After that rousing speech, we chat idly until the bell rings. Indigo and Magenta head off to class, but Vermilion hangs back.

"What's up, V?" I ask. At fifteen, she's the youngest of us and a freshman here at Forest Park Academy.

"I've got a piano lesson this afternoon," she tells me.

I nod. "I remember."

"It's with Mr. Alexandrov."

"What time do you need me to be there?" Vermilion has been having issues with her piano teacher for a while now. Over the summer, she studies with a jazz pianist, but Alexandrov is the best classical teacher in the state and is the devil incarnate. I'm not being biased when I tell you she's a musical savant in piano. It became her refuge after her best friend died four years ago. After Dean's death, she threw herself into the piano, outgrowing teacher after teacher until Mr. Alexandrov came out of retirement to take her on. It was clearly a vanity exercise for him, to have one of the best classical pianists in the country under his tutelage, but we make do.

From the start it was clear he hated Vermilion, but he's the best in the state, and if Vermilion wants to be the best, get into the best school, and continue to grow as a musician, Alexandrov is her only option. His tactics have ranged from demeaning to downright cruel. Because of this, we try to always make sure one of us is with Vermilion at her lesson.

"Straight after school." She sighs. "I hate that you have to do this for me."

I play with her blonde ponytail, the color the exact shade as my own. "It's absolutely no problem. I *want* to be there with you."

"Do you think he's gotten any better?"

"I hope so," I reply, but know there's a snowball's chance in hell that he has.

"Me too," she says, sighing. It's a testament to just how much she loves the piano that she doesn't let this dickhead and his antics get in the way of her playing.

"Don't worry, if he tries anything. I'll be there, okay?"

She nods. "Thanks, C."

I give her a smile and a quick hug. "Don't worry about it. Now go to class before you're late."

We both hurry off to class, but that discussion and the earlier one with my sisters get me thinking. Our mother left us ten years ago. People will say she abandoned us, but it never felt like that to me. I should've been too young to understand why she did it, but I wasn't. She sat all four of us down and told us she was going to work in Switzerland and that it was her opportunity to make a difference and show the world what women are capable of. She said that for too long women have left positions of power for men to fill and she wanted to change that. She kissed each of us on the forehead and told me to protect my sisters. I don't know why she chose me specifically. Maybe she saw something in me or had a feeling I was the more protective one. Regardless, I took her words to heart and worshipped my mother as my idol. Sure, there were times I wished she was here: when we got our periods, when we went shopping for training bras, with Magenta when she had Emily last year and Vermilion when Dean died, but I look at what she's achieved and I can't help but be awed at that. Plus, we made out all right. Our great aunt stepped in to help at times, but for the most part we relied on ourselves. We're strong, independent women who don't need anyone.

Our mother is the type of woman we need more of, ones who will turn around and tell the men who think they're running the world to fuck off and let them know who really runs this shit. *That's* why I won't take any shit from any of the guys around here, the ones who think they're all that. They think they're top shit, but *I* know better, and if Captain Dick thinks—

"Thoughts, Miss Tremont?" Mr. Cahill asks, interrupting my reverie.

"Huh?"

"*Pride and Prejudice*, Miss Tremont, the book we are currently studying. I asked a question and I would like to know your thoughts on the matter."

A piece of paper with a hastily written message flutters onto my desk.

He wants to know about the different relationships portrayed in the book the note says.

"I don't need your help," I snap at Harley, from whom the note came.

He holds up his hands. "My bad, sorry."

"Miss Tremont?" Mr. Cahill asks again, but I ignore him.

"I've told you to leave me and my sisters alone. We are not helpless damsels and you are not some white knight riding in here to save us. We don't need you, we don't need anyone, got it?"

"Miss Tremont," Mr. Cahill snaps. "That's enough. I know you have a class after this, so see me after the final bell."

For the rest of the fifty-minute class, I sit and stew, shooting daggers at Harley, who studiously ignores me. I can't even tell you what happens in my final class of the day, my thoughts changing from rage to panic. Vermilion's lesson starts straight after school, and I can't be late. I can't even ask M or I to go instead, both with their own commitments after school.

I rush back to Cahill's room, hoping we can get this lecture over and done with, but of course he's nowhere to be seen. The urge to leave is strong, but I know if I do, it'll cause more trouble than it's worth.

Finally, an agonizing seven minutes after the bell rang—yes, I kept track—Cahill finally shows his old, wrinkled face, a cup of coffee in hand.

"Ah, Miss Tremont," he says, taking a seat behind his desk.

"Can we get this over with?" I ask. "I have somewhere I need to be like ten minutes ago."

He shakes his head. "That's the youth of today's problem, always in a hurry, always wanting to be somewhere else, some*one* else. You think having this purse or that phone and driving one of those cars will turn you into who you want to be, like all those celebrities you see in the movies."

"With all due respect, sir, I couldn't give a shit about all that, but I really do need to be somewhere urgently."

He tsks at me and takes a sip of his coffee. "Something distracted you in my class today, Miss Tremont. That is not something I tolerate."

"I know, sir, and I'm sorry. I promise it'll never happen again." I really am sorry too. Daydreaming or getting lost in thought is *not* something I do. The pills, my little white saviors, are supposed to ensure I'm completely, one hundred percent focused. I guess I'll have to up my dose.

"You are a good student, a promising student," Cahill tells me. "I'd hate to see all of that evaporate because of behavioral issues."

"Again, I apologize and promise it was a one-off. I'm coming up on my period so my hormones are going haywire. I know it's not an excuse, but you know how us women can get." The words taste like ash coming out of my mouth but if there's one surefire way to end a conversation, it's bringing up your menstrual cycle.

"Ah, yes, well, just make sure it doesn't happen again."

"I will."

He nods. "Good, you may go."

I race out of the classroom, not caring about

propriety or going to my locker. Alexandrov no longer has a studio and there's no way in hell I'd let that dickhead in *my* house, so the school allows us to use one of the studios here. It's convenient as well as practical. I make a mad dash to the fifth-floor music rooms, where I can already hear a male voice raised.

It's only when I get closer I realize voice *isn't* Alexandrov's.

CHAPTER SIX

"DO you treat all your students like that?" Harley rages as I stand in the doorway.

Vermilion sees me and rushes to my side.

"Are you okay?" I ask as I brush back her hair from her face.

She nods. "Where were you? You're late."

"I know, V, and I'm *so* sorry. I had to deal with some bullshit from class." I shoot Harley a glare. I expected him to be apologetic, seeing as though he's the reason I'm late, okay *partly* the reason, but there's a wrinkle in his brow, like he's trying to figure out some impossible math problem.

I turn from him to Alexandrov. "You're getting sloppy if you let him catch you." I nod to where Harley stands.

Alexandrov folds his arms over his chest. "Just remember I do not have to be here. I came out of retirement to teach. I can just as easily go *back* into retirement."

Vermilion whimpers and clings to my side harder.

"Threaten my sister and her future one more time and I'm sure our mother would love to have

Vermilion live with her. I hear there are plenty of schools for the arts in Europe. Never mind the fact my sister will also be the last *minor* you're allowed within fifteen hundred feet of. She goes away, so do you." I arch an eyebrow, and Alexandrov flinches. Yes, I know all about his penchant for the barely legal. Thankfully, he's never come onto my sisters or me but I know of others who haven't been so fortunate. There's also no need for him to know Vermilion would never in a million years, leave us to go live with our mother. Yes, she's talented enough to get into one of those schools, but after Dean died, she clung to us something fierce. The last thing we'd ever do, especially after going through such a traumatic situation is send her away. She's one of us, she *belongs* with us.

"Are you serious?" Harley explodes. "You're letting your sister continue her lesson?"

"*Outside*," I spit at him. I brush a kiss on Vermilion's forehead. "I'll be right back, okay? Don't move." She nods and lets me go. I grab Harley's well-toned forearm and drag him across the hall.

"What the fuck are you doing here?" I hiss at him.

"I was on my way to the library when I walked past and heard him berating your sister. He's a maniac." He shakes his head.

"He's also the best classical piano teacher in the state. Vermilion's grown out of all her other teachers. He's the only one who has something to teach her and her best shot at the National Conservatorium. He's a monster, but one we have to put up with so she can reach her full potential."

"She shouldn't be alone with him," he warns.

"And she wouldn't have been if I didn't have to

deal with Cahill. Don't worry about this, Captain Dick, this is a family problem. We've got it under control."

He laughs. "Captain Dick? Yeah, okay. But just remember who was here for your sister when you weren't."

I don't think, just react, grabbing him by the throat and slamming him up against the wall. I can't imagine I'd be able to do this if he was expecting it, but I'll take what I can get. "Don't you *ever* imply I'm not there for my sisters. I'd do *anything* for them. I'd *die* for them if need be. I know I was late. Trust me, it was *killing* me every single second I wasn't here for her."

"Okay, okay," he chokes out.

"I've told you before and I'll keep telling you until it finally gets through your thick head. Leave. My. Sisters. Alone."

He nods, his face rapidly turning red. For the life of me I don't know why he isn't pushing back. It's not like he couldn't flatten me if he wanted to, but I'm never one to give up an advantage.

"Good," I say as I let him go. "Alexandrov," I call, turning back to the studio. "If you think this counts as part of the lesson, you're mistaken." I'm almost at the door when a large, warm hand wraps around my bicep. The look I give Harley has him dropping his hand instantly.

"Look, I know you've got this handled, but that guy.... There's something not right about how he treats your sister. If you want, I could say something to my dad—"

"Running to Daddy might be how you fix things

in your world, but in ours *I* take care of them, and I have this one handled." I head back into the studio.

"Cerulean," he calls, following me. It's the first time he's used my name, and I don't want to examine what it does to me. "I know you've got this handled. That's more than clear. But if there ever comes a time where you don't or it's too much—"

"If, and that's a big fucking if, I ever need help, you're the last person I'd come to."

He holds up his hands. "Fine. Whatever."

He walks away but stops. "Vermilion." My little sister's head snaps up. "If anything like this happens again and in the unlikely, but still in the realm of possible, event that your sister isn't here, you can call me, okay?"

She nods.

"Give me your phone," he orders. The idea that there may come a time where I'm not there for Vermilion is laughable, but I am slightly touched by the fact that he's looking after my sister. Not that she needs it. And in the case that Indigo and Magenta are also unavailable, it *might* be a good idea for Vermilion to have some backup. Even if that backup is Captain Dick.

She hands it over, and his fingers fly over the screen, presumably inputting his number and sending hers to him. Finally he points to Alexandrov. "If I get wind of you mistreating this girl again, you'll have a lot more to worry about than just Cerulean." With that, he's gone.

FOR THE DURATION of Vermilion's lesson, I

wouldn't say Alexandrov is on his best behavior, because he doesn't know what that is, but he's fine, normal. He's a narcissistic, evil son of a bitch, but he's the best in the state and will be the one to take Vermilion where she wants to go.

The lesson wraps up, and Vermilion packs up her things before escaping into the hall. I follow her but again I'm stopped by a hand on my bicep, this one cold and clammy.

"You need to watch yourself, girl," he spits.

I look down at his hand with disdain. "And you need to remember *yourself*. I've been told you like to be called Daddy. Truth or amusing lie?"

He drops his hand from my arm.

"I also hear you're into role-play. Something involving an adult diaper, a pacifier, and a bonnet?" His face pales. "That's what I thought. How about *you* remember *your* place, and I'll keep mine, right here, holding your reputation and freedom in the palm of my hand?"

The blood comes rushing back to his face at an alarming rate. "Listen here, bitch—"

"No, *you* listen. You're my sister's teacher. You're here to train her to be the best pianist she can be, which is pretty damn good. All we ask is you do your job and not cause her to break down. In return, you get the accolades for having her under your tutelage. You want to bring other stuff into that room, fine, but just remember, she is more than a timid freshman. She is a Tremont, which means she has me. You can threaten to go back into retirement all you want, but we both know you won't do that—"

"And we both know *you* won't do anything to jeopardize your sister's future."

"Exactly," I say. "So you do your part, I'll do mine, and everyone gets what they want."

"Fine," he huffs.

"Good." I take a few steps out the door. "But just a reminder that Indigo is graduating this year, Magenta and me next year. We'll be going to all corners of the country. Vermilion won't be anchored here. Our parents would have no problem with her moving with one of us, especially if she finds a better, nicer piano teacher near us. Just remember that when you think you have me where you want me."

"IS every lesson this year going to be like that?" Vermilion asks in the car on the way home.

I grab her hand and give it a squeeze. "No. Alexandrov was just testing us today to see if we'd backed off over the summer. He was sorely disappointed."

She nods.

"But I want you to do one thing for me. Don't start your lesson or even go into the studio until whoever is coming with you is there. If Alexandrov has a problem waiting, remind him Indigo is graduating this year, me and Magenta next year."

"And then what will I do?"

"If you want, you can come and live with one of us. Alexandrov is good, but he isn't the only piano teacher in the country. I'm sure wherever we end up we could find one who's just as good as, if not better than, him near our new places."

"Okay," she mumbles.

"No matter where we are, there will *always* be room for you, okay? We won't leave you here by yourself."

"I know."

"You're a Tremont," I remind her. "One of the 'Hued Hussies.'" She giggles at the asinine nickname the idiots at school have given us. "We bow to no one."

"We bow to no one," she repeats, a smile on her face I'd do anything to keep.

HARLEY

CHAPTER SEVEN

I KNEW CERULEAN HAD ISSUES, but I had no idea the extent of those issues. Knowing what I do, they kind of make everything else fall into place. She carries the world, or at least that of her and her sisters, on her shoulders. She may not be the eldest; that's Indigo, with whom I have homeroom and History, but she's assumed the responsibility for them and all that entails. But I can see how much it weighs on her, how much time and effort she devotes to worrying about her sisters. She can't shoulder all of this and worry about herself too. She was flustered today, something I wouldn't associate with her. And even though she hated I was there, that I've seen behind the curtain, I think she was relieved too. Of course, this will probably give her more reason to hate me, but it's given *me* a reason to watch her a little closer. Not that I needed a reason, but there's something about Cerulean Tremont that pushes all the right buttons for me.

A little later than I anticipated, and with a whole lot more on my mind, I arrive at the library. Naturally, in a school like Forest Park, the library is huge. It's old, but in a grand way. Dark wood bookcases stand tall and proud, each book stacked neatly, all in prime condition, all exactly where they should be. If I was a different type of person, I'd be in awe. Instead, it's just another example of how pretentious this school is.

"Can I help you, young man?"

I jump and turn to face the person who addressed me. She's tiny—barely five foot, if that. She has purple-gray hair, but it doesn't look clichéd. It's styled into a sleek, lopsided—asymmetrical?—bob, and her makeup could rival any of those people on YouTube who do those videos. Green eyes sparkling behind frameless glasses.

"Well, aren't you a fine specimen of soon-to-be manhood?" she says, her Georgia accent as thick as the air on a hot summer's day.

"C-can y-you say something like that to a student?" I splutter.

She waves me away and walks back toward the front desk. "Oh, sugar, I've been here since the revolution. They know they can't change me; can't get rid of me neither."

I laugh. "And that gives you the right to say sexually suggestive things to students?"

She sighs as she sits down. "If you can get away with it, why not? I figure, at my age, it won't be long before I forget my name, so when the good Lord puts a specimen as fine as yourself in my path, I may as well enjoy it."

I laugh again. "I guess I can't argue with that."

"Or course you can't," she counters. "It's rude to argue with your elders, and I'm old enough to be your great-grandmammy. So, what can I do for you Mr....?" She trails off.

"St. James," I tell her. "Harley St. James."

She sits up. "The headmaster's son. Interestin'." She looks me up and down again. "You going to win us a championship this year?"

I stand a little taller. "Sure as hell going to try."

"You curse at all your elders, boy?" she asks.

Shit. I duck my head. "Sorry, ma'am."

"Ma'am!" she exclaims. "Just how old do you think I am?"

I open my mouth to repeat what she told me about being old enough to be my great-grandmammy, but she holds up a hand. "Wait, don't answer that. I am no ma'am. I'm not a Mrs. or a Ms. I am Miss Violet, that's it."

I nod.

"And for shit's sake, don't worry about your language. I may be old but I'm not dead, and life is too short to worry about offendin' anyone."

I take a step back, her language and attitude catching me unawares. That's twice in the space of half an hour that's happened. I'll have to pay more attention to what's going on around me.

"Now, for the third time, what brings you to my domain?"

"I'm, ah, here to get a start on my history assignment. It's on the history of segregation in Georgia."

When I say that, she stiffens, but relaxes before I can make more of it.

"And you don't want to consult Google like the rest of your classmates?"

"I thought a fine establishment such as this might

have some newspaper articles on file or access to the State or Federal libraries. They would have what I'm looking for." I shoot her my best smile.

She leans back in her chair. "Fine establishment," she says, shaking her head. "Do the girls out there"— she nods to the door—"know how much trouble they're in with the likes of you?"

I laugh. "I hope not, otherwise I'm off my game."

She throws her head back and laughs. It's full and rich. She gets up and heads toward a bank of computers. "Let's see what we can find, shall we?"

EVEN THOUGH FOREST PARK does indeed have access to the State and Federal library archives, Violet is almost as much help as the articles we find.

"Those were dark times," she says as we look at the headline of a newspaper from 1958. "So many people fightin', so much tension. It seemed like at any moment anythin' could set somethin' off and it would grow from there."

"Sounds terrifying."

She nods. "And for what? Because people had different color skin? It was needless. Cut us and we all bleed the same."

"Right."

"I was fourteen, don't do the math, when things started to change. It felt like a monumental thing at the time, but really, *has* much changed?" She shakes her head. "The important thing is, they did change, even if there are some backwards hicks who want to go back to the good ol' days."

I laugh.

"It's up to the young ones like you to not let them take over. White, black, brown, yellow, red, who cares?"

"Exactly."

"So, is this a good start?" she asks.

"It's a *great* start. You've been a massive help."

She flicks her hair. "I aim to please."

"And that you have," I reply.

We sit in silence for a while, both of us lost in our own thoughts before a clock chiming breaks our concentration.

Violet reaches into her pocket and pulls out a roll of Life Savers, taking one and offering one to me.

"Thanks," I say as I pop the candy in my mouth.

We sit for a little while longer before she speaks. "I know why I'm still sittin' here, but the question is, why are *you*?"

I run a hand through my hair. "Got a lot on my mind." A certain honey-blonde dynamite and all her problems, to be exact.

"Well yes, plans of how to bring us a state championship would take up a lot of that brain power, and rightly so."

I chuckle. Throughout our time together Violet has revealed herself to be quite the devoted football fan. "Yeah, that and some other stuff. Plus, I don't really want to go home."

"No?"

I shake my head.

"Why's that, sugar?"

"Just, um, family stuff." As much as I love Violet's straight-shooting ways, I realize unloading to her about my father, her boss, may not be the smartest thing in the world.

"That jackass of a father gettin' you down, huh?"

I almost choke on my Life Saver. To save me from dying—or our shot at state from failing, it's hard to know—she hits me on the back a couple times.

"No need to be surprised, sugar. The man came in here on his first day spoutin' on about how things were goin' to run, his expectations of me, and so on and so forth."

"Let me guess, you told him none of that would happen."

She looks over at me, her green eyes sparkling, and pats my cheek. "You catch on quick, that's good. A good QB needs to be able to adapt."

I laugh.

Sobering, she puts her hand over mine. "He doesn't matter. *You* do. What doesn't kill us and all that."

I nod.

"Good man. Now you best get home. It's probably *not* good to piss the old man off too much. No doubt our hero can take it, but why test that theory?"

That gets another laugh out of me. Truthfully, I haven't laughed this much in a while. A *long* while. "Thanks, Miss Violet."

"You are most welcome, sugar. You ever need anythin', and I mean *anythin',* you come to me, okay?"

"Okay, thank you."

"You can thank me by bringin' that trophy home."

"I'll do my best."

She nods before I gather my books and get out of there.

. . .

THE NEXT DAY AT SCHOOL, I'm ready for whatever Cerulean wants to throw at me, and I know she will throw something. She has to. Her pride, her ability to look after her sisters is at stake. What she doesn't know is that I'll let her have it. Her sisters are obviously important to her, and I would never take them from her.

Every day, the same scene plays out. I walk down the hall with TK and half the team at my back, then the crowd parts and there they are. I wink at Indigo and wave to Vermilion, who gives a timid smile back. But this time Cerulean kicks off the lockers and stomps toward me.

I hold my hands up, preempting her. "I didn't do anything, I was just being friendly."

She pulls me to the side, ignoring the hollering and whistling going on.

"Did you tell anyone what happened yesterday?" she demands.

"What? No! I said I wouldn't, and I didn't."

"Good."

"I get it, your sisters are your thing. I said I'd leave that up to you and I am."

She turns and walks away.

"But...."

She halts and marches back to me. "But what?"

"But if I catch wind that something's not right or that things are getting worse, I *will* step in, whether or not you like it."

"It's not your business," she grits out.

"I saw it, I stepped into it, it's mine if I want it."

"I can handle it," she insists. Her fingers stretch and contract, her eyes wide and blazing.

"All I'm saying is that if there ever comes a time you can't, I'm there." I shrug.

"We don't need you."

"Maybe not." I take a step closer, and her pupils dilate. "But you want me."

I lift a hand to run down her arm but the movement breaks whatever trance she was in, and she takes a step back.

"In your dreams, dick. I'll tell you for the last time. Leave. My. Family. Alone." With that, she spins on her heel, blonde hair flying out around her, and stomps off.

I go back to my boys, who are guffawing about what just went down.

"Oooh, boy," TK says. "You just got *told*."

I laugh. "Nah, we were just having a conversation."

"Yeah, a conversation where you were *told*."

I shake my head.

"Don't worry about it, man," he says, slapping my arm. "Many a man has tried and failed with her. You're not the first and you certainly won't be the last. The girl makes every Disney villain look like a Girl Scout. You've had your shot, you missed, now admit defeat and turn your attention to the many other *fine* women this hallowed establishment hosts." He nods to the numerous girls lining the hallway who smile, wink, or wave at his attention.

"Whatever," I reply, not really paying attention. We pass Kingsley, and I nod at her. She nods back and as she does, a plan starts to form.

CHAPTER EIGHT

I TURN and stomp away from Harley and push through the ever-present crowd that seems to swell whenever he's near.

"Get out of my way," I snap at some freshmen girls hoping to be noticed by Captain Dick or one of his band of merry men.

Finally, I reach the bathroom, my hands shaking, heart pounding. No matter how many or how deep the breaths I take, I feel like I can't get any air in my lungs.

I make my way into a stall and lock the door. Everything is out of control, and I *hate* it. This doesn't happen to me. I'm strong, I'm capable. I'm mother-fucking Cerulean Tremont, and *nothing* gets to me.

An image of Harley, his light brown hair adorably messy, his brown eyes clear, telling me I want him pops into my head.

No.

I shake my head. I will not let Harley St. James in. He can't get in. No one can *ever* get in.

Fumbling with the zip of my bag, I finally get it open and rifle through the contents, eventually locating the small tin with my savior inside. The pills will help keep me focused; they'll clear out all the clutter and just leave me.

The minute I swallow one, I feel my tension ease. I know it's a placebo effect, but still, the peace it brings is more than welcome.

I give it a couple more minutes before opening the stall and finding Magenta leaning against the counter.

"Feeling better?" she asks.

I place my bag next to the sink and wash my hands. "I am, thanks for your concern."

"That was some show you put on with Captain Dick out there."

I shrug. "He was interfering. I had to make sure he knew his place and didn't say anything."

"Looked a lot more than that to me."

I turn to face her, her hair a darker blonde than mine, her figure curvier than mine. "What are you getting at, Magenta?"

"Just that you two were looking awfully cozy, that's all."

"You can't be serious?" I ask. "Remember who you're talking to, M. It's me, Cerulean, not Indigo. You know me, you know who I am, how I am. You really think I'd throw all that away for a guy? Especially *that* one?"

"I'm saying you wouldn't be the first girl to be fooled by a charming guy."

"Oh, M." I take a step toward my sister and grab her hand. "It'll be okay, I promise."

She gives me a sad smile. "I know, I just worry."

I let go of her hand and bring her in for a hug. "I know you do," I say, squeezing her tight.

"Promise me you won't get carried away," she implores once we break apart.

"You know I won't."

"Promise me," she insists.

"I promise."

She nods, and we exit the bathroom. As we walk down the still busy hallway, the crowd parts. The guys give us hopeful and borderline leering looks, hoping we pick them for a bit of fun. That's all it is too. Fun. None of us have a boyfriend, and only Magenta has ever been in a serious relationship. With how that turned out, it's fair to say we've *all* learned that lesson.

The girls we pass on the way to class give us one of two reactions: simper or sneer. Love us, hate us, either way, we don't care. We know who we are, we know what we are, and we bow to no one.

Unfortunately, there's always one who wants to test our bounds. That person for me is Trinity Barnes.

"That was some show you and Harley St. James put on this morning," she says to me in Photography.

"Only an idiot like you would confuse a warning with a show," I retort.

She flicks her black hair over her shoulder. It's not even a natural black; it's got that totally devoid of any other color, one hundred percent fake black look to it.

"If you ask me, it looked more like you getting your panties in a wad because Harley turned you down. It's okay if it was, we all have to face rejection at some point. Well, *most* of us, anyway."

"And I suppose you're the exception to the rule?" I ask.

"Duh, of course I am."

I nod and pick up my camera, checking the settings. "Well, thank you for informing me of the facts of life. I'll sleep better now you've explained them to me."

"You really are a bitch, you know that?" she spits at me.

I shrug. "I could say the same thing about you, but my mama raised me with manners."

Trinity scoffs. "Your mama ran off as soon as she could. I don't blame her, I wouldn't want to be saddled with raising y'all either."

"Because your own mama did such a bang-up job with you." I arch an eyebrow.

She fidgets under my gaze, pulling down her blouse, but because of its length, all it does is push the boobs her daddy bought her for her sixteenth birthday in my face.

It's the shit-for-brains girls like Trinity who have made my and my sisters' domination over the school not only possible, but necessary. What these airheads don't realize is that aside from all of our family's wealth, we're sitting in a prime position for the rest of our lives. Our cards, if played right, could get us anything and everything we ever dreamed of. I, for one, fully intend to take advantage of that fact. But others aren't so focused on the future. No, they're too worried about getting the latest purse, or shoes, or jewelry or car or whatever. They're content to live their lives as the son or daughter of insert-name-here. And that's how they'll go through their whole lives.

Sure, they might reach some position of power because of it, but it won't mean anything because their whole lives they've scraped by and been allowed to get away with mediocrity because of their last name.

I'm determined that won't be me. They will *not* draw me into teenage stupidity and nepotism. Everything I achieve will be because *I* earned it. The only thing Trinity will have earned is a shot of penicillin and a course of antibiotics.

"At least my mama taught me not to be a frigid bitch. If you think you're gonna be able to hook a catch like Harley St. James with what you've got goin' on, you're doggone crazy."

"Yes, how crazy I must be to want to be the mistress of my own destiny instead of a brainless lemming without an original thought of my own. Then to be at the mercy of my 'good on paper' husband, who has the right name, right job, right amount in his bank account, but behind closed doors can't get it up for me because I've had so much plastic surgery I no longer resemble a human and runs off with his male business partner to live in California. My, what a life that will be."

With a huff, she turns and walks off.

FOLLOWING OUR PLEASANT CONVERSATION, it comes as no surprise that at lunch, Trinity is firmly encamped at Harley and the football team's table. No doubt she's flirting up a storm, trying desperately to show me what I'll never have.

"Looks like Trinity has reached a whole new level of desperation," Magenta comments as she sets her tray down.

"Skank," Indigo curses.

"Afraid of a little competition, Ind?" Magenta asks.

My eldest sister shoots Magenta a saccharine smile. "Never, sister dearest. I'm simply stating a fact."

I laugh at their antics. "She's trying to prove she's superior to me by getting Captain Dick's attention," I tell them.

"Ah, that explains it," Magenta replies, nodding.

"Why? That's the stupidest thing I've ever heard," Vermilion pipes up.

"Because that's how they teach girls like her to act and from what they derive their self-worth," I explain.

"Again, that's stupid."

"Just remember that when someone with drop-dead gorgeous looks wants into your pants and renders you useless with a look," Magenta warns her.

In response Vermilion glares at her before going back to her ever-present book. This time we all laugh.

"Well, Trinity can have Captain Dick and whoever else comes along. I have better things to do with my time and bigger fish to fry," I say.

"Keep reminding yourself of that," Indigo says, patting my hand. Beside her, Magenta gives me a look that tells me I'm not fooling anybody.

HARLEY

AS CERULEAN and her sisters enter the cafeteria, everyone stops and watches them. Unaware or not caring about that, they continue to their table, not a single shit given that they hold everyone captive.

"How do they do that?" I ask no one in particular.

"They're goddesses, man," Jon, one of my linebackers, says.

"You've seen them in action," David, one of our punters, adds. "Would you take them on?"

"He's our motherfucking QB, of course he would," TK says as he sits down, a girl with long black hair, clearly fake breasts pushed up to her ears, lips slathered in a garish pink lip gloss, and who is batting her fake eyelashes at me with him. "Didn't you see him this morning with Cerulean?"

"You were *so* brave," the girl coos.

"Ah, thanks?" I reply.

"I'm Trinity." She leans over to offer me her hand, giving me an eyeful of her tits.

"Nice to meet you." I take her hand and shake it, studiously trying to avoid looking at her cleavage.

"Trinity's like the anti-Hued Hussies," TK supplies as he stuffs his face.

"What does that even mean?" I ask after trying to work it out for myself.

She laughs, the high-pitched, overly flirty and fake sound grating.

"He just means I'm ten times the woman they all are," Trinity explains.

"Ten? Try a million," TK says, pulling her to him and rubbing his face against one of her boobs.

"I just don't get what it is about them that everyone finds so great," she whines.

"Er, the fact that they're smokin' hot might have something to do with it," Jon replies.

Trinity's face whips to his, her hair flying all over the place.

"I mean, if you're into that blonde ice princess sort of thing," he adds.

"Yeah, babe," TK says to Trinity. "You're *so* much hotter than they are."

"Were they always like this?" I ask.

"Ugh, *yes*," Trinity answers, twirling a lock of her hair around her finger.

"No one really likes them, but they fear them?"

"You've seen them in action," TK says.

"Yeah, but I'm trying to work out why you let them get away with that shit."

"They're the Tremonts," David says. "They practically helped build Savannah and this school. Add to that the fact that they're more than formidable opponents, and we just let 'em go."

"Plus, they're fine as hell," Jon repeats.

David nods.

"Ugh," Trinity says as she inspects her nails.

"You know it's true," TK argues.

"Just because they're okay-lookin' doesn't mean they can be royal bitches to everyone." She stops inspecting her nails. "I mean, look at you, you're the star wide retriever—"

"Re*ceiver*," TK corrects.

"Whatever, you're a star football player, rich, good-lookin', everyone likes you, shouldn't *you* be the one ruling this school?"

"I mean—" he starts before Trinity speaks over him.

"They think they're so great. They're so popular, so *powerful*. So their great-great-granddaddy helped build this school, so what? Why does that mean they're allowed to treat everyone like shit?"

"I don't think—" Jon starts, but Trinity silences him with a glare.

"Everyone thinks they're *so* perfect and can't do anything wrong, it drives me crazy!"

"Not everyone," TK says, pulling Trinity closer to his side and trying to get a look down her top.

"You see it, don't you?" she asks me. "You've only been here a few days, but you see how everyone fawns over them."

"I, er, don't know. They seem all right to me."

"Ugh." She rolls her eyes and goes back to inspecting her nails.

"They're trash, don't worry about them. All you need to focus on is you and me," TK says, bringing Trinity even closer to his side.

She laughs. "Oh, TK."

"You know we'd be good together," he presses.

"Eh," she says, twirling a lock of hair around her finger. "Maybe, maybe not. It would be fun to see them get what they deserve though."

I SPEND the walk to Chemistry and much of the lesson wondering about the Tremont girls. Trinity and TK and anyone else can say otherwise, but I *know* there's more to those girls than a desire to be bitchy. The whole concept seems so... *simple* for them. I'm sure it's what they want people to think, but I don't think that's the case at all.

I make my way to my final class of the day, Study Hall. I wave to Miss Violet as I walk in. She gives me one back as she helps a student.

Going to my usual table at the back left-hand corner of the study area, I see there's somebody already there.

"Hi," I say as I put my books down.

Vermilion's head snaps up. Her hair is the same shade as her older sister's, her eyes a lighter green.

She squeaks and bows her head.

Okay then. "How are you?" I ask.

She shrugs.

"How are your lessons going?" It's been a week since I came across her and Alexandrov. As much as I hope that if she needed help she would come to me, I'm not sure whether her loyalty to her sister would put an end to that.

"They're okay," she squeaks.

"That's good." I gesture to the chair I'm standing behind. "Do you mind if I sit here?"

She shakes her head.

"Thanks. I haven't seen you here before."

She nods. "Usually I use this as another practice period, but I have a geography test in a couple of days and I need to study."

"Want some help?" I ask.

Her mouth opens at my offer, her eyes wide. "Y-you'd d-do that f-for m-me?"

I shrug. "Sure. I don't have anything urgent, and I don't want to brag, but I've spent more than my fair share of time overseas, so I'm quietly confident I know my way around."

"You really wouldn't mind?"

I shake my head. "Not at all."

WE SIT for a while as I help Vermilion work out the complexities of Eastern Europe.

"You think you've got a handle on this now?" I ask as we near the end of the period.

"I think so, but with all the 'Stan's in there, it gets a bit confusing."

"I have no doubt if you put your mind to it, you'll be able to conquer it."

She smiles at me, and for once I feel like I'm doing some good at this school, that I'm finding my feet.

"You know, you're not as bad as I thought you'd be," she says, piling her books up while we wait for the bell.

I laugh. "How bad did you think I'd be?" I ask.

She shrugs. "I don't know. My sister—" She stops when she realizes she's about to spill a trade secret.

"Oh, go on, don't stop there," I encourage.

She shakes her head. "It's nothing, just ignore me. I'm socially stunted and have no idea how to interact with people."

"You've been doing just fine for the past forty-five minutes."

"Because we were studying, not because we were being actual human beings."

"We weren't human beings?" I ask.

"No, we were studying!"

"And that doesn't make us humans. Right."

She blows out a breath. "I'll lay it all out for you, all right?"

I nod and motion for her to proceed.

"My sister, well sisters, Cerulean and Magenta, don't like you."

I smile. "I figured."

She nods. "With us, we're basically all we've got. Sure, our dad is home, occasionally, rarely, but either way, he doesn't care about us, doesn't pay attention to us."

"And your mom?" I ask.

"Our mom is in Switzerland. She's the CFO of a large multinational corporation. She hasn't been home since she left ten years ago. We see her some summers, but not for very long."

"Wow."

She shrugs again. "It is what it is. We're okay with what we've got, and we've got each other so...."

"So it's you four against the world," I finish for her.

She nods. "Yeah, I guess."

"You know I'm not here to change that."

"*I* know that. So does Indigo, and *maybe*

Cerulean, but Magenta.... She doesn't trust anyone, especially those who are a threat to us."

"I'm a threat to you?"

She rolls her eyes. "You're the QB who's going to bring the school a state championship. If you're not a threat, then no one is."

I sigh and run a hand through my hair. "I'm just here to get a scholarship to go to college. Anything beyond that is just.... It's high school bullshit, is what it is."

Vermilion giggles.

"I have nothing against you or your sisters. For the most part you all seem like really nice girls. A little stubborn maybe, but I don't see that as a bad thing."

"Y'all," she says.

"Huh?"

"You said 'you all.' In the South, we say y'all. If you're going to be part of this community, you're going to have to speak our language."

"Y'all?" I ask.

"Y'all," she confirms.

"Y'all," I repeat, and she smiles.

The bell rings, and we gather our things.

"If you have any problems studying, you have my number," I remind her. "So gimme a call or text or whatever."

"Thanks, Harley."

I have genuinely enjoyed my time with Vermilion Tremont. She's timid, yes, and more than a little shy, but she has a fire inside her I suspect is a uniquely Tremont attribute. They're firebrands, and when that's not directed at me, it's quite enjoyable to watch.

"So what's this about you being socially stunted?"

I ask, her words from before coming into my mind. Lord help me, but there's something about these sisters I just want to find out more about.

Beside me, Vermilion tenses slightly.

"You don't have to tell me, but from where I stand, you're a great girl and everyone should clamor to get to know you."

She ducks her head, but I can still make out a slight blush on her cheeks. We get to her locker, and she methodically puts her books away.

"I just find it hard to socialize with people, that's all."

"And yet, you were fine with me."

She shrugs.

"Do you want friends?" I ask. "You're a freshman, right? What'll happen once your sisters graduate?"

She shrugs again, her bottom lip starting to wobble.

I grab her arm and spin her so she's facing me. "Look, I'm not saying this to be a dick, but you're a sweet girl and high school can be rough. Trust me, I've been to enough of them."

That gets me a small smile.

Across the hallway, I spot Kingsley and beckon her over.

"What's up?" she says as she bounces over.

"Have you met Vermilion?" I ask.

Kingsley rolls her eyes at me. "We live in Savannah, QB1, of course we know each other. The children of wealthy families all send their kids to the same places. We've known each other since we were in kindergarten. The correct question is have we spent any significant time together? That answer would be no." She turns to the youngest Tremont, her head tilted. "You're in my Algebra class, right?" she asks.

"Um, I-I t-think so," Vermilion stutters.

"Mr. Shorten is a total fascist, isn't he? As if algebra isn't bad enough, we get stuck with the devil incarnate as our teacher."

This time Vermilion laughs.

"So have you struck a deal with Harley too?" Kingsley asks.

"A deal?"

"Yeah." She shoves me, what is probably hard for her, but barely moves me. "This loser doesn't have many friends, so I agreed that I'd *pretend* to be civil to him when I feel like being anything but."

Vermilion's mouth drops open.

"But don't worry," Kingsley continues. "You look like a cool chick, so I'll be your friend out of the good-ness of my heart."

I laugh as Vermilion stares at the whirlwind that is Kingsley Lee.

"What are you doing this weekend?" Kingsley continues, totally oblivious to Vermilion's shock. "I was thinking of going to Atlanta, get some shopping in, but that's so clichéd. I'd kill to go to Miami or New York, but my parents won't let me. Anyway, I was thinking of going for brunch, see if we can't convince the waiter to serve us mimosas. What do you say?"

"Huh?" Vermilion asks.

"Brunch, Sunday. You in?"

"Y-you're in-inviting me?" Vermilion stammers.

Kingsley hooks her arm through Vermilion's. "Of course, you're my new BFF."

"W-why?"

"Why not?"

"Because y-you d-don't know m-me."

"No, but I can sense you, and I sense you need a good time and some friends. Am I wrong?"

"My sisters—"

"Your sisters will always be there for you, but sometimes it helps to get out of your family bubble and experience new things," Kingsley says.

"What do you say?" I ask.

"Um, okay," Vermilion agrees.

"Yay!" Kingsley says, clapping and jumping up and down. "Gimme your phone and I'll give you my number so we can coordinate our schedules."

Vermilion shoots me a look of half fear, half wonder as Kingsley enters her details. I give her what I hope is a reassuring smile.

"It's all sorted then," Kingsley says, handing Vermilion's phone back.

I lean down and place a kiss on Kingsley's cheek. "Thank you," I whisper in her ear.

She shoots me a blinding smile and pushes me away. "Kissing isn't covered by our agreement," she jokes.

"My sincerest apologies."

"For that, I expect some sort of payment."

"Let me know where you're going on Sunday. Mimosas on me."

Kingsley squeals again. I shake my head at her antics, but as over-the-top as they may be, they're exactly what Vermilion needs to come out of her shell a little. One day there will come a time when her sisters are no longer at this school, and I shudder to think what would happen to her then. At least now she has a friend, someone on her side who can help her navigate the choppy waters of high school.

At the corner of my eye, I see a flash of honey blonde hair coming toward us.

"Now that's sorted, I guess I'll leave y'all to it," I say.

"Ooh," Kingsley coos. "Look who's getting all Southern on us."

"A friend taught it to me." I send a wink Vermilion's way. "I'll see you lovely ladies later."

On my way to my locker, I pass Cerulean. Any hope my involvement with Vermilion may have gone unnoticed is dashed by the look of pure hatred she sends my way.

CHAPTER TEN

WHAT THE FUCK is Vermilion doing with Harley? And who is that girl with my sister? She looks vaguely familiar but I can't place her. Karen? Kate? Who the fuck knows.

"We're going to have *so* much fun," the girl trills.

"Who's having fun?" I ask, opening my locker and putting away the books I don't need.

"Oh." The girl turns to me. "Me and Vermilion are going to brunch on Sunday."

"You are, are you?" I ask, arching an eyebrow.

She nods, not backing down. Either she's stupid, or she's got balls of steel. "We're friends," she says.

"Are you now?"

She nods again while Vermilion stands there, her fingers twitching, playing some intricate piece on an imaginary piano.

"And just *how* did you and my sister get to be such firm friends?"

"Cerulean, don't," Vermilion says, snapping out of her trance.

I turn to her. "I'm just taking an interest in your life, sister dearest. Isn't that what family does?" The last real friend Vermilion had was Dean. They were as close as two kids could be and when he died she was devastated. I don't want that to happen again. I don't want people getting close to her only for them to leave once she's attached. I don't want them using her because of her name or to get to me or Indigo or Magenta. I don't want her to get hurt again. Am I going overboard? Possibly, but that's who I am.

"Harley was just being nice. He helped me study for my geography test, that's all."

"And you got a shiny new friend to boot," I add.

"He was just being nice," she repeats.

I turn back to the girl. "I'm sorry, I don't know your name."

"Kingsley, Kingsley Lee," she replies. Kingsley, that's it.

"Lee as in Douglas and Margaret's daughter?"

"That's them." Her lack of caring moves her up in my estimation. The Lees are a big deal in Georgia. Not as big as the Tremonts—we're old money while the Lees are relatively new—but I'm willing to bet the expectations on little Miss Kingsley are the same as they are on us.

"And just how did *you* get in with our Lord and Savior QB1?"

"He, um, gave me a ride home the other night." She shifts her weight from foot to foot and starts playing with the hem of her blouse.

"Did he now?"

"Look," she says, taking a deep breath. "Harley has nothing to do with me genuinely wanting to be Vermilion's friend. I know how hard it can be to have a prestigious last name in this school, this town, hell, in life in general. Shouldn't us girls stick together?"

I consider her words, then look at my sister. In her short life she's been through a lot, and friends would be good for her. I still can't help but worry, though.

"Vermilion's fine as she is," I tell Kingsley.

"And *I* think Vermilion can make up her own damn mind," she replies.

"Guys, stop, *please*," my sister begs.

Kingsley turns to her. "I'll be at the Peach Blossom at ten on Sunday. If you want to come, and I'd really love you to, I'll be waiting. If not, then I'll see you in Algebra, okay?"

"Okay," Vermilion says in a small voice, head down.

"Cerulean," Kingsley says to me, "I'd say it was a pleasure meeting you, but it's my guess you'd be offended by that, so I'll say it was everything I expected it to be."

I have to hide my smile as she walks off. The girl has spunk; I'll give her that.

VERMILION IS silent on the drive home.

"I know you're pissed I made a scene with that girl, but you don't need her," I tell my sister. "This is Harley trying to get to me, and he's using you to do it. It's pathetic, but what more can we expect from the likes of him?"

"He's nice," she says. "So is Kingsley. They're both nice to me and not because they have to be."

I shake my head. "That's just what they want you to think."

"How do you know?" she asks. "How can you know what's in someone else's head, Cerulean? You're not a mind reader, you're just a seventeen-year-old girl."

"I'm your sister and I'm looking out for you."

"And what happens when you and Indigo and Magenta go off to college? I'll be left here all alone, with no friends, no support system."

"It's like I told Alexandrov, you can come and live with one of us. We'll find a better piano teacher and then in a couple of years you'll move to New York to go to the Conservatorium."

"What happens if I don't want to live with one of you when you're in college?" she asks.

My head whips to the side so suddenly, my arms go with it and the car swerves. "Fuck!" I cry as I correct the steering, ignoring the honks from the surrounding cars. "What do you mean you don't want to live with one of us?" I ask when we're back in our lane.

She blows out a breath and starts tapping a rhythm on her leg.

"Vermilion," I say, snapping her out of her trance. "Why don't you want to move?"

"Come on, Cerulean. Would you even *want* me around? You'll be in college, off doing your own thing, finally getting to be the person you've always wanted to be. You won't want your little sister around, cramping your style."

I pull into our long drive and park my SUV next to Indigo's convertible. "I'll always want you around," I tell her. "You're my sister, my whole life."

"That's just it," she tells me. "Here, we're your

whole life, but at college you won't need to worry about us. Don't get me wrong, we appreciate the lengths you go for us, but your reward for doing that is going to college and being who you are, who you were always meant to be."

"I am and was always meant to be your sister," I remind her.

"Our sister, yes, but not our mother or even our father. I know because of... Dean you felt like you had to shield me from everything but there *will* come a time where eventually I will have to stand on my own two feet. Why not loosen the reins now? At least you're here if something goes wrong. If we wait until you're gone, it could all fall apart, everything we worked so hard to build."

I'm so shocked she actually said Dean's name that I'm momentarily silenced.

"You deserve a life too, Blue," she says, using my childhood nickname.

"I just don't want you to get hurt," I tell her.

"Isn't that a part of life?" she asks. "Besides, if I can live after... Dean, then I think I can survive anything."

"Of course you can." I take her face in my hands and press a kiss to her forehead.

"We bow to no one," she reminds me.

"We bow to no one," I repeat.

LATER THAT NIGHT, I sit at my massive, custom-built puzzle table. It's five feet wide, six feet long, with removable buckets on the edge so I can store the pieces I've separated into color groups, and a movable easel so I can see what I'm putting together. It might be a hobby someone's grandma does, but for me, it's relaxing. When I'm trying to piece together the thousand, two thousand, and three thousand piece behemoths, I don't think about anything except finding the next piece, then the next and the one after that.

In the background *90 Day Fiancé* is on and I can't help but chuckle when one couple's arguing breaks through my haze. I love watching all these saps who actually think their relationships will work out.

"Vermilion was in a good mood when she got home," Magenta says as she saunters into my room. She picks up a piece I've been trying to figure out for about half an hour and slots it in effortlessly.

"Hey!" I slap her hand away.

She laughs and takes a seat on my bed. "She said something about brunch on Sunday?"

I nod. "Douglas and Margaret Lee's daughter invited her."

"And you're letting her go?"

"I'm not her mother."

"No, but...."

I stand up, stretching my back. "But what?" I ask.

"Come on, C, you know what I'm going to say."

"And you know why I do what I do, so why are we having this conversation?"

"In amongst all the excitement of this brunch, a *very* interesting person was mentioned."

"I know. I'm not happy about his involvement either but...." I take a deep breath. "I don't know, maybe he's not as bad as we thought. He helped V study for her geography test, and Kingsley seems like a nice girl." What Vermilion said in the car really stuck with me. If she does decide to stay here when we go to college, she will be all alone. Being friends with Kingsley could be a good thing. At the very least there's time for us to get to know her, make sure she's not going to hurt Vermilion in any way.

"This is a slippery slope," Magenta warns.

"I know, but something V said stuck with me."

"And what was that?" She crosses her arms and her legs.

"What happens to V after we go off to college?" I ask.

"She comes with one of us."

"And if she doesn't want to?"

"Why wouldn't she?"

"She's afraid we'll forgo the college experience to look after her."

"That's just stupid, she's our sister."

"I know, that's what I said. But also...."

"Also what?"

"She has a point."

Magenta flops back on the bed. "When did she get so grown-up?"

I laugh and sit next to her, tucking my legs underneath my body. "I know, right?"

We're silent for a while before I speak again. "She said Dean's name. Twice."

Magenta sits up. "What?"

I nod. "I know. I didn't think it would happen either."

"Holy shit. She really is growing up," she says as she lies down again. I join her and snuggle into her side.

"Yup. Unfortunately, I think it's something we'll have to get used to."

"And Harley? Are we going to have to get used to *him*?"

"I'm not stupid, M. I'm not weakening my stance on him."

"Good. I know you like to think you're not," she continues. "But deep down, Cerulean Persephone Tremont, you are a romantic. It's why you watch this trash, secretly rooting for everyone to get their happily ever after."

I gasp. "I am *not*."

"You are," she insists. "But I love you anyway."

And that's why my family is everything.

CHAPTER ELEVEN

AT PRECISELY 9:55 A.M. I drop Vermilion off at the Peach Blossom café for her brunch date with Kingsley. Her excitement is palpable, and I know this is the right thing to do. As much as I want to protect her, eventually I *will* have to let her live her own life.

It's a nice day out, so instead of going straight home, I take a walk around the many squares that make up the Midtown area. It's what I love most about living in Savannah: all the beauty, the greenery, the old antebellum houses, the river. In the future I might move far away, but in my heart, I'll always be a Southern girl.

A while later I swing past the café. The girls are laughing and smiling and having a great time. I stand for a while and watch my sister. Truthfully, I can't remember the last time I saw her this happy. When Dean died, a piece of her died too, as clichéd as that sounds. But now, maybe we're getting some of the old Vermilion back.

I'm so busy reminiscing about the old Vermilion that I don't notice Harley until he's standing next to their table, two glasses of orange juice in his hands.

They're in champagne glasses, which make me think it isn't so much orange juice as it is a mimosa.

Kingsley squeals and jumps up and hugs him around the neck. He laughs and hugs her back, while Vermilion flashes him a genuine smile. With a nod toward the register and a quick wave, Harley leaves. I don't notice until it's too late that he's heading in my direction.

"Shit," I cuss as he sees me and smiles.

"Well, if it isn't Miss Royal Blue," he says as he approaches.

"What did you call me?" I ask as I try to shake off the fog from the past few minutes.

"That's what color Cerulean is, isn't it?" he asks. "A royal blue?"

"Technically, it comes from the Latin *caeruleus* which means sky blue, but whatever."

"Good to know. So, how are you?" he asks, shoving his hands in his pockets.

"Why do you want to know?" I fire back.

"I don't know, to be polite, or because I thought being nice to you might mean you'd stop biting my head off at every opportunity? Take your pick."

I sigh and wind the end of my ponytail through my fingers. "I'm fine," I say eventually.

Harley's eyes widen. "Really? I mean, that's, ah, good."

I nod. "How, um, are you?" This awkwardness between us is weird and has me off-balance, a feeling I'm not used to and certainly don't like.

"I'm good," he says, smiling. "Kingsley and Vermilion seem to get on well." He nods to where they're sitting, another round of mimosas just now being delivered.

"I hope you don't intend for them to get drunk," I scold.

He laughs. "That's their last one. I told Mike, the owner, that's their limit. Apparently being a star quarterback has its advantages."

"Why are you being so nice to her?" The words are out of my mouth before I can stop them.

He sighs and runs a hand through his hair. "Like I've said, she's a sweet girl; so is Kingsley. They're both kind of loners, so I thought they might hit it off. I was right."

"But why do you care if they hit it off or not?" I ask. "They're freshmen, and you're a senior and our Lord and Savior QB."

"So that means I can't care about anyone or anything other than football? I know it may not seem like it, but there are other things in life."

I snort. "Trust me, I know."

"But only you're allowed to care about them, is that it? I play football, therefore that's all I'm good for, the only thing I can do, and I shouldn't worry about anything else?"

"I didn't say—" I start, but he cuts me off.

"Or is it easier for you if no one else gives a shit about anything else? That way you can control us and have us right where you want us."

"That's not—"

"For your information, I'm all too aware of what it's like to be the odd one out. I saw two such lost souls and thought 'hey, maybe I can make a small difference in their lives. Maybe I can help them to not feel so alone.' I should've known you'd take it as me interfering. Here's a newsflash for you, *Cerulean*"—he all but spits my name—"I'm not interfering or trying to take your role or position or whatever you want to call it, I just wanted to do something nice for Kingsley and your sister. I care about them, just as I'd care about you if you ever let down those high-ass walls you've built around yourself."

With that he turns around and storms off.

All I can think is: *he cares about me?*

HARLEY

CHAPTER TWELVE

"GREEN FORTY-EIGHT, GREEN FORTY-EIGHT, HUT!" I call and clap my hands.

The ball flies into them, and I move into the pocket while TK sprints down the field. With the defense looming and a sack imminent, I let the ball fly. I'm "tackled"—that is, hugged, hands off the QB in practice—just as the ball finds TK's waiting arms and he strolls in for a touchdown.

There's a chorus of hoots and hollers as he jogs back to the rest of us.

"That's some fine-ass passing, my man," he says when he makes it back.

"It was all right." I shrug.

"*It was all right*," Jon mimics. "Shit, man, that was epic."

"Yeah, it was," I agree, breaking out in a smile for the first time since my run-in with Cerulean on the weekend. There's an avalanche of slaps on my helmeted head, back, and shoulders before we make our way to the sidelines for a well-deserved water break.

Friday's our first game of the season, and it

couldn't come at a better time. On the field the team is looking sharp, and off it.... Well, I could use the distraction.

Running into Cerulean on Sunday... let's just say it didn't go quite how I intended. Still, I can't say I regret what I said to her. I meant every word. And sure, some of that anger may have been a *bit* misdirected from my father, but with the aim of putting her in her place, I'm hopeful it did the trick.

The truth of it is, I'm tired. I'm tired of only being seen as a meathead who throws a ball well. Yes, it's fully how I intend to make a living, but football isn't the be-all and end-all for me. I want to be more, and I want people to realize that.

Plus, I'm sick of Cerulean's shit. I genuinely like Vermilion. Given what I saw with her piano teacher, she looked like she could use a friend. And if that friendship keeps Kingsley away from TK, then all the better. I'm still not sure why she was waiting for him, or what she was hoping to do with him, but I can hazard a guess it wasn't anything good. Sometimes, not all the time, I get a weird vibe from him. It's nothing I can put my finger on, and definitely not something I have any evidence of, but it is something I'll keep my eye on.

Speaking of TK, he slings an arm around me as we walk back onto the field.

"So, Trinity and I were thinking, party on Saturday to celebrate our impending win?"

"You don't think you're tempting fate by organizing this?"

"Nah, man, it's in the bag. Trinity has a hookup at

one of the clubs in town, says she can get us booze and everything."

"And how much is that gonna cost?" I ask.

"Don't worry your pretty little head about it, QB," he says, putting his helmet on and getting in position. "We got you covered."

I'M EXHAUSTED when I get home later that evening. As I open the door, Cookie unfolds himself off the bottom step of the stairs and comes to greet me.

"Hey, buddy," I say as I scoop him up.

"That mongrel cat of yours pissed on the floor in our bathroom, *again*," my father informs me as he comes out of his study and heads to the kitchen.

"Sorry."

"The smell was horrific. If you can't control it, I'll have it put down."

I want to ask him why it's such a big deal. He didn't have to clean it up, Mrs. Stark would have. Plus, if he kept their bedroom door shut, Cookie wouldn't go in there, but I value my head where it is, so I don't.

"Sorry," I say again.

"Hurry up," he says. "Dinner is ready, and we're waiting on you."

I nod and rush up the stairs to my room. I dump my gym bag and put Cookie on my bed.

"I know you like to explore, buddy," I tell him. "But it's probably best if you stay out of the old man's way. He's got an even bigger stick up his ass than usual."

Cookie purrs and rubs his cheeks on my hands.

"Good boy."

I empty my gym bag and grab my protein shaker so I can take it with me when I go downstairs. My parents are waiting for me when I make it down a minute later.

"Hey, Mom," I say, kissing her cheek before taking my seat.

"How was your day, sweetie?" she asks.

I shrug. "It was good."

"Good?" my father asks. "We've made too many sacrifices for your day to just be *good*."

I suppress my sigh and swallow a mouthful of grilled chicken and veggies. "Practice went well," I continue as if Dad had said nothing. "The team is looking sharp, and we're clicking, which is awesome."

My dad shakes his head at the use of the slang. I know what he's thinking. He's thinking I've been educated all over the world and I still speak like a common American. It was bad enough I never really lost my accent, but it damn near broke his heart when I started playing football. It was even worse when Mom helped find people to coach me, but she did it anyway. If he had his way, it would've been soccer, or football to everyone else in the world, and the chance to ply my trade anywhere.

"That's wonderful," Mom comments.

I nod. "Coach is pleased."

"So he should be," Dad adds. "He gets paid enough. Only in the South does a football coach earn as much as a principal. He does half the work and deals with less than a tenth of the students."

"Now, now, Cary," Mom says. "Remember, we

said when Harley started showing promise that we would do whatever it took for him to succeed. Georgia is a hotbed for football and is where Harley needs to be."

My father actually "humphs" like a child.

"Cary...."

"What, Heather? All I'm asking for is a bit of goddamn respect. Is that too much to ask?"

In response, she tsks. "I've seen your salary and benefits package, Cary. You're being well compensated. Besides, Forest Park Academy is the most prestigious private school in the state."

"Filled with the most entitled children in the state," he adds.

"And the International School in Switzerland wasn't?" Mom rebuts. She sighs and puts down her fork. "Look, I'm well aware that coming back here wasn't your preference, but it's what's best for Harley's future." I desperately want to butt in and ask, "remember me?" but I know better than that. "He is our only child, Cary, and we owe it to him to do everything in our power to ensure he has the best future he is able. Sometimes that means we as parents have to sacrifice. For years Harley and I have followed you around the globe at your whim. We have never complained, even when homesickness struck its hardest. I don't think one year here, just one, is too much to ask in the grand scheme of things."

Ladies and gentlemen, may I present Heather St. James, mom of the century and protective mother bear.

She sits there, arms crossed, eyebrow arched

while my father grips his cutlery, his knuckles white. Me? I shovel more broccoli in my mouth.

"I have feelers out to Dubai, Samoa, and England" is all he says.

"And come June next year, I will be by your side wherever you choose, but for now we are here, in Savannah, Georgia, and you will not say another word about it."

The stare down continues and ends with a curt nod from my father.

"Will there be any scouts at this game?" Mom asks me, switching gears completely.

"Ah, I'm not sure. I know Coach has said a few have contacted him, and he's trying to get a few more, but it's only the first game of the season."

My father goes to say something but Mom shoots him a look, and he remains silent. It's qualities like this that make my mom a great doctor. She'll go to the ends of the earth for her patients, and I admire her for that. I see a lot of her in Cerulean. Shit.

THE REALIZATION that a lot of what attracts me to Cerulean is what I admire in my mother rattles me a bit. But like any good QB, I roll with the punches. Seeing her with TK the next morning is strange, but I don't let it get to me. Much. They're standing close to each other, talking in hushed tones, eyes shifting all over the place. It's weird because they've made it more than clear how they feel about each other, so what could possibly bring them together?

"What was that about?" I ask TK as we walk to

class. So maybe I let it get to me more than I'd like to admit.

"Huh?"

"With Cerulean."

He side-eyes me. "Don't worry, QB, I'm not encroaching on your territory."

"She's not my territory," I snap. "And anyway, I thought you told me to stay away from her."

"And did you take my advice?" he asks.

"And do what?"

"Stay away from her?"

"I tried."

"And you got burned, right? I told you, man, that girl is something else. She's not made like other girls."

"You mean girls like Trinity who are only interested in your dick?"

He shoots me a cheesy grin. "What's so wrong with that?"

"I just hope you're wrapping it up tight, man. Wouldn't want you to catch something."

"Aww, QB, are you worried about me?" he asks as he slings an arm around my shoulders and messes with my hair with the other hand.

"I'm worried about what happens to our season if our star wide receiver can't run because some godforsaken STD swells his balls."

"You thinkin' about my balls, QB?" He flutters his eyelashes at me.

I push him away. "You're too pretty for my taste."

We laugh and continue on to class, whatever TK and Cerulean were doing now long forgotten.

.   .   .

IN MEDIA STUDIES, Cerulean is hyper-focused. Every question Ms. Victoria asks, Cerulean's there, hand in the air, answering before she even finishes the question. She reminds me of that chick from *Harry Potter*, but with better hair.

"You were on fire today," I say to her as we walk out of class.

She looks over her shoulder at me, her sleek neck and shoulders doing things to me such innocuous body parts shouldn't do.

"I'm sorry, are you talking to me? I didn't think such important, wonderful, and all-round good guys like you would stoop to associate with scum like me."

I scratch the back of my neck. "Yeah, I may have gone off a little the other day."

"Just a little?" she asks.

"What do you want from me? An apology? 'Cause I can do that."

She whirls around, her hair flying out, her signature berry smell strong in the air. "I don't want anything from you. I never have, never will. You're the one who keeps inserting himself in my life, my sister's lives. We don't need you and we certainly don't want you."

"Who said anything about wanting?" I ask, shooting her my best panty-melting smile.

"Ugh," she says before spinning around and storming off.

CHAPTER THIRTEEN

JUST WHEN I think there might be an actual human inside Harley St. James, he comes out with *that*, showing me he's exactly the chauvinistic caveman I always thought him to be.

English and Math are much the same way, except there are a few football meatheads in those classes, backing up Captain Dick and simultaneously egging him on. By the time I make it back to my locker, I'm exhausted. Unfortunately for me, there's two hyper freshmen waiting for me.

"Cerulean!" Vermilion cries.

"Hey, Red," I say as I deposit my books in my locker.

"How was your day?" she asks.

"Fine, why do you want to know?"

"You're my sister, can't I ask how your day was?"

"Of course you can, but very rarely do you do so, so why don't you tell me what it is the two of you want."

"Wewanttogotothepeprally," Kingsley rushes out.

"You what?" I ask.

"We want to go to the pep rally," Kingsley repeats, this time at normal speed.

"*Why?*" I ask.

"Because it's our first one in high school and it'd be cool to go, plus Harley's our friend and we really *should* go, you know, to support him as well as get in the school spirit."

"School spirit?" I scoff.

"Yeah, you know, supporting our team and thus school by wearing their colors and cheering them on, hopefully to victory," Kingsley explains.

"I know what it is, thanks," I say to her.

"You're welcome." She shoots me a smile so sweet it would give a lesser person a toothache.

"Can we go?" Vermilion asks.

I blow out a breath. "You *really* want to go?" I ask.

They both nod so fast and hard I'm afraid they might be at risk of breaking their necks.

"You don't have to come," Vermilion adds. "You can just drop us off and come back or stay in the car or whatever."

"Great, relegated to a glorified cab driver," I mutter.

"Come on, Cerulean, *please*," she begs.

"Fine, but you owe me one." Instantly I'm swarmed by the two of them, squealing and jumping around me.

Christ, what have I gotten myself into?

IT MAY COME AS A SHOCK, but I've never attended a pep rally. My desire to attend one now Captain Dick will be front and center is less than zero, but yet, here I am, walking the halls after dark, looking for something to do. I had hoped there would be a classroom or two left unlocked so I could slip in and stream the latest episode of 90 *Day Fiancé*, but it seems like I'm shit out of luck.

Walking around the gym, I find the girls' locker room is open. It's not ideal, but it's better than watching Captain Dick be worshipped and adored by the brainwashed masses. I reach out to push open the door—

"Well, well, well. Look what we have here," a voice says.

My shoulders tense and I take a deep breath before turning around. "Shouldn't you be upstairs being fawned over?" I ask Harley as he leans against the wall. I'm ignoring just how good he looks in his jersey and a pair of distressed jeans.

"They can wait."

I shake my head. "The arrogance never ends with you, does it?"

"Why should it?"

"I'm sure there's probably a million reasons and examples."

"But none you can remember off the top of your head, right?" he asks. He steps closer, his Viktor and Rolf cologne invading my nostrils. "I have to admit, you're the last person I'd expect to see at one of these things."

"Technically, I'm not *at* it, I'm under it."

His eyes blaze when I mention being under something.

"And what else are you under?" he asks, walking closer still.

"If you're implying I'd ever be under *you*, you have another think coming."

"I don't know," he says. He leans against the wall, his arms bracketed above me. "You look pretty good right here."

I scoff but make no move to escape him. I breathe in, his scent going deep into my lungs and making my knees weak.

"You see, I have this theory," he continues.

"Oh, please, *do* tell me this no doubt earth-shattering theory."

"You want me." He leans in further, speaking directly in my ear and sending shivers up my spine.

I sigh. "Haven't I heard this before? What, originality isn't in your repertoire?"

He chuckles as his nose runs up my neck. "I can't help it if it's true."

I shake my head. "Really?" Yes, there are tingles where his skin touches mine, but again I'm trying to ignore them.

"Uh-huh."

"Prove it," I say, my chin jutting out. Let him do what he wants to me, I won't break. At least, I hope I won't.

He pulls back to look me in the eyes. "What?"

"You think I want you *that* badly, then prove it. *Show* me how much I want you." I want to put this asinine theory to bed once and for all.

He laughs. "Show you how much you want me?"

I nod. "Afraid you're not up to it? That's fine, you're not the first guy I know who has problems in that department. Granted, you're a little young, but hey, shit happens."

"I'll have you know I have *never* had any problems in any department."

"Maybe, maybe not. I think that's still to be determined."

"You're something else, you know that?" he asks.

I scoff. "Of course I know. I'm Cerulean Tremont, and I always get what I want."

"And you want me."

"No, but I'm willing to let you have your shot. To try to convince me otherwise, however useless that may be. Once you realize what a fool you've made of yourself, you'll finally leave me alone."

"Oh, royal blue," he says, running his nose up and down my neck, his hand running up my leg and under my skirt. "It'll be my pleasure, and yours, to show you how much you want me."

I laugh but am cut off when he reaches my panties. I had thought this was a good idea, a surefire way to show him how much I *don't* want him, but now the time has come, I'm not so sure this won't backfire on me spectacularly. But it's too late to back out of it now.

"What will I find when I get there?" he asks. "Hmm? Will I find you wet, baby doll? Will I find you ready for me? What's your body saying that you won't?"

"Why don't you find out instead of yakking like an old maid?" I roll my eyes, anxious to get this over and done with. I know he won't let this go unless he sees for himself how much I don't want him. I hope.

He throws his head back and laughs. "An old maid? Really?"

I shrug.

He traces the edge of the material.

"Oh, for fuck's sake, just do it already," I tell him. It's hard to tell whether I do so because I want this over or because I just want him.

Without any more preamble he slips under the material, the edges of his mouth pulling upwards. "Why, Miss. Tremont, I do believe you are aroused."

"Do you want a medal?" I ask. Goddamn fucking body betraying me.

"No, I want this." He slides a finger inside me, and I gasp. "Yeah, that's right," he says. "God, you feel so good, just like I knew you would."

As much as I hate him inside me, I also crave it. Almost without realizing it, I widen my legs. He chuckles. "Yeah, you don't want me at all."

"Harley," I say, not knowing where I'm going, what I want to say, whether I want him to stop or if I'd kill him for doing so.

He slides a second finger inside me, and I moan. "I told you," he says. "We'd be good together, *great* even."

I try to push his hand away, but he uses his free hand to grab both of mine and pin them above my head.

"Do you want me to stop?" he asks.

Do I? I know I *should,* but God help me, I don't. I shake my head.

"That's what I thought." He adds a third finger, and it's not long before I'm coming hard. Traitorous fucking body. "There we go, baby doll."

As soon as his hand relaxes around my wrists, I break free and push him away. Shit. "That didn't mean anything," I tell him.

"No?" He sucks his fingers into his mouth. "Because it felt like you coming to me."

"It was an orgasm, you're a master of foreplay, so what?"

He shrugs. "You tell me. You're the one who doesn't want me unless I'm about to make you come."

"Would you stop saying that?" I ask. I don't need and certainly don't want a reminder of what just went down.

"What? Come? Come, come, come!"

I roll my eyes. "Seriously? Are we back in first grade right now?"

"Oh, baby doll, this isn't first grade anything." He palms the hard-on pressing against his jeans.

A smile pulls at the edges of my mouth, and I advance toward him. "No, it's not." He may think he got the better of me just now, and maybe for a *slight* moment I forgot myself, but not anymore. I'm Cerulean motherfucking Tremont; I bow to no one. "In fact, I'd say it's on the impressive side."

"Well, I don't want to brag...."

I laugh. "Isn't that what you jocks do in the locker room? Compare size? See who's the biggest, the toughest?"

I'm within his reach now, and he doesn't hesitate to pull me against him, my hands resting on his chest. "Royal blue, when it comes to me, there is no competition."

I run one of my hands down his chest and rub him through the fabric. He throws his head back and groans. "Because you're the best, right? The biggest man on campus?"

He nods. "That's right."

"No one can beat you, no one can best you, everyone bows to you, right?" I unzip his pants and slip my hand inside his royal blue boxer-briefs. He's thick and long in my hand.

"That's right."

I jerk him once, twice.

"Holy shit, Cerulean." His head drops to my shoulder.

"Does it feel good?" I ask.

He nods. "So good."

"Yeah?" I use my thumb to rub over the head of his dick, collecting the precum there. "Do you want me?"

"Like nothing else."

"More than state? Than Nationals?"

"More than anything." His breathing is fast and shallow. It won't be long now.

"Are you going to come for me?"

"God, yes."

I stop.

"Wha—what are you doing?" he asks.

I remove my hand from his pants. "The next time you think you know me, know who I am, *what* I am, I want you to remember this and the fact that you don't know shit about me. I bow to no one."

Screw the locker room; I'll wait for Vermilion in the car. Anything to get as far away from this place as possible.

HARLEY

EVEN THOUGH IT pains me to do so, I chuckle as I buckle up my pants. I've got to hand it to her; she knows how to play the game. She may think she won tonight, but she also gave away more than she thought she did. She wants me; I just have to prove to her I'm worth taking a chance on.

Cerulean

CHAPTER FIFTEEN

THE DAY after the pep rally, I expect to find Harley a lot frustrated, pissed-off, even hostile. What I *don't* expect is for him to be waiting for me at my locker.

"Can I help you?" I ask.

"Ladies," he replies. "Vermilion, Indigo, Magenta." He nods at all of them. Vermilion and Indigo titter and wave at him. Magenta scowls, shoving her messenger bag in her locker and storming away.

"What do you want, Harley?" I ask. I push past him to get to my locker.

"Oh nothing, I just wanted to say good morning."

While I was hoping he'd move altogether when I shoved past him, all he does is move to the side and lean against the wall.

"Good morning?" I ask.

"Yeah, it's a customary greeting said before midday. If you'd prefer, I can also say it in Swiss German, regular German, French, Arabic, Japanese, Setswana, Indonesian, and a couple of dialects."

"Ooh, say it in Setswana, that sounds cool," Indigo says.

He opens his mouth but before he can say

anything, I grab his arm and drag him into the nearest classroom.

"What the hell do you think you're doing?" I hiss.

"I told you, saying good morning."

I cross my arms and stare at him.

He chuckles. "You look really pretty today too, by the way."

"I look the same as I did yesterday and the day before that and every other day I've been here."

"Nah, something's different. You've got a glow or something."

"I do *not* have a *glow* and if I do, it's probably the new moisturizer I'm using."

He shakes his head. "You're something else, you know that?"

"Surely last night showed you that."

"You mean when you came on my fingers?"

My thighs clench at the reminder. "No." I take a few steps toward him and play with a button on his shirt. "When I got you so hard you were seconds away from coming, then I left you with blue balls."

He picks up a strand of my hair and plays with it. "Blue like the girl who caused them," he murmurs. He looks up, drops my hair, and takes a step back. "I don't know, I think blue might be my color."

I scoff.

"I know it definitely looked good on me," he continues, eyes flashing. "I know it definitely *tasted* good on me."

I bite back a moan.

He laughs, making me think I didn't do as good a job as I thought I did of hiding my reaction.

"Anyway, I was waiting for you for another reason as well."

I nod. I *knew* there was some smart-ass—

"I wanted to thank you," he says.

"You *what?*" I shriek.

"I wanted to thank you," he repeats.

"What the ever-loving fuck for?" Is this guy for real? I left him with a raging case of blue balls and he's thanking me?

"In case you haven't realized, and I know sports and school-related activities in general aren't really your thing, but I'm a star athlete here. There are a lot of expectations on me. That's fine, I can handle it. In fact, I thrive on it. So you doing what you did last night not only got my bodily fluids flowing, it also started my competitive juices."

"I, er, you're welcome?"

"I mean, what you did was go above and beyond in order to get me fired up, so I just wanted to let you know I appreciated it."

"Ah, yeah, sure," I reply.

"That's not to say me coming all over your hand and that cute-ass skirt you were wearing wasn't my preferred option, but I can work with this as well."

I swallow hard at the image of his cum being sprayed all over me.

He steps closer to me, and I back up, running into a desk. He picks me up, sitting me on the table, spreading my legs and stepping in between them. "You can tell yourself as much and as many times as you like that you don't want me," he says. "But we both know the truth."

I try to hop off the desk, but he grabs my hands,

sandwiching them under his as he leans over me. The change in angle pushes my boobs out, nipples hard, and brings his pelvis into contact with mine. Even through our uniforms, I can feel he's hard. He grinds against me, and a moan slips out of my mouth.

"You think you bested me last night, but you didn't. Yeah, you took me off guard, I'll give you that, but two can play at this game."

"This isn't a game," I say, trying unsuccessfully to wiggle out of his hold. The only thing I do is rub against him more.

"Oh, but it is, my royal blue. I'll prove to you I'm the only man in this school, hell, this town, state, goddamn fucking country who deserves you and can match you pace for pace, beat for beat."

"And if I don't want to play? Don't want you?" I ask.

"Oh, you do." He smirks. "Want to know how I know?"

"Sure. You've told me everything else, may as well go the whole hog."

"You want this because you're a competitor, just like me. Because you like being pushed, being challenged. It gets you wet. We're one and the same, you and I," he tells me. "You make me work for it, just like I push you to do the same, and guess what? We're one hell of a team."

"I'm not a team player."

"Not yet, baby doll, but you will be."

"What makes you so sure?" I don't know why I ask the question. It's out of my mouth before I even think about what I'm saying.

"Because that's what happens when you meet your match."

"And you're my match?" This guy.... I've got to hand it to him, he's really something.

He lets one of my hands go and cups my cheek. "Yeah, baby doll, I am. Just like you're my royal blue."

"And what, we're just going to run away into the sunset together?"

He shrugs. "I don't know what happens. All I know is we're meant for one another, and I'll prove it to you." With that, he walks out.

HARLEY

I DIDN'T MEAN to say all that shit to Cerulean, it just came out. *She* brought it out of me. I meant every single word I said though. She *is* my match, and we *are* meant for each other. I know it as surely as I know I'm gonna win state with Forest Park and bring home the national championship as well.

Cerulean is... well, she's everything. She's strong, she's fierce, she's protective. She's smart as hell and sexy as fuck and I want her in my life. I've lived all over the world, been with girls from all over the world, but none of them have *ever* made me feel as alive as she does. She gets my blood pumping like no other, not even football. I think I do the same for her. We feed off each other. She pushes, I push more. We're better together. I just have to prove that to her.

There's never been an opponent I've failed to beat, and I'll be damned if Cerulean Tremont, my royal blue, will be the first. She's met her match; she just doesn't realize it yet.

CHAPTER SEVENTEEN

HARLEY MIGHT SAY, and genuinely believe, we're meant to be together, but the only people I'm meant to be with are my sisters. They are my world, and there's nothing I won't do to protect them. Which is why, once again, I spend my afternoon with Vermilion and that fuckwit Alexandrov.

"Again!" Alexandrov barks at my sister. "If you are to apply to the Conservatorium workshop, you must do better."

"What workshop?" I ask, putting down my book.

Vermilion stops playing and turns to face me. "The Conservatorium is holding workshops for potential students next summer."

"What needs to be done for the application?"

"A video recording of an audition piece, a written recommendation, and an application fee."

"And you've already written that recommendation, right, Alexandrov?" I ask, crossing my arms over my chest.

"If your sister can master this piece, then yes, it will be done."

"You want to rephrase that?"

"No." He continues to hold my stare.

"My sister *will* be going to that workshop," I tell him. "Whether it's as your student is up to you."

He huffs and turns back to my sister. "Again. We are wasting time."

AN HOUR LATER, Vermilion's lesson wraps up.

"I want that recommendation emailed to me by the end of next week," I tell Alexandrov as we leave. "And God help you if it's anything but glowing."

"If and when she masters the Mozart, then she will have her recommendation, not before." He slams the door of the studio and walks away.

"When does the application have to be in?" I ask Vermilion, my arm around her shoulders, playing with her braid.

"In a couple of months. Do you really think I'll get in?" she asks.

"I think if you don't then you don't want to go because they obviously don't have an eye for talent."

She giggles, and it warms a part of my black soul I *never* let anyone see.

"He was hard on me today," she adds.

I sigh. "I know, but you handled it well."

"I wish he wasn't my teacher."

"I know, Red, so do I. But he's the best and so are you."

It's her turn to sigh. "I know."

"You know I'd be all for finding a teacher from outside Georgia for you, but Daddy will never go for it." Even though I offered to do all the leg work, just the thought of having to deal with the logistics of moving someone here to teach Vermilion was too much for dear ol' Dad.

"It sucks," she says.

"It does."

I smell him before I see him, that Viktor and Rolf cologne that seems to imbed itself in my nostrils and wind its way to my brain.

"Ladies," Harley says. He's obviously just finished with practice, his gym bag slung over his shoulder, his hair wet and curling slightly at the ends.

I groan while Vermilion shoots him a beautiful smile. I love my sister with all my heart, but this friendship she has with him has got to end. If for no other reason than my inability, even with the help of the pills, to stay focused around him.

"Did you just get done with practice?" she asks, walking out of my embrace and over to Harley's side.

"Yup. You?"

She nods.

"How was it?" he asks.

She shrugs. "It was okay."

"Is your teacher still being an ass?"

"Yeah, but Cerulean's there to make sure he doesn't get too bad."

"I'm sure she does," he says, shooting me a smile over Vermilion's head.

I roll my eyes and continue to walk toward the parking lot.

"You ready for the game tomorrow?" Vermilion asks.

"Sure am. Are you gonna be there?"

"Ummmm," she says. "Probably not."

"How come?"

"It's, ah, not really our thing."

"But is it *your* thing?" he asks.

"I don't know."

Their footsteps stop. "I know you and your sisters are close, that's great, but it doesn't mean that you have to do what they do, like what they like."

He's right, but fuck me, I do *not* want to go to a football game. Neither will Magenta. Knowing Indigo, she'd be up for it, but will probably sneak away after a few minutes to hook up with some random guy under the bleachers. And yes, Vermilion is old enough to go by herself, or even with that friend of hers, but I'm a control freak and don't want to deliver my sister into an environment I know nothing about. Sue me.

"Kingsley has been bugging me to," she concedes.

"I'm glad you guys are friends," he says, smiling.

"Me too. She's a lot of fun, even if she is a bit... out there."

Harley laughs, the sound going straight between my legs. It's husky and rough, but warming at the same time. Ugh, I need to get out of here. I turn to leave, but his voice stops me.

"And what about you, royal blue? Are you wanting to come to our game?"

I whirl on him. "One, *don't* call me that, and two, if I want to go to the game, I'll go. I don't need to be goaded into it."

"So you're going then?" He smirks, and I'd love nothing more than to slap it off his beautiful face. Or kiss it off. No, definitely slap.

"I'll be wherever the hell I want to be tomorrow night," I say before walking away.

. . .

LET it never be said I won't do anything for my sisters. Climbing up the bleachers, Vermilion, Kingsley, Indigo, and I find our seats.

"Who would've thought there were so many good-looking guys here?" Indigo says, looking around.

"If you ditch me, I will melt your favorite lipstick," I threaten.

She laughs, and the sound makes every guy in a ten-yard radius stop and stare at her. "Oh, baby sis, I've got the manufacturer on speed dial. So melt all you like, it won't make a difference."

"I hate you," I hiss.

In response, she leans over and kisses my cheek. "Love you too, C."

I roll my eyes as the team runs out—to warm up, I assume. I don't know, I've never been to one of these stupid things before. "I can*not* believe I'm here," I groan.

"And I can't believe I've never been here before. Those boys are cut!"

"Right?" Kingsley agrees.

I shoot her a look, and she sits back in her seat.

"Can you not?" I ask my eldest sister.

"But it's *so* much fun to rile you up, C." She turns to me and giggles again. "And put away your 'I'm Cerulean Tremont, all bow to me and worship at my feet' look, it doesn't work on me."

It's my turn to sit back in my seat.

"This is fun," she says after a while.

"Are you feeling all right?" I go to feel her forehead but she smacks my hand away.

"Of course I am. God, when did you get so uptight? You need to get laid, girl."

"I've always been like this, and I do *not* need to get laid."

"How are things between you and Captain Dick, anyway?"

Just then the crowd claps and cheers as the team runs off the field.

"There are no 'things' with me and Captain Dick," I tell her.

"Are you sure? 'Cause from where I stand, y'all look pretty cozy."

"No. Nope. No way. There are no things, we don't look fucking cozy, and I do *not* need to get laid," I insist.

"In that case," she says, inspecting her nails. "Why not? He's hot, you're hot. Go post genetically blessed selfies on Instagram."

"You know why that's not a good idea," I remind her.

"Because of Magenta?" she asks. "Look, I love the girl and I know she's been through hell and back, but that was her choice. Why should we be bound by her experience? Not every guy is the same as Beckett."

"She was heartbroken, Ind. I thought you of all people would be sympathetic to that."

"Sympathetic? Yes. Let it dictate my life? No." She looks around, catching the eye of a guy, I'd say in his late twenties, early thirties, blond hair, blue eyes, built like a tank. He smiles at her and she smiles back. "Now if you'll excuse me, I'll prove that right now."

She gets up, the guy eagerly following her as she makes her way down the bleachers.

"You owe me a hundred bucks," I tell Vermilion as she and Kingsley giggle.

I know Indigo has a point, that I can't let one person's single bad experience dictate my life, but Beckett really did a number on Magenta. I can't, and won't, ever forget the pain and hurt she went through because of him. Besides, isn't it natural to avoid things that aren't good for you? Sure, stuff like chocolate or fried foods might taste good, but eat too much of them and you get fat, which then leads to all sorts of health problems.

Confession? I wish I was as fearless as Indigo. Her "I don't give a fuck" attitude seems so freeing. Out of all of us she seems the most... content, I guess you could say. Not that we're *un*happy with our lives, it's just hard with responsibilities and whatnot. And yeah, my responsibilities may all be superficial and idiotic, but keeping Forest Park in line isn't stupid, at least not to me.

I don't want to be worshipped and adored; I'll leave that to Captain Dick. The only thing I want is a place free from teenage stupidity and a misplaced sense of importance. I shudder to think what the school would be like if someone like Trinity Barnes, who by the way is majorly slutting it up on the sidelines in her role as cheerleader, was in control.

ONCE AGAIN THE team runs out, tearing through a paper banner the cheerleaders no doubt spent hours upon hours creating.

The game starts, and although I don't really have a clue what's happening, I can tell Harley's in control. He marches the offense down the field, gaining yard after yard. Even I can admit it's impressive, the surrounding voices echoing my thoughts.

This time when the ball is snapped, I know that much, and Harley drops back, the guys in front of him form a semicircle around him while TK and another guy sprint down the field. Just as it looks like the defense is about to break through and get to him, Harley lets the ball fly. I swear the whole stadium holds its breath until the ball is safely in TK's hands and he runs it in for a touchdown.

"Ho-ly shiiiiiiiiiiit," one guy says, behind me. "That musta been about fifty yards."

"Sixty," Kingsley corrects. "He was on our thirty-five and TK ran it five."

The guy just shakes his head. "Kid's got an arm on him. State's a certainty."

THE GAME CONTINUES MUCH how it started, with Forest Park running out fifty-four to three winners. The crowd is buzzing as people make their way down the bleachers and to their cars.

"Come on," Kingsley says, grabbing Vermilion's hand and mine.

"And just where do you think you're taking me?" I ask as she shoves her way through the crowd.

"To wait outside the locker room, of course."

"And why am I doing that?"

"So we can congratulate Harley on, like, the best game ever."

"Again, why am *I* doing that?" I repeat.

She stops and gives me a no-nonsense glare. "Because your sister wants to."

I look to Vermilion. Her eyes are bright with an excitement I haven't seen in a long time, a flush on her cheeks.

I sigh and motion for Kingsley to lead the way. The crowd around the locker room door is almost as thick as that leaving the stadium, except this one is all female, all of them in varying stages of undress.

"This is pathetic," I mutter as we stand around. "You and you." I point to two girls I've never seen before and who can't be more than thirteen. They're dressed in bandeau tops and booty shorts, hair curled and makeup on point. "How old are you?"

"Old enough," one of them says, her hand on her hip, smacking her gum.

"For what? A statutory rape charge? Put some clothes on, take that makeup off, go home, and come back when you're sixteen." I know TK likes them young, the younger and dumber the better, but this is too low, even for him. Or maybe it's not, but I'll die before I let these girls lose their innocence to a sleaze like TK.

"Ugh," they say and look around for support, but get none.

"If I see you around here again, I'll call your parents and tell them y'all are pregnant," I threaten.

"You can't do that!" one of them, the one not obnoxiously chewing gum, says.

"Try me."

"Who the fuck do you think you are?" the gum chewer asks.

"Cerulean Tremont." They pale, even underneath all the layers of cosmetics they've got on. I nod. "That's right, now get out of here before I completely ruin your high school career before you even start it."

They turn and all but run to the parking lot.

"That was awesome," Kingsley says.

Just as the two run past the door, TK exits.

"Hey! Where are y'all going?" he asks.

Like the good girls they are, they don't stop to answer. He watches them until they've disappeared from sight, then turns back to the assembled masses, his eyes landing on me.

"Of course you're here," he says. "I better not have any problems gettin' pussy tonight."

"The fact that you'd have to stoop so low to find someone willing to sleep with you speaks volumes. But then again, they don't know any better, do they?"

TK and I have a... complicated relationship, I guess you could say, but that doesn't mean I'm willing to let him take advantage of girls who don't know any better. He scowls, while I arch an eyebrow and cross my arms. If he wants to cross me, then let the games begin.

HARLEY

CHAPTER EIGHTEEN

AFTER THE GAME, in the locker room, everyone is on a high. Savannah Public, our opponents tonight, are apparently one of our biggest rivals, so putting them to the sword like we did is a pretty big deal.

"Ho ho!" TK crows as he comes up to me. "That was some sa-weet passing tonight, brother."

"That was some sweet receiving," I counter.

He pretends to brush invisible dust off his shoulders. "Well, you know."

I shove him playfully.

"We going to get some hot young pussy tonight?" he asks.

"Young?" I ask, laughing. "We're eighteen, I'd hardly call that over the hill."

"Nah, but the girls are. They've been spreading their legs for years now. They're all stretched out and shit."

"That is one of the most fucked-up things I've ever heard, man."

He just shrugs. "I mean, the older girls are all right, they're total pill fiends, which makes them crazy as fuck in bed. But the younger ones, they need pills of a different kind. You know how it is. They pretend like they're not desperate for it, make you work your ass off to get them so you give 'em something to loosen them up a little. It's not like they don't know what's going down, but man, it gets me goin' just thinking about it. A girl lying there all pliant and shit, just waiting for you...."

I look at my wide receiver. He may have the safest hands in Georgia, but off the field? He's not right.

"That's, ah, not my scene," I tell him. "Plus, with all the hoops we have to jump through to play, do you really think that's the best idea? What if someone takes a photo and posts it online? There goes your hope of any colleges picking you up, and you can definitely kiss the NFL goodbye."

It's his turn to shove me. "It's all good, QB. You worry too much."

"And maybe you don't worry enough," I say under my breath as he walks away.

I SHOWER AND CHANGE, then head out, making sure I tell all the guys how much I appreciate their hard work tonight. Does that make me a suck up? Yes, but it also makes them feel appreciated, and guys who feel appreciated work harder for the team and for me.

When I get out of the locker room, I find Cerulean and TK having a stare down of epic proportions.

There are squeals from some of the girls waiting when I appear, but they do nothing to break the deadlock between my receiver and my royal blue.

Bursting between them, I sling an arm around

Cerulean and one around Vermilion, who is standing next to her.

"You came," I say.

She sends a final glare at TK before turning it on me and trying to wiggle out of my hold.

"Uh, yeah."

"Hmm, interesting." As I talk, I turn us and start walking toward the parking lot. I'm not sure what TK's deal is, or what Cerulean's deal with TK is, but I've had my fill of him today. Plus, his adrenaline is probably still pumping, and that coming up against Cerulean's fire is a recipe for disaster.

"Let me get this straight. You don't like me, you don't like football, but yet here you are, waiting for me after a football game?"

"Vermilion and Kingsley wanted to come," she replies almost robotically. I've got to admit; I'm liking this more *cooperative* side of my royal blue.

"I'm sure they did." I turn to the girls. "Thanks for your support, ladies. I appreciate it."

They both giggle.

"You were awesome tonight," Kingsley says.

"Well, thank you. It was great to start the season off with a W."

As I'm talking, Cerulean tries once again to slip out of my grasp.

"Uh-uh," I tell her, pulling her back to me. "We've discussed why my number-one supporters are here, but nowhere in that sentence did it explain why *you,* my royal blue, are here."

"Yeah, *royal blue* why are you here?" Vermillion asks, a twinkle in her eye.

Cerulean shoots her a look. "Whose side are you on?" she asks.

In response Vermilion giggles.

"Aw, don't be like that," I tell my girl. She rolls her eyes but doesn't say anything else.

"*There* you are," Indigo says, coming up to us, adjusting her tank top and jeans. "I've been looking everywhere for you." She looks up, a smile on her face. "I should've known to head straight to the locker room and our star QB."

"Ugh," Cerulean says, once again trying to escape my hold. This time I let her. "I don't care what the rest of y'all do, but I'm going home. If anyone cares to come with me, I'm leaving now."

"Thanks for your support," I call as she stomps away from us, flipping me the bird.

I chuckle as Indigo shakes her head. "Do you have a death wish?" she asks.

"Not particularly, but your sister is just so much fun to rile up."

"Boy, you are gonna get it one of these days."

"As long as your sister is the one who's bringing it, I'm more than fine with that."

"Is that so?" She arches an eyebrow.

I shrug.

"He calls her royal blue," Vermilion supplies.

Indigo's eyes open wider. "Does he now?"

"Anyway," I say, attempting to change the subject. "There's a party tomorrow night at one of the clubs. You guys should come."

"And I suppose Cerulean is included in this invitation?" Indigo asks.

"Of course. Magenta too."

"And what's the motive behind this invite? What are you hoping to get out of this? 'Cause I feel I've got to tell you, if you're hoping to get closer to Cerulean, to see if alcohol will loosen her up a bit, it won't."

"I—"

"Don't get me wrong," she continues, cutting me off. "You're a nice guy and my sister tolerates you, which is *way* more than she does for any of the other losers in this shithole of a school, but no one is getting through that wall of hers. It's a yard wide and a mile tall. Not even you, Mr. Fantastic QB, are getting through that."

"So I'm supposed to give up and let her go through life alone? Not talking to anyone, not connecting to anyone?"

"She's not alone," she says as Cerulean pulls up beside us. "She has us."

With that, the girls get in and drive off, leaving me to think over Indigo's words.

I heard what she said, but I also know what I feel, and I *felt* Cerulean coming on my fingers. I *felt* her opening up to me. Indigo might say it's impossible, but she's never seen a competitor like me. I *will* win Cerulean over.

Cerulean

CHAPTER NINETEEN

THE RIDE back to our house is silent, and I know it's not because no one has anything to say. It's so Indigo can pick her moment. Well, fuck that.

"Just say it," I tell her.

"Say what?"

"Whatever smart-ass comment you have about me and Harley."

"I didn't know there *was* a you and Harley."

"There isn't, but I know you think there is, so just say whatever you're going to say and get it over with."

"I like him," she says, which is in no way what I was expecting her to come out with.

"You what?" I ask.

She shrugs. "I like him. As a person, I mean. He seems... different, not at all like the other fuckheads around here."

"I like him too," Vermilion says. "And he *is* different."

"He's awesome," Kingsley adds.

"You're not involved in this conversation," I snap at her.

"And you're an idiot for not acknowledging how awesome Harley is," she snaps back.

I pull into our driveway and park in my spot next to Indigo's convertible. "Well, if y'all like him so much, y'all can go after him."

"He doesn't want any of us," Indigo says, opening the door and hopping out. "He wants you." She shuts the door after dropping that truth bomb, then opens it again. "Oh, there's a party at one of the clubs in town tomorrow night. I get the feeling he'd *very* much like it if you were in attendance." She shuts the door again and walks into the house, Kingsley and Vermilion following her.

Fuck my life.

AS I GET ready to go to this stupid party, I'm still not clear on *why* I'm going.

"Don't wear that," Indigo says as she comes into my room and straight to my closet. She flips through the hangers until she finds a light blue silk cami. "Wear this."

"It's practically lingerie, Indigo," I tell her, but change anyway.

"Uh-huh, and when Harley sees you in it, he'll lose his mind."

"I don't want him to lose his mind," I mutter.

"No? Then why are you going?" she asks.

I flop on my bed. "I have no idea."

She sits next to me. "Tell me honestly, do you like him?"

I blow out a breath. "I don't want to."

"But you do." It's not a question.

"Maybe. I don't know. He's just always there, you know? It's like I can't escape him."

She nods. "He's playing it well."

"I don't *want* him to play it well. I just want to be left alone."

"I know it may seem like it but letting someone in isn't a weakness. *Wanting* to let someone in isn't a weakness."

"I know that, it's just...."

"We've been so used to doing everything on our own. Mom's off plotting world domination, and Daddy's never here and if he is, he doesn't give a shit anyway."

"Yeah." I sigh.

"From what I've seen, Harley's a good guy," she adds.

"No, I know that. He's been great with Vermilion. I just.... Do I even want a boyfriend?" I ask and wonder just how the fuck I got here.

"Fuck buddy?" Indigo suggests. I shove her and she laughs. "Not all relationships have to be romantic."

"They can also be more than just sex," I counter.

"They can, but why bother with all that frou-frou shit when you can get straight to the good stuff?"

I laugh, and she joins me.

"Are you coming tonight?" I ask.

"Oh, I'll be coming, it just won't be at the party."

"Who's the lucky guy?"

"Joe, the guy from the game. As thick as a board but he does this thing with his tongue that made my eyes roll back in my head."

She laughs as I shove her again, sending her off the side of my bed.

"You're worthy of love, Cerulean," she tells me as she gets up.

"So are you."

She smiles, but it doesn't reach her eyes. "Maybe one day I'll find that's true."

"Hey," I say as she reaches my door. "You know you always have us, right?"

"Of course, and y'all will always have me."

"We bow to no one, remember that," I remind her.

She nods and walks out.

WALKING into the club where the party is being held, I feel... nothing. High school and everything that comes with it are a necessary evil for me, a means to an end. I have no interest in really being here, but since I have to be, I'll take what's offered and do what I can to ensure my experience is as pleasant as possible. If that means taking *some* of what Harley St. James is offering, then so be it. Life's meant to be fun, right? And maybe Indigo is right and there is fun to be had.

Looking around, I see girls grind on guys, guys feel up girls, drinks being drunk by the gallon, and yup, I check a few of the booths lining the perimeter of the club, drugs are being taken. I'd caution against it, but while I'm a lot of things, a hypocrite isn't one of them. While I prefer my pharmaceuticals to give me an academic edge, I know others prefer a more casual high.

I nod to Kingsley and Vermilion as they stand with a group of freshmen girls, some guys standing nearby obviously trying to work up the courage to approach them.

I chuckle as one finally does, walking up to Vermilion. Her eyes widen when he taps her on the shoulder, mouth dropping open. He says something to her, and she shakes her head while Kingsley pushes her toward him. With a bit more pleading, he takes hold of her hand and brings her onto the dance floor.

"They look good together," a voice in my ear says, his cologne washing over me.

I nod, turning to face him. "They do. What?" I ask as he raises his eyebrows.

"I thought you'd say something nasty about how he's not good enough for her, for sure."

I shrug. "He may not be, but she deserves to have a little fun. Right now it's harmless, but if he does something to her and hurts her, then I'll cut his dick off."

Harley chuckles. "There's the protective sibling I know."

"She's my little sister, I'm going to do everything I can to shield her from harm."

"And does that leave you with any time to enjoy yourself?"

I shrug again, a small smile playing at the corners of my mouth. "Maybe. Depends on who's asking."

He looks around. "At the moment, it looks like I'm the only one." He holds his hand out.

"Well, then." I place my hand in his and let him lead me out onto the dance floor, not too far away from Vermilion and her suitor.

It shouldn't surprise me that Harley's a good dancer, but it does. He spins me so my back is to his front, his hips flush against me.

"First a football game, now you're at a football party. Aren't you turning into quite the jersey chaser, royal blue?" he says right in my ear.

I scoff. "Hardly. Vermilion had a tough lesson the other day, and I wanted to take her mind off things. She had mentioned the game, so I thought, why not?"

"She had a tough lesson?" he asks. "Was she all right?"

His concern for Vermilion makes it hard, *really* hard for me to hate him. "She's fine. I just wish there was someone else we could take her to. Alexandrov.... He's the best, but he's a fucking horrible person. It takes all I've got to keep him on track."

"You're like a lioness protecting her cub," he says.

"She's been through a lot already in her life. If I can ease a bit of it, then I've done my job as her older sister."

He swings me around so I'm facing him and takes my face in his hands. "You're doing fine. Look at her." He turns my head to where Vermilion is laughing and dancing, now surrounded by a large group. "I don't know what's gone on with her and I'm not going to ask, but I know it has to be something deep, something major. She's a great kid, and I have no doubt she'll go far. Alexandrov will get his."

"I wish I could be so sure," I tell him.

He cocks his head to the side, eyes exploring.

"What?" I ask.

"That's the first time I've ever seen you express doubt."

"Don't get used to it," I retort and try to look away, but he grabs my chin and directs my face back to his.

"I like it," he says. "Not because you're showing a weakness, which it's not," he adds, preempting my comeback. "But because it tells me there is something underneath that armor. Sure, I know you have a great sense of protectiveness over your sisters, but sometimes I wonder if you ever stop to think about *you*?"

"Me, them, it's *all* I think about. I think about what I need to do to make their lives easier, what I can do to make school easier, not just for them but for everyone. I just want...." I stop and consider.

"What? What do you want, royal blue?"

I shake my head. "It doesn't matter."

"I disagree. Now tell me, what do you want?"

I look up into his big, brown eyes. He lowers his head, eyes focused on my lips. I lick my own, knowing he's going to kiss me and, God help me, I think I want it too. Our lips are almost touching—

"Cerulean!"

My head snaps to the side, Vermilion's standing there, wringing her hands, brow creased. "What is it? What's wrong?" I ask.

"We need help."

HARLEY

CHAPTER TWENTY

WHEN I WALK into the club, Cerulean is the first person I see. It's like my eyes automatically search her out without me even realizing. She stands off to the side, oblivious to the fact everyone's eyes are on her, taking their cues from her. People might bitch about her, call her that and worse, but they also respect her. She has a quiet strength that resonates from her. She doesn't have to yell and scream and carry on, she can simply comment on something and her judgment is made. She's incredible.

The crowd parts as she moves through the club, and again, it's something she's oblivious to.

Vermilion's off to the side with a group of friends, and Cerulean smiles as she passes. It's that reaction to seeing her sister that gets me to approach.

Pulling her out onto the dance floor, I feel like a god, and it has nothing to do with what she is to the people around us—their leader, their queen, their *sovereign*—but the fact she's allowing *me* to dance with her. I try for small talk but, like everything with us, things go awry. It's when I'm an inch from pressing my lips against hers, an inch from sliding my tongue in her mouth to tangle with hers, that we're interrupted.

Vermilion appears beside us.

"We need help," she tells us.

"Help? With what?" Cerulean demands.

Vermilion grabs both of our hands and drags us towards the bathrooms. "Karlie was dancing with us when she started acting weird. None of us are drinking, so we got worried and took her to the bathroom. We barely managed to get her inside before she passed out."

We open the door. A girl, Karlie, I presume, is on the floor, her head in Kingsley's lap. "She just passed out," she says, looking up at me. Cerulean shoos all the girls hovering over Karlie out.

"Is she breathing?" I ask as Cerulean kneels down to check.

She nods. "Her heartbeat feels a little fast, though."

"Did she take anything?" I ask the freshmen.

They both shake their heads. "We were only drinking Cokes too. She was talking to TK, but he wouldn't do anything, would he?"

"Did you see him mess with her drink?" Cerulean asks. "Or anyone else?"

They both shake their heads.

"You think someone slipped something in her drink?" I ask. What I really want to ask is if she thinks TK did this, but I don't want to go pointing fingers, especially not without any evidence.

She shrugs. "If the girls said she didn't willingly take anything, and she wasn't drinking, her breath doesn't smell like alcohol, then what else can it be?"

"Does she have any medical problems?" I ask.

"I don't think so," Kingsley says. "She's not wearing one of those medical bracelets. She would if something is wrong with her, right?" Her voice is high and tight, her eyes wide.

I squeeze her hand. "I'm sure she would." I lean over and get my arms behind Karlie's back and under her legs.

"What are you doing?" Vermilion asks.

"We're going to get her out of here and to the hospital. If she has been drugged, they can run a test and see. If not, then that's definitely where she needs to be." I get to my feet; the girl in my arms doesn't stir.

"Can someone get the door? Then we just need to figure out how to get her out of here without the whole school seeing her."

"Take a right out of here, instead of left," Cerulean says.

I arch an eyebrow.

She shrugs. "What? A girl's gotta have an escape plan," she tells me.

"I thought you'd rather bulldoze your way through than slip out the side door."

She shrugs again and holds open the bathroom door for me.

I take a right, head down the hall, and push through a door that leads us to the alley beside the club. Luckily TK got the football team parking in the lot behind the club. I stop beside my car.

"My keys are in my left pocket; can someone get them for me?"

"And how exactly are you going to fit everybody?" Cerulean asks, eyeing my Mustang.

"Everybody?"

"You seriously didn't think we'd leave you to deal with this by yourself, did you?" she asks.

"Ah...."

She turns and heads to a silver BMW SUV and unlocks it. She opens the back door, folding down the back seats. "You two get in here. We'll lie Karlie down in front of you. Harley, you stay with her in case anything happens. What's her last name?" she asks her sister.

"Jamieson," Vermilion replies as, like the good subjects we are, we snap to and follow our sovereign's orders.

As I pass her to get in the car, I press a kiss to her cheek.

"What was that for?" she asks.

I shrug. "Because I can, because we got interrupted before, because you're here helping this poor girl. Take your pick." If it were anyone else, I'd swear they were blushing, but this is Cerulean Tremont we're talking about, so it *must* be a trick of the light.

I get in the car, Karlie in my lap, Cerulean shutting the door after me.

THE RIDE to the hospital is quick but silent. Behind me, Kingsley and Vermilion huddle together, holding hands like their lives depend on it. Up front, Cerulean is cool, calm, and focused. If I didn't have a girl who's probably been drugged on my lap, I'd find that a total turn-on. I'd also be pissed as fuck we were interrupted earlier, but only a tool curses some girl needing help over finally getting his lips on the woman of his dreams. And she is. Cerulean, I mean. She *is* the woman of my dreams. I'm not too proud to admit it, and why should I be? Who are all these guys who run around thinking it's weak to admit their feelings? Shit, if Cerulean would let me, when we finally stop dancing around each other, I'd shout from the rooftops that she's my girl. *That's* what a real man does. He's man enough to admit his feelings and not be afraid to show them.

The car turns sharply, and I realize we've pulled up to the front of the ER. Cerulean jumps out to open my door, the girls in the back right behind me.

"You take her in. I'll park and be there in a minute," Cerulean tells me before getting back in the vehicle and driving away.

When I walk in, Karlie in my arms, there's a flurry of activity.

"We think someone slipped something in her drink," I tell the doc as I place her on the gurney. "She was only drinking soda and didn't take anything willingly," I continue.

He nods. "We'll run some tests. She's in good hands," he tells me before following her back into the treatment area.

The three of us take seats in the waiting room.

"Do you think she'll be okay?" Vermilion asks.

"You heard the doc," I tell her. "She's in good hands, and y'all did the right thing by coming to get us." I get a small smile when I say "y'all."

She rests her head on my shoulder. "I'm sorry I interrupted you and Cerulean though."

I chuckle. "It's all good."

"Is it really?" Kingsley asks.

"Guess it's got to be," I reply.

"Do you like my sister?" Vermilion asks.

I nod. "I do. She's a ballbuster, and she's fierce and hot as fuck." That gets giggles from both girls.

"I think she likes you too."

"I think she's *getting* there," I counter.

"Trust me, if Cerulean didn't like you, there's no way she'd let you get as close to kissing her as you did."

I laugh. "Thanks for the vote of confidence."

"Just remember me when y'all move away and get engaged and married and start having babies," she says sleepily.

"I thought you would move when your sisters did?" I ask.

She shrugs. "They'll have their own lives. I don't want to impose."

Just then Cerulean comes through the doors. "How is everything?" she asks.

I go to shrug but realize Vermilion's asleep on my shoulder, Kingsley on hers. "They took her back but didn't say much, just that she was in good hands."

"Someone should call her parents," she says, taking a seat on the other side of me.

"How would we even know where to look? Are phone books even a thing anymore?"

"We could always call your dad, ask him to look up her record," she says, scrolling through her phone.

"I'd rather knock on every door in this town to find her parents."

She looks up from the screen. "Really?"

I scratch the back of my neck. "My father and I don't, um, really get on," I tell her.

"Well, there's something I didn't see coming."

"Cary St. James had very specific career goals in mind for his son. Throwing a football around a field was not one of them."

"So he doesn't support you?" she asks, fingers flying over her screen now.

"In private? No. In public? He's the model of a supportive parent and of his school."

"And your mom?"

I smile. "My mom could give you a run for your money in the overprotective stakes."

She arches an eyebrow and holds her phone to her ear.

"What are you doing?" I ask.

"Calling Karlie's parents."

"How?"

"Have you forgotten who I am?" She asks before turning her attention to the voice on the other end of the phone. "Mrs. Jamieson?" she asks. "My name is Cerulean Tremont. My sister Vermilion is friends with Karlie. I don't want to alarm you but she was at a party tonight. We think her drink may have been spiked."

"No, ma'am," she says, "she wasn't drinking alcohol."

Mrs. Jamieson says something else before Cerulean continues. "Anyway, she passed out, so we brought her to Savannah General to get her checked out."

The voice on the other end is frantic.

"They haven't told us anything yet, I think they're still evaluating her, but yes, getting down here would be a good idea."

There's more back and forth before she ends the call.

"Tell me," I say when she puts the phone away. "Do you have *every* Forest Park student's details or just those who are friends with your sister?"

She chuckles. "Neither. I have a contact within the staff, and they get me any info I might need."

"Sometimes, just sometimes, you really impress me, royal blue."

"Oh, yeah?" she asks, leaning closer to me.

I nod. "Oh, yeah."

Again our mouths are only inches apart—

"Harley?"

I groan and drop my head to Cerulean's shoulder.

"Harley," my mom says, hurrying towards us. "Dr. Garcia thought that was you. Did you bring in a girl who's been drugged?"

I nod and look up at my mother. The light brown hair she passed down to me is held back by a blue headband, her makeup impeccable, and she's wearing horrible apricot scrubs. "I forgot you were on call tonight," I say.

"You forgot?" Mom and Cerulean say at the same time.

My mom looks to Cerulean, then to Vermilion asleep on my shoulder. "You always did do well with the girls."

I groan and cover my face with a hand.

"Heather St. James," she says, I assume to Cerulean.

"Cerulean Tremont."

"So you and my son are...."

"Just friends, Mom, Jesus."

"Right."

"I'm sorry," Cerulean says. "But did you say someone drugged Karlie?"

"Are you the girl's family?" Mom asks.

"They're on their way," Cerulean tells her. "My sister," she gestures to Vermilion, "is friends with her and came and got us when she passed out. Is she okay?"

"All I can tell you is that she's in a stable condition and we expect her to make a full recovery."

"So she's okay?" I ask.

Mom nods. "She will be."

I blow out a breath.

"Now, do you want to tell me how you forgot your mother is on staff at this hospital and about your failure to inform her of your presence here?" She crosses her arms over chest and taps her foot. Cerulean does the same.

"It's not like *I'm* the one being admitted. I'm just doing a good deed and helping a friend of a friend."

"How do you forget your mom's on staff at this hospital?" Cerulean asks.

"Ah," I say, scratching the back of my neck again. "We're new here?"

Both Mom and Cerulean shake their heads. The similarities between the two really are disconcerting. Thankfully, the automatic doors whoosh open and two people hurry in, the woman an older, heavily operated on version of Karlie.

"I think Karlie's parents are here." I nod to where they stand at the reception desk.

Mom goes over to update them while Cerulean shakes her head again.

"What?" I ask.

"Really? Forgetting your mom works here?"

"Hey! We've lived in a lot of places and she's worked in a lot of hospitals. Sooner or later they all get jumbled. Plus, she works weird shifts. How am I supposed to know when she's working?"

"You're an idiot."

"Yeah, but you like me anyway." I shoot her a cheesy grin and get a small one back.

I'll take that as a win any day.

Cerulean

CHAPTER TWENTY-ONE

MONDAY MORNING I'm waiting for TK at his locker.

"Need a refill already? You really should—"

He stops talking when I slam him against his locker. You know, I shouldn't be able to do that to big, strong football players. I guess there's something to be said for taking people off guard.

"What the fuck?" he wheezes.

"Karlie Jamieson," I say.

"Nice rack, legs for days, freeeeeeeshman I *think*, if memory serves me correctly."

"You can add drink spike victim to that list," I tell him.

"So?"

"Her friends say she was talking to you on Saturday. Tell me you had nothing to do with it." We went back to the club yesterday to try to get hold of the security footage but were told that because of the nature of the event, the age of the patrons, and the various activities taking place in the venue, the security cameras were turned off. As if I believed that bag of bullshit. But the manager wouldn't budge, no matter how much I offered in order to change his mind.

"I had nothing to do with it," he parrots, and I relax my hold. "Although—"

I slam him up against the lockers again. He holds his hands up. "Relax. Jesus. Fuck, girl, uptight much?"

"I know you," I spit. "I know what you do, how you operate, but never did I *ever* think you'd stoop this low."

"I just told you it wasn't me," he says.

"Maybe I don't believe you. Maybe I think this is *exactly* the sort of thing you'd do if you were desperate." I look to his pants. "Having problems getting him working?" I ask.

In a blink, our positions have been reversed, my back now pressing against the bank of lockers. He's a freaking wide receiver; of course he was only humoring me before.

"Shut your mouth, bitch."

I laugh. "What would all those jersey chasers say if they knew the great TK Thomas can't get it up? Is that why you drugged Karlie? Less pressure to perform? Plus, she would've been passed out, she wouldn't know how long it took for you to get hard or that you couldn't stay that way."

He shoves me again, a lock digging into my back, but I don't care. TK's a coward; he prefers subtle methods to get his prey, not out-and-out intimidation.

"You know, there are pills you can take to help with your... problem. I would've thought with your pharmaceutical connections that wouldn't be *hard* at all." TK's parents own a pharmaceutical company, hence the amazing drug hookup he has. Anything he wants, he can get straight from the source.

"Like you can talk," he says, bits of spit flying all over the place. "How's your studying going, Cerulean? Are you able to concentrate? Stay awake, alert enough to get all your work done?"

"You think you have something on me—" I say but he cuts me off.

"I *know* I have something on you, and you know it too. Who sells you those pills, huh? Not very smart to threaten your dealer now, is it, *royal blue*?"

My eyes snap to his at the use of Harley's nickname for me.

He chuckles. "Oh yeah, I know *all* about you two, although it'd be hard not to. You play a good game, but him? Guy's got *no* game whatsoever."

"Who gives a shit about what is or isn't happening between me and Harley?" I say.

"No one, really," TK says, waving his hand. "But I know you. I've known you since kindergarten, and I know how much you'd hate for your identity to be taken over by a guy. Add to that the drama that would be sure to ensue once your little... dependency is exposed, and what's left of little Cerulean Tremont then?"

"And let me guess, all of that gossip is just going to magically start spreading if I try to do anything to stop you?"

He smiles and pats my cheek. "See? You don't need Ritalin after all."

"My need for Ritalin has nothing to do with my intelligence, fuckhead."

"Don't you have pre-acceptance to some fancy school in D.C.?" he asks.

"The Carver Institute," I grit out.

"That's it. Just what would they think if one of their star recruits was found to be abusing prescription pills?"

"And what would colleges or even NFL teams say if one of their highly ranked targets was lost in a plague of date rapes?" I counter.

"Plague is going a bit far, isn't it?" he asks.

"Are you telling me that if I ask around, Karlie will have been the only one this has happened to recently?"

He stares at me and I stare back.

"I lose Carver, I can go somewhere else," I tell him, hoping he doesn't hear the catch in my voice. "It gets out you're drugging girls? No one *ever* is going to touch you. You'll be lucky if your mama and daddy can keep you out of jail."

He literally growls in response.

"You be a good boy, take your magic blue pills, get girls the old-fashioned way, and I won't let *your* secret slip. In return, you keep my business private. Do we have a deal?"

"*Fine.*"

It's my turn to pat his cheek now. "There's a good boy, run along now."

He steps back, releasing me. I step around him, head held high. A little further down the hall, Harley is standing with a bunch of his teammates. I give him a small smile as I walk past him. His brows are furrowed, the corners of his mouth turned down, but that changes when he sees me. I nod to him, and he shoots me what would usually be a panty-melting smile. My panties haven't melted but they *might* be just the slightest bit damp. The guys hoot and holler, and I can't help but laugh and shake my head. I wouldn't normally be this open with a guy at school— in fact, I wouldn't normally be with *any* guy in school —but Harley's different. I don't know what it is about him. Maybe it's the fact we both know this place is only a means to an end, but there's something there.

Yes, I've hooked up in the past, dated a college guy or two, but never for long. TK might be seven kinds of shady with an erectile dysfunction problem, but he was right about something. I *would* hate for my identity to be taken over by a guy. I'd hate for my position at this school to be watered down because of it. I'd hate for my achievements to be discounted because of it.

I keep my smile in place until I get to the bath-room. My hands are shaking, sweat on my brow as I close the lid of the toilet and take a seat.

I can't have everything I worked for go down the drain. I've put in too much work, too much effort for it all to go to waste.

What would everyone think if it all went to hell? What would my mother think? She trusted me to get shit done, and I have so far.

I *will* live up to her expectations. I'm Cerulean Tremont, and I bow to no one.

HARLEY

SHE TRIES to hide it as she ducks into the bathroom, but something is eating at my royal blue, worrying her. Something isn't right.

I excuse myself from the guys, more hoots and hollers coming my way, and wait for her outside the bathroom. She appears several minutes later.

"Hey," I say, bending down to kiss her cheek.

She stiffens underneath my lips.

"Are you okay?" I pull back to look her in her jade green eyes.

"I'm fine," she replies, the smile she pastes on not meeting her eyes.

"Uh-huh, sure."

She huffs, popping her hand on hip. "What do you want, Harley?"

"I want to know what's going on," I say, ignoring how good my name sounds coming out of her mouth. "I also really want to know what's going on between you and TK. Y'all looked *awfully* chummy."

"Are you jealous?" she asks.

"What?" I rear back. "Of course not."

"Good, because TK Thomas is the least of your worries."

I take a step closer to her and cup her cheek. "I saw the look on your face just before you went in there. Something's wrong. Tell me, and maybe I can fix it. We can fix it together."

"Are you going to be my knight in shining armor?" she asks, looking up at me, her eyes bright.

"I'll be whatever you need me to be if you just tell me what's wrong."

She opens her mouth just as the bell goes. "We better get to class," she says and moves around me.

"Hey," I say, getting her attention once again. "I promise. Whatever it is isn't as bad as you think."

She gives me a smile that looks almost... sad. "Maybe. Maybe not."

THE DAY PASSES SLOWLY until I can get to Cerulean in Media Studies. Unfortunately, one might say deliberately, she engages Ms. Victoria in an in-depth discussion so I'm not able to start a whispered one with her.

It's clever, but it's only putting off the inevitable. That comes at lunch in the cafeteria. I load up my tray and instead of heading for my usual football table, I slide in next to Cerulean.

"What are you doing?" she hisses.

"I'm eating lunch." To demonstrate just that, I take a huge bite of my chicken salad sandwich.

"I can see that, but why are you doing it *here*?"

"Where else am I supposed to eat? The classrooms are off limits, you can't eat in the library, and eating in the bathrooms or locker rooms is unhygienic."

"I meant what are you doing at *this* table?"

"Am I not allowed to sit here?" I ask. "Am I negatively affecting your lunch experience?" I look to Vermilion, who smiles, then to Indigo with a massive hickey on her neck, who winks. Magenta huffs but says nothing. "See?" I say through a mouthful. I swallow it and put an apple in front of Cerulean, who only has a bottle of water. "Here."

"What's this?" she asks.

"An apple, what does it look like?"

"I know what it is, what I want to know is why you're giving it to me?"

"You're not eating, so I thought I'd share 'cause I'm nice like that."

"Thanks," she says, putting it back on my tray. "But I'm not hungry."

I put it back in front of her. "You don't have anything to eat. You need food." I poke at her side. "You're all skin and bones, so just eat the fucking apple."

She puts it back on my tray. "I said I'm not hungry, and keep your fucking hands to yourself."

I arch an eyebrow. "You really want me to do that?" I slide my hand under the table and start walking it up her leg. Leaning over, I whisper in her ear. "You know what these fingers feel like inside of you, how much pleasure they can bring you. Are you *sure* you want me to keep them to myself?" I slip under her skirt, her breathing hitching, and yup, nipples poking through her blouse and bra.

I've just reached her panties when Magenta slams

her hand on the table. "For fuck's sake, Cerulean, get a hold of yourself."

With that reproach, she pushes my hand away.

I chuckle and return to my sandwich. "Tell you what," I say before taking a bite. I chew then swallow. "I'll keep my apple and my hands to myself if you want me to, if you tell me what was eating at you earlier this morning."

"Grr," she says, standing up, grabbing my arm, and forcing me to follow her. She drags me to a classroom and pushes me in. "What's your deal?" she asks once the door has closed behind her. "Why can't you leave me alone?"

I walk up to her, crowding her against the wall. "I can't leave you alone because you don't want me to," I tell her.

She throws her hands up, almost hitting me in the face. "I have seriously lost count of how many times I've told you to fuck off."

I run my nose along her neck, inhaling her sweet berry scent. In my pants, my dick springs to life, pushing painfully against my fly. "I think we both know that if you *really* wanted me gone, you would've given me no other option but to leave you alone." I nip and lick her neck, a moan slipping out of her. "But you don't want that, do you, royal blue?"

"N-no, I-I d-do," she stutters.

"Really?" I ask. I slide my hand under her skirt again, this time making it to her panties, which are damp to the touch. "The state of your underwear says otherwise." I move the material to the side and push a finger inside her.

"Oh, God," she moans as I thrust.

"This doesn't seem like someone who wants me to leave her alone."

"It's just...." She trails off.

"It's just what, baby doll?" I ask, pressing kisses to her neck.

"I can't...."

"Can't what?" I add a second finger, and she moans louder.

"I have things.... Oh," she says as I thrust a little harder.

"What things do you have, royal blue?"

"I need...."

"What do you need?" I add a third finger, her juices running down my hand.

She moves her hand to mine, pressing my palm against her so I'm rubbing her clit. "I need you," she says, grabbing the back of my neck and pulling me to her, our lips meeting.

Hers are soft and full, and when she opens her mouth for me, my tongue tangling with hers, she tastes like peppermint. I thrust my fingers into her harder, faster, grinding her clit against my palm, and it isn't long before she tightens around me.

"That's it," I encourage. "Come on my fingers, baby doll."

She throws her head back, exposing her throat. Wanting to mark her perfect skin, I lean down and bite where her neck meets her shoulder. The pain sets her off, and she comes on a rush. I keep thrusting as her shock waves subside, until she opens her eyes.

"That wasn't meant to happen," she tells me once she's back to herself.

I take my hand out from underneath her skirt. "Yet, it did," I say as I lick my fingers clean.

She runs a hand through her honey-blonde hair. "Shit," she curses and starts pacing.

"Hey," I say, grabbing her by the shoulders when she passes me. "What's going on? What's wrong? Why can't we do what we just did?" She looks up at me, her brow furrowed. I smooth it with my finger. "We're good together, baby doll."

"I know," she replies, shoulders slumping.

"Why is that a problem for you?" I ask. "That's it, isn't it? This," I wiggle my finger between us, "is a problem for you, isn't it?"

"This isn't who I am," she says.

"And just who do you think you are?"

"I don't know, some two-bit whore who can't go an hour without getting off, maybe?"

I can't help but laugh. I grab her hips and walk us to a desk, pulling her between my legs when I sit on top of it. "Royal blue, you're anything but a whore, and unless you're going out every night, you've gone *way* longer than an hour without getting off."

She rests her head on my shoulder. "I can't do this, Harley."

I brush her hair away from her exquisite face. "Do what, baby doll?"

"This, us, a relationship."

"Okay."

"I can't lose who I am, everything I've worked for, everything I stand for."

"Okay," I say again.

"I just can't be one of *those* girls."

"What girls?" I ask.

She looks up at me. "The ones who forget themselves in favor of their boyfriend."

"You won't."

"I can't do a relationship," she repeats.

"So we don't," I say.

"Huh?"

"We don't do a relationship. We're both busy, we've both got a lot on our plates, plus, relationships are so 2010 anyway."

She laughs. "I've never done, well anything with a guy I've gone to school with."

"Consider me honored," I tell her. "But hear me when I say this, I never want to change you or force you to do anything you're not comfortable with. You're you, and I wouldn't want you any other way."

She smiles. "You know, you make it pretty hard to hate you."

"It's all part of my charm," I tell her before kissing her.

"And this?" She brushes her hand over my erection once we break apart. "Is this part of your charm too?"

I nod. "A very, *very* big part."

She pulls me to the edge of the desk and undoes my pants. I make life easier for her by lifting my hips when she moves to pull my boxer-briefs down. When she lowers herself to her knees, I all but lose it. Her warm mouth wraps around my crown, and I recite stats and run plays in my head. As she sucks me, she hums and moans, little noises that drive me wild. It's when her hand slips between my legs and plays with my balls that I lose it, emptying myself down her throat.

As long as she keeps doing that, I'll do whatever she wants.

CHAPTER TWENTY-THREE

THINGS WITH HARLEY have been good. Surprisingly. We've been doing whatever we're doing for a couple of months, and so far, the sky hasn't fallen, the world hasn't ended, and everything is just... good.

The football team has two games to go and is sitting at 8-0. More and more scouts are coming to the games, and offers for Harley are rolling in. Listen to me, I sound like an airhead girlfriend. I am *not* Harley St. James's girlfriend. I'm not his fuck buddy either. That would imply he's being fucked. He's not. Therefore, that makes me his... whatever.

His scent wraps around me as he takes a seat next to me in the cafeteria, then presses a kiss to my cheek. Like always, he picks up his apple and places it in front of me, and like always, I put it back on his tray.

"I don't like this not eating thing you do, royal blue," he says.

"And I've told you, I don't care what you think."

Across from us, Indigo chuckles. "Good luck trying to get Cerulean to do anything she doesn't want to do," she says. "She's bitten the heads off people for less."

He slings an arm around my neck, pulling him to me. "You wouldn't do that to me, would you, baby doll?"

"Only if you asked for it," I reply.

"Maybe later," he says, pressing a kiss to my lips.

"You two are sickening," Magenta says, throwing her fork down. Needless to say, she still hasn't come around.

"M...," Vermilion says.

"No. I've held my tongue, for the most part, for two months while you two are fawning all over each other, and I'm sick of it."

"What do you want from me, Magenta?" I ask.

"I want you to be the hard-ass our mom raised you to be. I want you to not fawn over Captain Dick here. I want you to rule this school like you have been. I want—"

"You want me not to be happy," I tell her, cutting her off. "And how dare you say I haven't been ruling the school like I have been. What's changed in two months, M? Harley and I aren't harming anyone. My grades aren't slipping, no one is stepping out of line, nothing has changed except—" I cut myself off before I say something I'll regret.

"Oh, no, don't stop there," she says. "Finish the rest of your sentence."

"It's fine, Magenta. You've said your piece, I've said mine, let's just leave it at that."

She shakes her head. "No, I want to hear whatever it is you were going to say."

"M," I warn.

"Tell. Me. What. You. Were. Going. To. Say."

I sigh and my shoulders drop. "I was going to say

that the only thing that has changed is your unwill-ingness to support my decisions."

She nods. "And I don't have a good reason?"

"No, you don't."

Indigo and Vermilion both gasp, while Kingsley picks at her salad.

"Not everything turns out badly," I tell her. "And really, did it turn out badly for you? Isn't Emily worth more than anything?" I ask. We don't usually talk about Emily in public. Sure, people know she exists, that was a bit hard to hide, but we don't like to make a big deal out of it. This is the South after all and unwed, teen mothers aren't seen as all that worthy of respect. Especially if your baby daddy isn't around and *may* not know about his child's existence. "I know things ended badly between y'all, but isn't your daughter worth the heartache?" I ask.

She shoves away from the table and storms off.

"Shit," Indigo curses and runs off after her.

I sag onto Harley's shoulder as he rubs mine.

"I know that was rough but I agree with what you said, the last bit anyway."

"Thanks," I say.

"You're right," Vermilion says. "It's time she gets over how her and Beckett ended."

I shrug. "Maybe. I still feel like shit saying all that though."

"You shouldn't," Harley says, pressing a kiss to my forehead. "That's what siblings are for, telling the hard truths. I suspect they come from you more than anyone."

I nod.

"She knew what she was walking into," he continues. "She demanded you tell her what you stopped yourself from saying. I'm sure she knew where it would end up too."

It's Vermilion's turn to nod.

"And just quietly...." He stops, and I look up at him.

"What?" I ask.

"Could it be that she's, I don't know, jealous?"

Vermilion leans back in her seat.

"No, no way," I say, shaking my head and sitting up. "Magenta's even more cold-hearted than I am, there's no way she's *jealous*."

"I don't know, Blue, he could be right," Vermilion chimes in.

I shake my head again. "Nope, absolutely not."

"Think about it," Vermilion urges.

I sigh and run a hand through my hair. "*If*, and that's a big fucking if, she is, what am I supposed to do about it?"

"I don't know if you *can* do anything," she replies. "I think it's something Magenta has to figure out on her own."

I slump back on Harley. "See? You're nothing but trouble."

He laughs and presses another kiss to my forehead. "Sorry, baby doll."

"So you should be."

"Don't worry about Magenta," Vermilion says. "Or don't worry *too* much," she corrects after a glare from me. "She has to work out her own shit."

My youngest sister swearing has me giggling, which was her point.

"Besides, I like the two of you together, doing whatever it is you're doing. You take care of so much, Cerulean, you deserve to have your own happiness, too."

"It's just, we know how heartbroken she was," I argue.

"And she has to get over it. You were right, she has Emily who is the best thing ever; she can't keep being angry over how things ended."

"Mmm."

The bell rings, and we all get up.

"Hey," Harley says, tugging on my hand and holding me back. "Are you all right?"

I shrug. "I feel like shit, that's all. I hate fighting with my sisters. Sure, we do it, but not a lot and never over something so big."

"Is there anything I can do?"

I shake my head. "Nah, we'll work it out. Eventually." *I hope*, but don't say.

He draws me into his arms, his hands resting on my butt. "I may not be able to fix things with your sister, but I can do this." He lowers his head and takes my lips. His mouth owns mine, and when his tongue demands entrance, I don't hesitate to give it to him. He tastes like apples, and it drives me crazy how much I like it.

His hands move lower, and he bends to pick me up, my legs wrapping around his waist, his hard-on pressing against my core.

"We need to get to class," I tell him when lack of oxygen forces us apart.

"Education is overrated," he says, trailing kisses up and down my neck.

"You may be one of the hottest QB's in the country, but colleges will still look at your transcript."

He sighs and puts me down. "You're a real hard-ass, you know that?"

I shrug and bat my eyelashes at him.

He laughs and takes my hand. "C'mon, let's go to class."

As we walk, he adjusts the bulge in his pants. He catches me staring.

"This is your fault, you know."

I smirk. "You'll survive."

He backs me against the wall and grinds against me. A moan slips out before I can stop it.

"Yeah, that's what I thought," he says, stepping back.

"You ass." I shove him. He doesn't go far. "Do you think I'm soft?" I ask as we walk down the deserted hallway.

"Royal blue, neither of us are soft here." I shove him again. "But seriously, the situation in my pants is proof that you haven't changed. Need I remind you of our encounter at the pep rally near the girls' locker room?"

I chuckle as my insides clench at the memory. "That was fun."

"Baby doll, you got me so hard and so worked up and left me hanging. I'm not saying you're doing the same now, but I will say I've gotten girls in bed faster."

I stop. "Is that something you—"

He cuts me off by putting a finger over my lips. "I told you when we started this thing that I would never force you to be anything other than who you are. I'm more than fine with what we've got going on. If you're ready to take this further, then so am I, but as long as you keep sucking my dick, I'm a happy man."

"So romantic," I say as I start walking again. Honestly, I don't know why I haven't slept with Harley yet. I *think* it's because I'm not ready to give him that last piece of myself. He's already gotten in so much further than anyone else, and sleeping with him won't just be a casual fuck. It'll mean something, and that terrifies me. Magenta might think I've forgotten the lesson from her experience, but I haven't. I can't and I won't forget; I just won't let it ruin what I think Harley and I are building here.

"But you like me anyway," he says as we head to class.

I think I might *more* than like him, but I'll be damned if I admit that anytime soon, if at all.

"HEY," I say, knocking on Magenta's door later that night.

She looks up from the book she's reading.

"Can I come in?"

She sighs and puts the book down. I take that as a yes and perch on the end of her bed after checking on Emily in her crib.

"If you're expecting me to apologize for what I said at lunch, I won't," she says, crossing her arms over her chest.

I smile. "I don't and I would never ask you to."

She slumps a little against her pillows.

"But I do want to *talk* about what happened at lunch," I say.

She nods. "I figured."

I take a deep breath. "Harley isn't the enemy," I start. "He's not forcing me to do anything or act any differently. He's happy I am who I am."

"And who are you?" she asks.

"The same person I've always been, just... happier."

"And he makes you happy?" She arches an eyebrow.

I nod. "He does. As crazy as it seems."

She shakes her head. "I still don't like him."

"You don't have to," I counter. "But please respect what he means to me."

"Just what *does* he mean to you?"

I stop and consider for a second. "He's someone I can be myself with, whom I don't have to act or pretend with. He's someone who makes me laugh and who also pushes me to be better."

"You don't *need* to be better."

"We could all do with being better," I say. "I don't mean being a better person, Christ knows *that* will *never* happen, but he pushes me to be the best I can be in whatever I'm doing."

"Whoopee for you."

I shake my head. "What more do you want from me?" I ask—plead. "Do you want me to be single for the rest of my life so you can feel better? How about Indigo? Or Vermilion? Do you want all of us miserable and alone so it makes you feel better? Because you're *not* alone. You *have* love, a total and unconditional love that the rest of us don't."

"Stop," she says, closing her eyes.

"I know things didn't turn out the way you wanted them to, and I'm sorry for that. I wish with all my heart they did, but you can't keep us miserable just because you are."

A tear rolls down her cheek.

"We deserve happiness too, Magenta," I say. "And so do you, if you let it."

HARLEY

CHAPTER TWENTY-FOUR

BEING WITH CERULEAN, in whatever way it is that we're together, is awesome. We're together when we can be and when we're not, it is what it is. It's honestly one of the most laid-back relationships I've ever been in.

"I saw you and Cerulean getting cozy after lunch today," Jon says as we change before practice.

I shrug. "You have a girl like that, you try keeping your hands off her."

"Tell me, is she as wild in the sack as I think she'd be?"

I slap him over the head. "What the fuck, man?" I ask.

"What? It's not as if everyone here isn't wondering the same thing."

"And what makes you think I'll tell you?"

"You're all chasing ghosts," TK says as he swaggers in. "He'll never tell because he can't."

Jon stares at me, eyes wide, mouth open. "You haven't tapped that yet?"

"No, he hasn't," TK answers for me. "The ice princess has literally got our star QB by the balls."

"Shit, TK, if I knew you were so concerned with my balls I would've had you fondling them and sucking me off these past months," I retort.

There are hoots and hollers all around the locker room.

"She's never going to give it up," he tells me.

"So she never gives it up. Seems like that's my problem rather than yours."

"Why are you wasting your time with her, man?"

"Why are you worried about who I'm wasting my time with?" I counter.

"I just don't want to see you left heartbroken and fuck up our season."

"I'll be fine," I say, doing up my cleats.

"I'm just looking out for you, man."

"Looking out for me or trying to cause trouble? I noticed Trinity has moved on. What happened with her, huh?" For a while Trinity was hanging around like a bad smell, then suddenly, after the party where Karlie was drugged, she developed a sudden interest in the wrestling team.

"Pfft," he says. "Girls like that, once they realize you're not gonna give them what they want, they go looking elsewhere."

"And why didn't you give her what she wanted?" I ask. "She's hot, she's easy. I would've thought that was right up your alley."

"I told you, man, old, stretched-out pussies don't do it for me."

I laugh. "If a woman's vag can bounce back after pushing a baby out of there, I'm pretty sure your dick ain't gonna do a whole lot of damage. And correct me if I'm wrong, but I don't think Trinity has any kids?"

By now the rest of the team has stopped what they're doing and is listening in on our conversation. There's a chorus of oohs and ahs.

TK turns a bright red, his eyes narrowed, jaw clenched.

"All right, you idiots," Coach calls. "Enough of the gossip, let's get out there and work on keeping our perfect season that way."

The locker room empties, but I stay behind, as does TK.

"You start talking shit about me and Cerulean or her in general, as well as her sisters, and I'll make you look so bad community colleges won't even want you to play for them," I threaten.

He shakes his head. "You're a fool, man. She's going to have a party on the ashes of your grave."

I shrug. "I might be, and she may do that, but it's none of your business. The only concern you should have is making sure you're exactly where I need you to be on the field."

"I'll do my job," he says, grabbing his helmet.

"Good." I run out onto the field and take my place as we warm up.

I trust TK on the field, but off it? He's shady as fuck.

COMING HOME AFTER PRACTICE, like always, Cookie is there to greet me when I walk through the door. Neither Mom nor Dad's cars are here, so it looks like it's just the cookie monster and me.

"Hey, buddy," I say, picking him up and nuzzling him.

In return, he butts his hard little head against mine.

"Did you have a good day?" I ask. "Get enough naps in? Hopefully, you didn't pee in Mom and Dad's bathroom again. The old man will go ape shit if you did."

Cookie purrs as I stroke his head, his eyes closing.

"Yeah, it's a tough life."

I'm just about to go upstairs when Mrs. Stark comes out of the kitchen.

"Hey," I say, pressing a kiss to her cheek. "I didn't realize you were home."

She laughs. "I'm always home."

I look at her. Her once brown hair is now gray, and the lines around her eyes are deep, but the eyes themselves are still strong with life.

"Well, I'm glad that you are."

She takes my arm and leads me to the kitchen. I sit on a stool and Cookie wakes from his nap, pawing at me to let him down before walking over to his food dish.

"That cat," Mrs. Stark says as she shakes her head. "Either eating or sleeping. A few times I've even seen him asleep, his head in his bowl."

I chuckle as she gives him a few of his favorite treats.

"So, what's going on with you?" she says, leaning on the counter in front of me.

"Not much. Football, school, the usual."

"And does this usual include a girl, perhaps?"

I don't even try to hide my smile. "It may, yeah."

"Are you treating her well?"

I glare at her.

"You haven't been in my life for a very long time. I want to make sure you were raised right."

I reach over and cover her hands with one of mine. "If I was, it was because I had the best foundation. What happened after we left built on what you'd already done."

She nods and tears well in her eyes. Pulling her hands out from mine, she wipes at them, then clears her throat. "So, what is this girl like?"

"Her name is Cerulean, and she's incredible. She's tough, and fierce, and smart, and beautiful."

"And you're being careful?"

"Jesus," I curse.

She swats at my hand. "Language! This *is* the South, you know."

I chuckle. "I know, but damn, Mrs. Stark, way to intrude in a guy's privacy!"

"I changed your diapers, Harley. I was there when you were being toilet trained and when you discovered you could wiggle your hips and your willy would dance. There's nothing of yours I haven't seen."

"That may be true, but a lot of time has passed since then. I'm not the same boy obsessed with making his 'willy'"—I make air quotes—"dance."

"Just make sure if it's dancing in this girl's vagina it has a condom wrapped over it."

"Yes, ma'am."

"And football's good?" she asks, thankfully moving on.

I nod. "It is. We're eight and oh, going for win number nine on Friday."

"That's good, that's good. I see those thick

envelopes come in, all those fancy college crests stamped all over them."

"It's definitely a trip. Plus, it gives validation to Dad. Proves that it was worth coming back here."

"I'm sure—"

I cut her off with a look.

She sighs, her shoulders slumping. "He was always tough on you."

"Tough? Tough I can handle, but you try being a ten-year-old boy in Japan, wanting to play on an American football team. I thought for sure he'd feed me to Godzilla."

It's her turn to send me a look.

"What? You know it's true!"

She tuts and turns around to get stuff out of the fridge. "Any of the schools catch your eye?" she asks.

"A couple. South Bend and Charleston are really hard to go past."

"But...," she prompts.

"I might be waiting for a couple of other schools."

"Such as?"

"Birmingham and Savannah."

She nods. "And Cerulean, what's she doing?"

"She's a junior, so she's still got another year after this."

"Do you think you have a shot at Birmingham or Savannah?"

"Coach thinks I do. He said they're both sending someone this week. They both want to have a chat with me."

"You know not to commit to anyone before you think it through, right?"

"I know."

"What happens if you get offers from both?" she asks.

I shrug. "I'll have to see who offers me the best deal, where I'll get the most game time, scholarship, that sort of thing."

"Scholarship? You don't need one of those."

"Do you really think my father would *pay* for me to go to college and play ball? Even if I don't make a career out of playing football, I still hope to make a living off it, whether that be coaching or commentating. Whatever happens I won't be getting an MBA or PhD like Dad would like."

She sucks on her teeth and nods. "Despite that, you are happy, aren't you?"

I smile, thinking of my life right now. "Yeah, I am."

HARLEY

IT DOESN'T MATTER what's going on in my life off the field, once I step foot on it, everything disappears. This is my domain, my kingdom. Off the field I may not trust TK as far as I can throw him, but on it, he's a magnet for my passes. And as much as I hate to admit it, he makes me look good.

"Blue forty-two, blue forty-two," I call. Yes, we changed the color of our calls. It's purely coincidence what color we chose; it's not like I'm obsessed with it or anything.

Looking left, then right, I know where my guys are; I know where the defense is, so I clap my hands for the ball to be snapped. Going nonverbal like this takes a lot of practice, and sometimes when we're playing away from home it's problematic, but here, on our field, in front of our fans, they know what to do.

Once the ball is snapped, it's like someone turns the volume all the way up. The ball is in my hands but the defense rushes up faster than I expect, my own defense doing their best to prevent guys from getting to me. I search downfield, but they cover all our receivers. The choice is there: get sacked and take the loss of yardage, or pass the ball, risking an inter-ception or possibly pulling off a throw that'll make my highlight reel long into my NFL career?

I look to TK again, now covered by two guys, but he nods and points to the sky.

Hoping and praying like nothing, I pull my arm back and launch the ball. The guys on TK jump, but mistime it. But TK doesn't. Just as he hits his peak, the ball flies into his outstretched hands. He brings it down, ball cradled tightly to his chest. The play is completed, and they move the chains.

In the stands, the crowd is going nuts. The guys running on and off the field all pat me on the back or slap me on the helmet as they pass. As TK makes his way off, he's swamped by our teammates. Yes, there's no denying he's one hell of a player, but that's where the accolades end.

We rush the next few plays, steadily marching down the field, before Coach sends TK on again. This time, the guy covering him slips, leaving him an easy catch and a stroll into the end zone.

Eventually we end up thirty-two to seventeen winners, but our "miracle" play, as it's being called, is all anyone is talking about.

"Hell of a game, son," Coach says as we run off the field.

"Thanks, Coach."

"I know you're probably eager to go celebrate, but there are some guys here who want to talk to you."

I nod.

"Go shower, and I'll have them escorted to my office."

As expected, the locker room is on a high. The

cheers get louder when I walk in. I hold my hands up and everyone quiets down.

"I just want to say that that was some fine-ass football tonight, gentlemen." More cheers follow. "You worked your asses off out there tonight and I'm damn grateful. I couldn't have done it without y'all."

I slap all the guys I can on the back on my way to my locker.

"Inspiring speech, man," TK says.

I shrug. "I was just acknowledging hard work."

"And yours is being acknowledged too, right?"

"You talking about the scouts?" I ask.

"Of course I'm talking about the fucking scouts. I heard Birmingham and Savannah?"

"Yeah."

"Must be nice."

"I'm sure you're getting interest, offers."

He shrugs. "Not Birmingham and Savannah."

"I'm sure they'll take a look after tonight."

"Everything just comes easy for you, doesn't it?" he asks. "Scouts, offers, scholarships, Cerulean."

"So that's what this is all about. It's got nothing to do with football; it's all about my girl. What, are you jealous she picked me? Or is it the fact you've known her for her whole life and she's never looked at you twice? Then I come in and sweep her right out from under you?"

He grits his teeth and bunches his fists.

I laugh. "You going to hit me, TK? Make me look bad in front of the guys who are waiting for me in Coach's office?"

He stands there, flexing and clenching his hands.

"You know it won't make a difference, right?" I tell him. "With the scouts, or with Cerulean."

Finally, he makes up his mind, pulling his arm back and swinging at me. Unfortunately for him, I'm expecting it and duck out of the way, sending him into the locker beside mine.

"Whoa!" Cries go up, heads turning our way.

I laugh as TK collects himself. "You just kissed goodbye to *both* of your dreams," I tell him as I walk to the showers.

THE MEETING with the scouts goes well, both offering me full scholarships and the promise of plenty of game time. They both seemed a bit stunned when I asked about their international business and political science programs but recovered well. Yes, I know Cerulean has a lock on a place at the Carver Institute, but it can't hurt to ask around, right? A lot can happen in a year and a half. Who knows, maybe she'll want to stay closer to home, closer to Vermilion. Birmingham or right here in Savannah are a lot closer than D.C. Plus, it's more than likely I'll be red shirted, so that means we could end up graduating at the same time.

I know I'm getting ahead of myself, but there's something about this girl that makes me want to make all the plans in the world.

Speak of the devil, she's waiting outside the locker room when I finally get out.

"Hey," I say, grabbing her by the hips and pulling her to me.

"Hey," she echoes, stretching up to kiss me.

"Sorry I took so long, I had a couple of meetings and I didn't realize you were waiting." It's a very girl-friend-y thing to do, I mentally add, but do not voice. I like my balls where they are, thanks.

She shrugs. "It's Friday night in Savannah, what else could I be doing?"

I kiss her neck. "Probably a few things. What did you used to do before I came along and turned you into a jersey chaser?"

She shoves me, but I bring her closer, my arms winding around her.

"You said you had meetings?" she asks.

I nod. "Scouts from Birmingham and Savannah."

"Wow."

"Yeah," I agree.

"They make offers?"

I pull back and stare at her.

"How good?" she asks.

"Good enough."

"Which one?"

I shrug. "I haven't decided yet."

She nods.

"You know, both have decent poli sci and international business programs," I say, tracing the collar of her sweater.

"Do they now?" She arches an eyebrow.

I nod. "They do. I asked."

She laughs and stretches up to kiss me again.

"I know they're not the Carver Institute, but I thought maybe they could be a backup option if...."

"If something goes wrong?" she asks, pulling out of my arms.

I run a hand through my hair, gripping the roots

and tugging. "No, of course not. I would *never* wish that on you. I just thought...." I kick at the ground. "I don't know, just in case it ever crossed your mind to maybe, you know, stay closer to home."

Her shoes stop inches from mine, her finger coming under my chin, lifting it so I'm looking her in the eyes, a smirk on her beautiful face.

"And in doing so I just *happen* to go to the same college as you?"

I shrug.

She nods. "Right."

"Look, it was just an idea, a thought. It doesn't mean you have to go there or even consider it. I just thought I'd ask."

"Do you want me to go to the same college as you?"

"I want you to go wherever you want to go. Would it be nice to be close? Sure, but a lot can happen in a year and a half."

"Such as?" She pops her hand on her hip.

"You could get sick of me, decide you can do much better with some stuck-up twat who is the fourth son with that name in his family and is destined to be a senator or something."

She nods. "It's entirely possible."

I bring her close to me. "And I could always fall in love with an extremely flexible cheerleader who can bend in half and stick her feet behind her head." She tweaks my nipple as I laugh. "It's just a thought, royal blue. Nothing more, nothing less. The ball, as always, is in your court."

"Is it?"

I nod.

She takes my hand and drags me toward the field. Because it's so long after the game, the cleaners are gone, lights are off. The only light is provided by a three-quarter moon. I follow my girl until she stops right where I was when I threw the "miracle" pass.

"That was some pass tonight," she says, wrapping her arms around me.

"Thanks," I reply, my arms winding around her as well.

"Really, it was very impressive."

I shrug. "I aim to please."

"Is that so?"

I nod. "Yup."

"So if I told you seeing you out here, in your element, completely and utterly in control, made me wet, what would you do?"

"Well, first things first, I'd want to see." I keep one arm around her while the other slips under the hem of her skirt. God bless this girl for always wearing a skirt, no matter the weather. This may be Georgia, but it can still get fucking cold. I reach her panties and find they are indeed wet. I push the material to the side and rub her lips.

"Once you had firsthand proof, then what would you do?" she asks, chest heaving.

"I'd want to experience it, play it with it," I tell her. I put the other hand under her skirt, pulling down her panties. She steps out of them, and I stash them in my pocket.

"How would you play?" she asks, eyes closed.

I get down on my knees, one hand running up her thigh and around to grab her ass, the other parting her lips and inserting a finger. She moans as I gently thrust into her.

"You like that, baby doll?" I ask.

She nods.

"How about this?" I add another finger, her moans getting louder. I pull her closer to me, and stick my head up her skirt, licking up her juices.

"Oh fuck," she cries out.

"Let me know if you're not okay with this," I tell her, the hand that's covered in her wetness going to her ass. She tenses when I run a finger around her rim but relaxes when I suck her clit in my mouth. I circle her a few more times before inserting the tip of my finger. "Okay?" I ask.

She nods.

I push a little more, and she moans again. I continue to lick and suck at her pussy, my finger working in and out of her ass, her hips moving to the pace I set.

"How's that, baby doll?" I ask. "Want me to stop?"

"Stop and I'll kill you."

I chuckle and keep at her. It isn't long before she's coming hard, her knees not able to take her weight, falling on me, my back on the ground, her straddling me, head on my chest. I pull my finger out of her ass, the other hand running up and down her back.

"You okay?" I ask.

She nods. "Just give me a minute," she pants.

"And to think you used to hate football," I say.

"God, Harley, that was.... I don't think I've ever come that hard."

My already hard dick pulses painfully in my jeans. "Humph," I grunt.

She pulls back at looks at me. "Did you just grunt?" she asks.

"Fucking A, I did. When a girl tells you she's never come that hard, you take that badge."

She laughs. "You're a dick."

I nod. "I know. He's hard as fuck for you too." I lift my hips to prove my point.

"Aw, poor QB. He's got a boner and no one offering to take care of it."

"Oh, there'd be girls willing to take care of it, I just don't want them."

She looks in my eyes, her own green eyes wide. "No?"

"No," I confirm. I lean forward and take her lips. "I want you and only you for as long as you'll have me."

CHAPTER TWENTY-SIX

"FOR AS LONG as you'll have me." Harley's words echo in my head. It's not them that scare me though, it's my response, the one I didn't voice.

"I want you forever," I think but don't say, and am terrified by the fact that this sentiment doesn't scare me.

"Well then, I guess I should probably do something about your hard-as-fuck dick then," I say as I slither down his body.

MENTALLY, I might be freaking out after the events of Friday night, but I'm still Cerulean Tremont. I bow to no one, not even cocky quarterbacks who bring me to my knees, literally.

But I put all of that out of my head as I watch Alexandrov put Vermilion through her paces on the same piece she's been working on for months. I listened to a recording, and she sounds almost the same, but Alexandrov still isn't satisfied.

"Again," he barks. "You are getting sloppy,

spending too much time at Waffle House and not enough time practicing."

I clench my fists and go to tear strips off him, but Vermilion stops playing and takes her hands off the keys.

"What I do in my spare time is none of your business," she tells him. "And regardless of what you believe, my playing has *not* suffered because of my social life. Just because you're miserable doesn't mean everyone else has to be."

We sit silent for a second, all three of us in shock that Vermilion said that. I hide my smile as he shifts his weight.

"Shall we continue?" she asks.

He nods.

"By the way, Alexandrov, I *still* haven't received the recommendation for the Conservatorium workshop. She's mastered the piece, and I'm still waiting. The deadline for applications is just a couple of weeks away," I remind him.

"I'll get it to you," he mumbles.

I nod. "See that you do."

"YOU WANT to tell me what that was all about?" I ask Vermilion as we walk to the car after her lesson.

She shrugs. "I was just sick of his shit. His dig about me spending too much time socializing got to me. I don't! Plus, I'm having fun, having a life."

"It's not a bad thing," I tell her. "To have a life, I mean. I know Magenta may think otherwise but we have to blow off steam every now and then, escape our lives for a little bit."

She nods. "Is that what you're doing with Harley?"

My thighs clench with thoughts of what I'm "doing" with Harley. "Maybe. Mostly I just like being with him, as weird as it seems."

"Why is it weird? You're single, he's single; isn't that what's supposed to happen?"

I laugh and muss her hair. "It's just weird."

"Why?" she presses.

I sigh and lean against the car when we get to it. "Because it doesn't feel like *me*, like the me I've spent all these years cultivating."

"But you like being with Harley?"

I nod. "Yeah, I do."

"Why?"

"I don't know. With him I feel... free, I guess."

"And yet, it doesn't feel like *you*," she says.

I poke my tongue out at her. "Sometimes you're too clever for your own good," I shoot back, climbing into the car.

"You being with Harley, feeling the things you feel, they're not bad things."

"No?" I ask.

"No, they're not," she confirms. "Yes, you have a reputation here, but people change, they're *allowed* to change. I dare say people even expect it in high school. You've been who you've needed to be, *wanted* to be even, but now you want something different, some*one* different. That's not a bad thing, that's growing up."

I glance over at my sister. "When did you get so wise?" I ask.

"About the same time I let Cameron Bray get to second base."

"V!" I all but scream.

"What?" She shrugs. "Like you and Harley aren't doing that and more. I know Indigo and Magenta aren't virgins either."

"I know, but we don't talk about things so... openly."

She shrugs again. "It's 2019. If we can't, then who can?"

"Okay, I get your point, but you're also my sister, my *younger* sister. I don't need to know about your sex life, just like you don't need to know about mine."

"Fair enough. Just a word of advice though? You're going to need to be prepared to be ravaged when Harley wins state."

"Oh, Jesus," I curse as Vermilion laughs.

THERE'S two minutes left in the final regular season game and we're down by three. While it's not disastrous if we lose, we will lose our number-one ranking going into the playoffs. Look at me, "we" like I'm some part of the team.

The defense is on the field and everyone holds their breath as the Georgia Prep QB airs the ball. Hands go up for it, but it's hard to see who brings it down.

Once the guys get up, it's one of ours who has the ball in his hands. The refs call the catch completed and the intercept good. I'm not ashamed to admit I go just as crazy as the crowd around me.

For a minute and a quarter, Harley marches the

team down the field, getting them twenty yards from the goal line.

With ten seconds to go, it's fourth and ten, still twenty yards out.

"Come on, baby," I chant under my breath.

Harley calls something out, blue seventeen? Then waits a second or two before clapping his hands. The ball is snapped, but no one is open and he's too close to the goal line to try another "miracle" pass.

Six seconds left, five, four.

Seeing an opening, he tucks the ball under his arm and runs. He spins past one defender, then another, jumping over a third. He's tackled a yard out from the line, but sticks out a hand and the ref's arms go up, signaling the touchdown as the clock hits one.

I slump back in my seat, certain they can hear our cheering in Atlanta.

The extra point is added, and the ball kicked off. With the return safely in TK's hands, Harley takes the field, the ball snapped, and they take a knee.

The crowd swarms the field, while I stay in my seat, watching it all, taking it all in. Savannah, Birmingham, South Bend, Charleston, whenever Harley ends up, their football team is in good hands.

I consider what he said the other day about maybe following him to college. For as long as I can remember, the Carver Institute has been my dream. It *still* is my dream, but Harley is becoming increasingly important to me as well.

HALF AN HOUR later and still no closer to working

out what the fuck I want in life, Harley walks out, a massive smile on his face, hair curling at the ends.

He walks up to where I'm sitting and takes a seat. "Hey."

"Hey, yourself," I reply.

"Good view."

"Good game."

He smirks. "It was, huh?"

I shove him lightly, and he reacts by pulling me on his lap. Normally I wouldn't allow this, but seeing as though we're alone, I'll go with it. "Mmm," he moans as he nuzzles my neck, biting gently.

"Good thing you have such *talented* hands," I comment.

He chuckles and slides one of those talented hands under my skirt.

"Yo, QB!" one of the players yells as he strolls past. "You coming to TK's or what?"

Harley looks up at me. "Whaddya think?"

I shrug. "Whatever you want to do."

"I want to do *you*," he says, burying his head where my shoulder meets my neck.

I chuckle and push off him before standing. "Come on, QB," I say, holding out a hand. "This is one of your crowning moments, let's go celebrate that."

He stands and draws me into his arms. "What did I do to deserve you?" he asks.

"Fingered me outside the girls' locker room," I reply, and he growls.

"If memory serves, *you* left me hanging that night."

I shrug. "You deserved it."

"And do I still deserve it?"

"That's still to be determined."

"Oh, yeah?"

I nod. "Uh-huh. I mean, tonight *was* an impressive display of athletic ability, I'll give you that, but what else can you do?"

"I'll show you what I can do," he says, bending down and throwing me over his shoulder. "Let's go see our people."

HARLEY

TK'S HOUSE is packed when we get there, but the crowd parts when we make our way through.

"Well, if it's not the King and Queen of Forest Park Academy," TK says, coming over to us when he sees us.

"Good game, man," I say, holding out my hand for him, but he slaps it away.

"Fuck you and fuck your slut of a girlfriend. Say, you ever wonder how she's so peppy all the time?" he asks.

"Careful, TK," Cerulean warns. "We wouldn't want people to think you're *soft*, coming after a woman, now would we? I mean, you'd never do that, would you? Come after the helpless, the defenseless?"

He huffs and walks away. I take Cerulean in my arms.

"On the field, he's one hell of a wide receiver, but off it, he's a total fuckhead."

She reaches up and pushes my hair off my forehead. "Let's forget about him, shall we? He's nothing, he's nobody, and tonight we're celebrating."

I kiss her, hard and fast. She meets me thrust for thrust. That's what I love about this girl. In every way, she's my equal—or more like I'm hers. We balance each other out, and despite her insistence we're not dating, which I'm fine with, we're perfect.

"Come on, let's dance," I say, grabbing her hand and dragging her to the makeshift dance floor.

For I don't know how long we bump and grind on each other, each touch progressively driving both of us crazier.

"Let's take a break," I yell in her ear.

She nods, and I take her hand to lead her outside. On the way, we swing past the kitchen where I snag a couple of bottles of water. We head outside to the pool area, where people are gathered in groups. I spot some of the guys on the team by the deck chairs, so head in their direction. There's only one free, so I take a seat, pulling Cerulean down on top of me.

"Mmm," she purrs, rubbing her ass on my now rock-hard dick.

"Stop it," I tell her, biting her earlobe.

She laughs and grabs one of the bottles of water, chugging half of it before handing it to me. I chug the rest, putting the empty bottle on the floor beside the chair.

"So are you guys like, a legit thing?" David asks.

"A legit thing?" I repeat.

"Yeah." He nods. "Like, official and shit."

Cerulean laughs. "Official what? Badasses? Hard-asses? Bitch and boy? What?"

"Like, a couple," he specifies.

"A couple of what? People? Why, yes, we are."

I laugh as David's brow furrows.

"Don't worry about it," I tell him.

"Y'all are weird," he says, taking a sip of his beer.

"Are we weird, baby doll?" I ask, running my hands over her sides and stomach.

"Hmm, I don't think so," she replies, wiggling against my hard-on again.

David rolls his eyes again and drains his beer. "That was some fine-ass play tonight," he says.

I tip my head. "Thanks, man. I couldn't have done it without you, though."

"Ah, always the team man," TK says, joining our group and tipping one of the JV players off a chair so he can sit.

I sigh. "I'm just recognizing and acknowledging the team's efforts, TK, nothing more, nothing less."

"Because you're the perfect Harley St. James, right?"

"I'm far from perfect."

He shakes his head. "You've got the perfect life, the perfect arm, the perfect girl. No matter what you do, you still come out smelling like roses."

"I'm betting right about now, he smells like sex," someone says.

"Nah, not yet," Cerulean says. "Later, though."

There are hoots and hollers all round. She spins in my lap to face me.

"He's jealous," she tells me. "Want to give him a show?"

"Don't you think that's a little cruel?" I ask.

"Don't you think he deserves it?" she counters.

"You're a bad influence," I say as I grab her bottom lip with my teeth.

She laughs, grabbing the back of my head, pulling

me to her. Her legs slip outside of mine, her heat rubbing against my dick. There's a loud crash and footsteps stomping away. When we break apart, the chair TK was on is vacant and on its side a few feet away.

"You guys are evil," Penn, a cornerback, says.

I shrug. "The guy's got an issue with me, but I have no idea why. I've done nothing to him but help him look good on the field."

He shakes his head. "Some guys just can't take others' success."

"I guess." I look to Cerulean. "Want to get out of here?"

She nods and gets up.

"I mean it when I say I couldn't have done anything tonight without y'all," I say to the guys.

"We know," David says.

I nod. "Have a good night, fellas."

"YOU WANT me to drop you home?" I ask when we get in the car.

"No, I don't." She leans over and rubs her hand over my still-tented jeans. "You've been semi or fully hard since we got here. I'm sure it's getting painful."

I shrug. "If you're offering to blow me, I won't say no."

She chuckles. "Blow you? No. Fuck you? Sure."

"Seriously?" I ask.

She nods.

"You're sure?"

"I'm sure." She leans over, teeth grazing my jaw. "Get me to a bed, baby," she whispers.

.   .   .

IF SOMEONE WERE to ask me how the fuck we got back to my place, I'd have no idea. We tiptoe through the house, hoping not to wake anyone, but all bets are off once I close and lock my bedroom door.

I pick Cerulean up and throw her on the bed, sending poor Cookie flying, scratching and hissing.

"Oops, sorry, buddy," I say. "Here." I make a pallet on the floor for him.

"He's cute," Cerulean says from the bed. I toe off my shoes and bounce onto it, lying on top of her.

"I've had him since I was one. Our housekeeper, Mrs. Stark, kept him while we were away and brought him back when she moved down here."

"What's his name?" she asks, running a hand through my hair.

"Cookie." She smirks. "I was one when we got him," I remind her.

"Was he your best friend growing up?"

I pause for a moment. "I guess. I mean, I had friends, but we moved when I was young and I don't have any siblings, so that left the cookie monster."

"What's it like being an only child?" she asks.

I shrug. "What's it like having three sisters?" I counter.

"Chaotic," she replies, and I laugh. "My sisters are my world. They're whom I do everything for. They're my strength, my support."

"And where do I fit into all of this?" I ask.

"You're a distraction," she replies.

"A good one?"

A smile breaks over her face. "I'm pretty sure."

I grind myself into her core. "Does that help you make up your mind?"

She shrugs. "Eh."

"What about this?" I dip my head and bite her nipple through her clothes.

"Meh, it's okay."

I growl and she laughs. "*Fine.*" I sit up and take off my shirt. Her laugh cuts off when my chest comes into view. "Yeah, that's what I thought."

She runs her nails over my abs, my dick jerking in my jeans.

"A good enough distraction?" I ask.

She nods. I sit her up and pull her sweater and top off. I unzip her skirt and get her out of that too. "Blue lace," I say, appreciating her body. "Very nice."

She shrugs. "I thought it was appropriate."

"Mmm." Her body is almost perfect. I still think she's too skinny, but fuck. She's long and lean, her legs going on for days.

"Are you just going to sit there all night or are you actually going to do something?" she asks, arching an eyebrow.

"Shh," I tell her. "Perfection like this needs to be appreciated." She rolls her eyes but I grab her chin and direct her gaze to me. "I mean it, you're perfect in every way. You're my perfect match, and I'm going to devour you."

Cerulean

CHAPTER TWENTY-EIGHT

"UNDO MY PANTS, BABY DOLL," he orders.

My hands shake as I tackle his belt. I'm not usually nervous during sex, but this isn't _just_ sex. It means something.

"Hey," he says, his hands covering mine. "If you don't want to do this, we don't have to. I'm more than fine with a hand job or something."

I chuckle and rise on my knees on the bed. "I'm more than okay with what we're about to do," I say, my lips almost pressing against his. "It's just.... It means more, what we're about to do, than it usually does. It's not just sex, you know?"

He lifts my chin so I'm looking him in the eyes. "Believe me, I'm more than aware this is more than sex." He swallows. "This is making love."

My eyes go wide.

"I love you, Cerulean."

I laugh, resting my head on his shoulder.

"Okaaaaaaaaaaaaaaay," he says. "That wasn't quite the reaction I was expecting."

"I'm sorry." I wipe my eyes. "I really didn't mean

to laugh, and I'm not laughing at what you said. I'm laughing because I'm relieved."

"Relieved?" he asks.

I nod and pull back so I can look him in the eyes. "Yeah."

"So I'll bite. *Why* are you relieved, baby doll?"

I slide my hands up his chest, over his strong, wide shoulders, and cup his neck, his pulse steady under my palm. "I'm relieved because you just showed me I'm not alone with what I'm thinking, feeling." I blow out a breath. "I've never done this, been in a true relationship, made love, caught feelings in general. I know they call me the ice princess at school, and they're right. I don't feel. Since our mom left, I've been the strong one. I've been the one to look after them, to do what she would've done. By doing that, there was never room for me to have feelings for anyone else."

"But you do now?" he asks, brow furrowed, eyes tight.

I nod, and his shoulders drop, all the tightness leaving his body—well, except for one area. "I do. I have many, many feelings for you."

"And what, pray tell, exactly *are* these feelings?"

"Well," I say, moving even closer to him. "I'm definitely fond of your fingers."

He smirks as I thread my fingers through his. He brings them up to his mouth and kisses each one before sucking my pinkie in his mouth.

I groan as the sensation goes straight between my legs, while his eyes flash.

Letting my finger go with a pop, he says, "What other feelings do you have for me?"

"Your mouth is, um...." I trail off as he leans over me. I collapse to my butt, and he keeps coming, crawling over me before finally settling himself between my legs.

"What about my mouth, royal blue?" He lowers his head and nips and sucks at my neck.

"It's, ah, good," I say.

He chuckles. "Just good?" He moves down my body, taking a lace-covered nipple in his mouth.

"Oh, God," I moan, my hands flying to his head, back arching.

Suddenly he stops.

"Wha...?"

"Tell me, Cerulean, how good is my mouth?"

I slap his chest and move to get off the bed, but he catches me by the waist and rolls us so we're right back to where we started.

"Uh-uh, you're not getting away."

I cup his face. "I don't want to."

"Good," he says, lowering his face to mine and taking my lips with his.

For I don't know how long, we just lie there, making out, hands wandering.

He hooks my leg over his hip, his hand running up and down my thigh to my ass, him grinding lightly against me.

When my lips are long past bruised, I pull back. "I do love you," I tell him. "I don't want you thinking I don't, or that I'm saying it just because you said it, or because of what we're going to do, but because it is genuinely what I feel."

"I know," he says. The corner of his mouth ticks up. "I also know you never say something because you have to, and I know you'd never do it just because you were obligated to. You're your own woman, Cerulean Tremont, and I wouldn't have you any other way."

I fumble with the waistband of his boxer-briefs. He helps me get them off. I run my hand up and down his length and he groans, resting his head on my shoulder.

"Fuck, that feels good."

"What'll it feel like once you're inside me?" I purr in his ear. He jerks in my hand, and I chuckle. "Knowing I affect you like that gets me *so* wet," I tell him.

He pulls back to look at me. "Oh, *really*?"

I shrug. "See for yourself."

He arches an eyebrow before leaving a trail of kisses over my chest and stomach. He gets to my panties and slides the material down my legs before running his nose up the inside of my thigh.

"Harley," I moan as he presses a kiss to my pubic bone.

"You're soaked," he says as he runs a finger through my folds.

I nod. "You going to do something with it?"

"Woman, are you testing me?" he asks.

I shrug again. "Merely wondering what your intentions are."

He crawls over me again. "My intention," he says, kissing one side of my neck, "is to make love to you." He kisses the other side. "All night long."

I grab his face and bring it to mine. "So do it already."

His mouth takes mine at the same time as one of

his hands sneaks behind me, undoing the clasp on my bra. I pull it off and fling it away.

"Goddamn, I love your body," he says, pulling back, his hands squeezing my boobs, thumbs flicking my nipples.

"Harley," I whine.

"You need something, baby doll?"

I look him in the eyes, my green to his brown. "You," I tell him. "I need you."

He leans over and opens the top drawer of his nightstand, pulling out a box of condoms. He rips it open and tears off a foil square. I snatch it out of his hand, opening it and rolling the latex down his length.

"Fuck, your hands feel so good on me," he curses, throwing his head back.

I rise to meet him, kissing him briefly before pushing him to the bed. Like a good boy, he moves to his back while I straddle him.

"I should've known you were going to take charge." He chuckles.

I smirk as I position him at my entrance, slowly lowering myself onto him. "You like that about me."

He grabs my hips as I raise and lower myself, his hips coming to meet me as I slip down. "No, I *love* that about you."

God, his words.... The sight of a guy has never made me giddy before, but yet, here I am, indeed giddy over Harley St. James of all people. What's even more surprising is me professing my love to the man underneath and inside of me, making love to him, *with* him.

I swivel my hips, and his eyes roll back, his head

going with them. The veins in his neck are popping out, and I know he's close.

"Shit," he groans.

"Aww," I coo. "Is poor little QB1 going to blow?"

Without warning, he picks me up and rolls us so I'm on my back. It's my turn to curse as he grinds against my clit and thrusts into me, hard. The headboard is probably banging against the wall, but neither of us care. He hits me deep, and I cry out.

"Just there, huh?" he pants, sweat dripping off his brow.

I nod and pull him into me, my nails digging into his back.

My orgasm is close, my pussy clenching around him.

"That's it, baby doll, squeeze me good."

"Harley!" I all but scream as I come hard.

Vaguely I hear him call out; feel him jerk inside of me.

"Holy fuck," he says, collapsing on top of me but keeping most of his weight off me.

"Mmm," I purr, kissing his neck.

Gently he pulls out of me, taking the condom off and disposing of it in the trash.

"That was something," he says, lying back on the bed, arm out.

I take the invitation, snuggling into his chest, tracing his nipple with my finger. "Yeah, it was," I agree.

He presses a kiss to the top of my head. "So what now?"

I blow out a breath. "I don't know." I look up at him. "But in the meantime, I think we should catch our breath and, whenever you're ready, we do that again and again until we're exhausted."

He arches an eyebrow and I shrug, giving him a wicked smile. He leans down to kiss me, rolling me to my back, where he grinds his rapidly hardening dick against me. "You good?" he asks.

I nod. "*So* good."

HARLEY

CHAPTER TWENTY-NINE

I GROAN as the morning light shines in my eyes. Beside me, Cerulean buries her head in my shoulder. Looking at the clock, I realize we've only had about two hours sleep.

Utilizing his spidey-cat sense, Cookie jumps up on the bed using the step I built him when I realized his age and arthritis meant he couldn't really do it on his own. He walks up the bed before plonking down in the tiny gap between Cerulean and me.

She groans before popping her head up. "Hi," she says, a blush coloring her cheeks when she notices me staring.

I lean over and give her a chaste kiss, making sure I don't squash Cookie. "Hi back."

She stretches, the move exposing her perfect breasts. Sure, they're not the biggest, but they're hers and there's not one bit of her I don't think isn't perfect. Well, except for her temper maybe.

"I'm sore in the best of ways," she purrs.

My morning wood jumps as I groan. "Don't tell me that," I plead.

She laughs and starts scratching Cookie's head. In response, he closes his eyes and purrs.

"We never had pets growing up," she says.

"No?"

She shakes her head. "Both my parents were too busy to help us look after one, and now.... Well, it's just not something any of us stopped to think about, I guess."

"What else didn't you have when you were growing up?" I ask.

She laughs. "God, so much. We never had birthday parties or sleepovers. We never went camping or on vacation together, or just on vacation, period."

"So you've never been on vacation?" I ask.

"I have, just not with my parents, as a family."

"I know your mom's in Switzerland, but what's the story with your dad?"

"My dad...," she says, still patting Cookie. "My dad is a complicated person."

"Like father, like daughter."

"Ha ha," she replies.

I shrug.

"I think if you were to ask him, my dad would say he's busy, focused."

"And if I'm asking you?"

"I'd say that he's... lonely, maybe? I mean, he and my mom were married for a while before they had us, then ten years later she takes off for bigger and better things."

I nod.

"Not that I begrudge her doing that, but...."

"She's your mom," I finish.

"Yeah."

We lie there for a while; the only sound is Cookie's purring.

"I miss her sometimes," she whispers.

"That's to be expected," I tell her. "When was the last time you saw her?"

"A little over two years ago. We all met her in Paris for a week."

"I love Paris."

She smiles. "It's one of my favorites too."

We're silent again before I break it this time. "It's okay to miss her, you know."

She gives a wry chuckle. "Try telling my mom that."

"She's a bit of a hard-ass?" I ask.

"Calling Cyan Tremont a hard-ass is like saying Georgia's only mildly interested in football."

I chuckle. "Again with the colors, huh?"

She shrugs. "It's a family thing."

"Something you think you'll continue?"

"I'm not planning on having kids, so fuck no."

I shift so I'm looking at her better. "You don't want kids?"

She shakes her head. "I've done my child-rearing with my sisters. They can carry on the tradition, or not."

"What about marriage?" I ask. If someone were to ask me where this is coming from, I'd honestly tell them I have no fucking idea. I know it's *way* too early to be having this conversation and the likelihood of Cerulean bolting is high, but I can't deny I'm dying to know the answers.

"You asking?" she counters.

"Fuck, no," I tell her. "I'm just... curious."

She laughs. "I'm not sure about marriage. I mean, if I met someone and he felt strongly about it, maybe, but otherwise I'm not sure one way or the other."

I nod.

"What about you?" she asks, playing with the edge of the bedsheet.

I smile. "I'm all for marriage," I say. "When I find a woman I want to spend the rest of my life with, I'd definitely want her to have my name and have the entire world know she's mine."

"Caveman."

I laugh and shrug. "There's just something about knowing the woman you love shares your name and is legally part of your family, I guess."

"What if she wanted you to take her name?"

"That could work too. I'm a flexible guy."

"You've definitely got staying power," she says through a yawn.

I bring her closer to me, careful of Cookie between us. "How about we go back to sleep for a while and then I can demonstrate my staying power a little later?"

"Sounds good," she says, eyes already closed, sleep taking its hold on her.

WHEN WE WAKE AGAIN, the sun is high in the sky. After a shower, a long-ass shower where I take Cerulean against the wall, we make it downstairs, our stomachs threatening to eat themselves.

Unfortunately, that's where my good mood ends.

My father is seated at the kitchen table, several news-papers spread out in front of him.

"Oh, hi," I say when he looks up.

"It's about time you got up," he replies. "It's well past noon. You've slept half the day away."

"I had a big night," I offer.

"So I heard." He stops when Cerulean comes into view, Cookie in her arms, wearing one of my jerseys that absolutely drowns her. "Miss Tremont," he says.

"Principal St. James," she replies, not at all intimi-dated by his gruffness, setting Cookie down in front of his bowl. The way she makes herself so at home in my home warms a part of me I thought would be buried for years to come.

My father turns back to me. "Let me remind you that the reason we are here is so you may excel at that ridiculous sport you love so much and obtain an offer at a suitable university."

"And I've done that," I remind him, going to the cupboard and pulling down some cereal and treats for Cookie.

"And how would those schools feel when they learn your focus is distracted by some high school fling?"

My eyes fly to Cerulean, who looks... amused? Her eyes are twinkling, a small smile on her lips.

"I'd remind them that even Tom Brady has a wife, kids too. Aaron Rodgers is dating; Eli Manning's wife had a baby on Super Bowl Sunday this year."

"Those are professionals," my father grits out.

"They're men, just the same as me," I argue.

"They are at the top of their game," he yells. "They've done the hard work."

"And I'm doing mine!" I all but yell, Cookie running off. "I've been seeing Cerulean for a while now and nothing has changed. My performance hasn't suffered, my grades haven't slipped." I pick up the cereal but put it down again. "Come on," I say to Cerulean. "Let's get out of here." She takes my offered hand, and we go upstairs to get changed and go.

"WAFFLE HOUSE," she says as I pull into the parking lot. "Fancy."

"We can go somewhere else," I say.

She smiles and undoes her seat belt. "I happen to *love* Waffle House."

The smell of grease and waffle batter hits us as we walk inside.

"Sit anywhere," the waitress says from behind the counter.

We take a booth by the window.

"Your dad's even more of a dick at home than he is at school," Cerulean tells me.

I laugh and twine my fingers with hers. "That he is."

"Seems like both our dads leave something to be desired, huh?"

I give her hand a squeeze, appreciative of what she's trying to do.

We order, and it's not long before we're diving into waffles, hash browns, and sausage.

"I never would've taken you for a Waffle House fan," I say, pushing my empty plate aside and wiping my mouth.

She shrugs. "Our mom used to take us here when we were little. She said she worked at one throughout college, and coming back made her thankful for all her hard work."

"She sounds like an incredible woman."

She shrugs.

"I mean, she raised, or part-raised, four incredible daughters, so she must be special, right?"

Cerulean laughs and throws her dirty napkin at me.

"What?" I ask.

"You've already got me into bed, you can stop working for it," she tells me.

I pick up her hand and kiss the back of it. "Never."

She rolls her eyes, but smiles nonetheless.

I look at my watch. "My dad should be gone by now, you wanna head back?"

Without saying a word, she reaches into her purse and throws a couple of bills on the table before getting up. I do the same and quickly usher her out of the restaurant and to the car. I unlock it, and we get in, pulling on our seat belts before I tear out of the parking lot.

"In a hurry?" she asks, a small smile playing on her lips.

I grab her hand and put it on my dick, already pressing against my fly. "What do you think?"

"Fuck," she curses, massaging me through the material. "Hurry."

I put my foot down, my Mustang surging forward.

CHAPTER THIRTY

EVENTUALLY HARLEY and I managed to separate ourselves long enough for me to go home and get ready for school today.

"Oh, hey," Indigo says as she comes into the kitchen where I'm making a cup of tea.

"Hey."

"I didn't see you all weekend."

"I was with Harley," I say, dunking my tea bag.

"Uh-huh, and, ah, how was it?" she asks, making herself a cup of coffee.

"It was good," I reply. It doesn't escape me that that's also how I described Harley's mouth on Friday night.

"The blush on your cheeks says different," she points out.

"It was pretty perfect," I concede.

She smiles. "Good, I'm glad. You deserve something of your own."

"Along those lines, could you do me a favor?" I ask.

"Sure," she says, blowing on her drink.

"Could you chaperone Vermilion's lessons this

week for me? Because of the playoffs, Harley won't have as much time to study, so I told him I'd help him."

"Is that what you crazy kids are calling it these days?" I throw a dishtowel at her. She laughs. "It's totally fine, you've done more than your fair share so I'll take my turn."

"Thanks, Ind," I tell her, kissing her cheek. "You're the best."

"Just remember that when you're having so many orgasms you can't see straight."

I laugh. "Oh, I will," I say with a wink.

THE MOMENT I step through the wide oak doors of FPA, strong, large arms come around me, a cloud of Viktor and Rolf surrounding me.

"I missed you," Harley whispers in my ear.

I chuckle. "You mean you missed getting laid," I correct.

He spins me around and pins me against the closest wall, one arm propped above me, the other cupping my face. "No, baby doll, it's all you."

I'll die before admitting it, but I kind of melt a little. I stretch up to kiss him. I intend for it to be brief, but the moment our lips touch, that's it. Our tongues battle, his hands go to my hips, bringing my body flush with his, his erection pressing against my stomach. It's only when someone whistles that we break apart.

"I may have missed you, too," I say as I wipe my lip gloss off his lips.

They kick up in a smirk. "*May?*"

I shrug. "What? You think now that I've let you into my pants I'll let you off the hook? I don't think so."

He laughs and takes my hand and kisses the back of it. "I'd expect nothing less from my royal blue."

This girl, the one who swoons or professes her love for a guy or, hell, who laughs on the regular, isn't me, but well, maybe it is. I thought being with someone, *loving* someone outside of my sisters would make me weak, split my focus. I was wrong. As we walk hand in hand down the hallway, people still clear a path for me, they still respect me. Sure, there are more looks and whispers, but let them stare, let them talk. It doesn't mean shit to me.

IN THE CAFETERIA AT LUNCH, Harley pulls me onto his lap.

"Seriously?" I ask.

"What?" he replies, his mouth full.

"We are *not* that couple," I say as I scramble off him. Sure, I've sat on his lap before, but that's when we weren't in public or there weren't any other chairs available.

"So you guys *are* a couple then?" Kingsley asks.

I glare at the sprite. "Who invited you to sit here, anyway?" I ask, despite the fact that she's been a regular at our table since the brunch she and Vermilion had all those months ago.

"I'm Vermilion's BFF, where else would I sit? And don't change the subject."

"Yeah, Cerulean, don't change the subject," Harley echoes, eyes bright, a wide smile on his face.

"Do you ever want to get laid again?" I hiss at him.

He scoffs. "Like you could turn down the awesomeness that is me. Besides," he pulls me closer to him and whispers in my ear, "you love me." For good measure he bites my earlobe too. I push his face away.

He laughs. "Am I wrong?"

"No, but you'll be sorry when I stop putting out." I cross my arms over my chest.

"I'm sorry," he says, bottom lip sticking out. "Will you forgive me?" He nuzzles my neck.

"You're such an ass," I tell him, tilting my head to give him more room.

"I love *your* ass," he says, giving it a squeeze with one hand, the other making its way up my thigh and under my skirt.

"So, couple? Not a couple?" Kingsley asks.

I get up, grabbing Harley's hand, and give her a wink as I drag him out of the cafeteria. "Where are we going?" he asks as I drag him down the hallway, out the doors, and into the parking lot.

"Unlock it," I order when we get to his car. I look around, and even though it's deserted, the probability that it'll stay that way is slim. "Drive," I tell him when I get in.

"And where exactly am I going?" he asks, doing as I say.

"Follow that road."

He does so, the road running along the side of the forest that gives the school its name. We come to the back of the school where the maintenance sheds are.

"Park there," I tell him, pointing to a hidden spot just large enough for a car.

When he does, I whip off my seat belt and straddle his lap, feeling for the lever to lower his seat.

"Comfortable there?" he asks as I finally find it and drop the seat back.

"Mmmm, I am now," I reply, leaning down to kiss him.

"Just what did you have in mind?" he asks when we break apart.

"Simply finishing what you started, baby," I tell him, grinding against him.

"Good plan," he says, reaching up and pulling my face toward him again.

While we kiss, I undo his belt and fly, shoving my hand in his boxer-briefs and giving him a squeeze.

"Shit, baby doll," he pants. "I *love* your hands on me."

"The feeling's mutual," I reply, grabbing one of his and placing it between my legs.

"You get so wet for me," he says, slipping beneath my panties and sliding a finger inside me.

"Mmm," I moan as he pumps his finger in and out. He adds a second finger, and I ride his hand.

"You like that, huh?" he asks.

I nod.

"Good," he says before stopping.

"Seriously?" I huff.

He laughs, pulling his pants and underwear down before reaching into the center console and pulling out a condom.

"Oh," I say as he holds it out to me.

"That was your plan, right?" he asks as I roll the latex on him.

"What do you think?" I ask, pulling my panties to the side and positioning him at my entrance.

"Fuck, nothing will ever feel as good as this does," he says once he's fully seated inside me.

"Not even bringing home state?"

He opens his eyes and cups my face. "Baby doll, the world could end right now and I'd die a happy man."

I groan, and not just because he lifts his hips to meet me. "That was corny."

"You like it," he says before kissing me once more.

"I really do," I tell him as I grind on him.

"Yeah, that's it, baby doll," he encourages. He throws his head back, the veins in his neck straining. I never thought a neck would turn me on, but then again, I never thought I'd be having sex with the school's quarterback in his car on our lunch break either.

I lean forward, one hand on his neck, the other resting on his shoulder, and bite down hard.

"Oh fuck," he yells, jerking inside me.

I giggle, actually fucking giggle as he looks down at where we're joined.

"What the fuck was that?" he asks, either his dick or me, I'm not sure. He looks up at me. "I didn't mean to do that."

I shrug. "I kinda like that you did. Makes me feel all womanly and shit."

"Oh, babe, you're definitely all womanly and shit." He thrusts his still-hard cock in me.

"Well, how about you be all manly and shit and make me come?"

He chuckles. "Will do," he says, and starts pounding into me with a vengeance.

It's not long before I'm coming hard. "Oh fuck, yes," I breathe, coming down from my high.

I rub my thumb over where I bit him. "It's going to leave a mark."

He grunts. "Good. I like the idea of you marking me. It gets me even harder than knowing I'll smell like you for the rest of the day."

"Shit, that's hot," I tell him, my head falling to his shoulder.

He pulls me back so he can look me in the eye. "We've got something here, don't we?" he asks.

"Of course we do."

"And it's not just sex?"

I cup his cheek. "We've only been sleeping together for four days; I think it's safe to say it's more than just sex."

"Good," he says.

"But just in case not everyone gets the message...." I lean down and suck on his neck, leaving a hickey for everyone to see.

"And you call me a caveman," he says, laughing.

I shrug. "What's mine is mine."

He pulls my blouse aside and sucks just above my left breast. No one will be able to see it, but I think that's the point.

"Come on," he says, fixing my top. "We should probably get to class."

. . .

WE'RE fifteen minutes late when we walk into English, but neither of us care. There are whistles and porno noises galore and one of the guys on the football team says, "Check out the hickey she left on his neck."

I chuckle as Harley pulls down the collar of his shirt, showing it off even more.

I get to my seat but look up when I feel someone staring at me. All alone in the back corner, TK sits draped over his desk, eyes narrowed, jaw working back and forth. I give him a smile and a wave. His eyes narrow further. Blissfully unaware, Harley wraps an arm around my waist, kissing my temple before taking his seat. I smile and take my own. TK can scowl as much as he likes, but while he's got one of my secrets, I also have one of his.

THAT'S ALL WELL and good until I see Ron Graham, head of admissions for the Carver Institute, leaving the office, TK right behind him.

"It was good to see you again, Mr. Graham," TK says. "I'll tell my parents you send your regards."

He nods and smiles. "Please do."

"Mr. Graham," I say, going up to him, my hands clammy. "How nice to see you. What brings you down to the Empire State of the South?"

His shoulders drop when he sees me. "Ah, Cerulean."

"I have to tell you, I am so incredibly honored to be attending your prestigious institution in eighteen months' time."

"Yes, about that, might we talk somewhere in

private?" he asks, cupping my elbow and trying to steer me toward the office.

I wrench out of his grasp. "How about we do this right here," I say.

"I really think we should go somewhere private and chat."

From the corner of my eye, I see TK smirk. "What has he told you?" I ask.

"Mr. Thomas has brought some... troubling rumors to our attention."

I nod. "And you're rescinding your offer based on *rumors*?" I ask, crossing my arms over my chest.

"Miss. Tremont, please understand the Carver Institute cannot have any shadows of doubt cast over its students."

"And if this rumor is based on nothing more than Mr. Thomas's jealousy and bitterness on his part?"

"I have known the Thomas family for many years. His father and I used to spend summers together on Cape Cod."

"Of course you did."

He cups my elbow again and pushes me closer to the door of the office. "The allegations Mr. Thomas makes are *very* serious. Not just in terms of what it means for your academic future, but also for your health. He is merely concerned for your well-being."

I laugh. "Of course he is."

"Drug use is a very serious problem, Miss Tremont."

I look to TK, a smug grin pulling at his lips, then back to Mr. Graham. "How much is he paying you to ensure nothing I say changes your mind?"

"The Thomas family are longtime supporters of the Carver Institute."

I scoff. "I'm sure they are. Just like I'm sure the donation they've given you will be put to good use."

"Miss Tremont—"

"Save it," I say, holding my hand up. "You've made your choice, sold your program. I'm out."

"I'm sorry."

"No you're not," I say, walking away from him and my future.

HARLEY

BY THE TIME someone told me something was going down between Cerulean, TK, and some old dude, it was already half over.

I arrive just in time to hear him tell her that drug use is a very serious problem. I want to butt in and say "no shit," but my bigger concern is why he's saying it to Cerulean.

TK sees me and comes over.

"Looks like your girlfriend's future is being flushed down the toilet right in front of us," he says.

"What did you do?" I grit out, unable to take my eyes off Cerulean.

"Nothing she wouldn't do to me if she were in my position."

I slam him up against the wall. "Why is he lecturing her about drug use?" I ask.

TK laughs. "Don't tell me you haven't noticed. The lack of appetite, the hyper-focus, her ability to concentrate beyond normal limits."

"What are you saying?" I shove him into the wall again.

"Your little girlfriend over there is addicted to

Ritalin, a lot of it too. I mean, that's great for my hip pocket, but not so much for her admission to schools who require their students to be squeaky clean."

"You're lying," I tell him, but as I do, things start lining up in my head.

He laughs again. "They're making sense, all those things you thought were just quirks. Suddenly it's becoming clear, isn't it?"

"Shut up," I tell him. "Just shut the fuck up." I let him go when Cerulean walks past me. "Hey!" I yell, but either she doesn't hear me or she's ignoring me. Either way, she doesn't stop.

"Hey," I say, finally able to reach to her and grab her arm, stopping her and pulling her to face me. "What the fuck just happened there?" I ask.

Her eyes and expression are blank. She shrugs. "TK played his card."

"And?"

"And my place at Carver, my future is gone."

I cup her face and direct her eyes to mine. "Your future is *not* gone."

"It may as well be. I've worked for that, for Carver my whole life."

"So you find a new dream."

She laughs. "If you woke up tomorrow and couldn't play football, could you find a new dream, just like that?" She snaps her fingers.

"Surely there are other schools besides Carver you can go to."

"It was the only one that mattered."

"What about me? Do I matter?" I ask.

The blank look disappears from her face. What

it's replaced with is almost worse. She tilts her head and cups my cheek, eyes soft. "Of course you did."

"Did? Why are you talking in past tense? We can take some time to grieve and then we regroup. This isn't over. *We're* not over. Your future isn't over," I tell her.

"Isn't it?" she asks.

"No! You're Cerulean Tremont," I remind her. "A Sovereign of Savannah, my royal blue."

She sighs. "I wish that could be enough."

"It is. I promise you, we'll make this work." In desperation, I press my lips to hers. She meets me, but not with the same fervor she usually does.

"Goodbye, Harley," she says once we break apart, backing out of my hold.

"No, Cerulean—" I reach for her again, but she holds up a hand.

"This was a mistake," she tells me. "I thought I could do this, be that girl, be happy, but I can't. It's.... It's not me, and I don't want it." She stops, takes a breath, then stares me in the eyes. "I don't want you."

This time when she turns to walk away, I let her.

CHAPTER THIRTY-TWO

AS MUCH AS it killed me to say those things to Harley, they were necessary. Look what our relationship has already cost me. I lost focus; I forgot what I am, *who* I am. I thought I could have it all. I got swept away in a daydream. Powerful women cannot afford to be distracted, and Harley distracted me in the worst, and I'll admit, best way.

"Ritalin?" Magenta asks, coming into my room and sitting on my bed.

"If you've come to tell me off or say 'I told you so,' you can save it. I already know everything you're about to say. I don't need to hear it from someone else."

She holds her hands up. "I wasn't going to say a word."

I flop back on the bed and throw a pillow over my face. "You were right," I say.

She sighs and lifts the pillow. "I was, and I wasn't." She tucks the pillow under her head as she lies down next to me. "I was right when I warned you about Harley and what could happen, but I was wrong to try to persuade you not to be with him in the first place."

"Huh?" I ask.

"You were happy with him."

"And I'll be happy without him."

"Will you really?" she asks.

"I tried to be one of those girls, M. One of the ones who has the boyfriend and the life and everything we're told we should have. Look what happened when I did."

"This wasn't Harley's fault," she tells me.

"Oh, I know. It was mine because I was weak, because I couldn't do it all."

Magenta sits up, grabs me by the shoulders, and shakes the shit out of me.

"Ow! What was that for?" I ask when she stops.

"That was for thinking like you aren't Cerulean Tremont."

"I may as well not be."

"Don't make me slap you," she threatens.

I sigh. "I fucked up."

"Yeah, you did, but can I tell you a secret?" She doesn't wait for my response, probably knowing I wasn't going to play along. "Everyone does. This doesn't make you special."

"But not everyone's are as monumental as mine," I counter.

"No, some of them are bigger. Need I remind you of who's in my room?"

"Emily isn't a mistake, M," I say, snuggling into her side. "She's a blessing."

She scoffs. "Well, maybe sometimes," she

concedes. She runs a hand through my hair. "You'll get through this, C."

"What if I don't?"

She pulls back. "Why wouldn't you? You have all of us to help you."

"But—"

"Sometimes I think you forget that this sister thing goes both ways. Yes, you've done a fuckload of stuff for us, but it doesn't mean we can't repay the favor."

"I never did it so you'd owe me."

"And we wouldn't be doing it to pay you back."

I sigh, and she continues running her hand through my hair. "What do we do now?" I ask.

"We take a minute, regroup, and then we take down TK."

HARLEY

SPENDING my lunch break in the library during is not something I thought I'd do my senior year, but here I am. There's absolutely no way I want to be anywhere near TK, and I can't even look at Cerulean without my heart wanting to jump out of my chest, so my options are limited. Add to that, Trinity has been trying to stick to me like glue, and I just... can't.

"Hey, Miss Violet," I say as I trudge through the doors.

"Uh-oh," she replies. "I know that tone. Come, sit."

She comes out from behind the desk and moves to a reading nook off to the side. I slump into a chair opposite her.

"Tell me, what's going on?"

"Have you ever had trouble in love?" I ask her.

She throws her head back and laughs. "Sugar, I've had so much trouble it'll make what you're goin' through look like child's play."

I sigh. "She told me she didn't want me."

Violet pats my knee. "Girls are stupid. Especially in high school. Overly dramatic too."

I run a hand through my hair. "The thing is, I don't even blame her. Her whole life, everything she's worked for has come crashing down."

"Shit happens," Violet says.

I look at her.

"What? It does. You can't stop it, you can't fight it, that's just how it is."

"I didn't do anything," I tell her. "I should've done something."

"Is there anythin' you could've done?" she asks.

I stop and think. "TK, my teammate, he orchestrated all of this. I-I goaded him, provoked him. I shouldn't have done that."

"*You* say you did that, yet it's your girl he went after?"

I nod.

"Then it sounds to me like it doesn't matter what you did, he was goin' to come after you one way or another."

I pull at my hair. "It didn't need to go down this way!"

"Life very rarely goes the way we want it to."

I look at her twinkling green eyes. "What happened with you?" I ask. "You know, your story."

She leans back in her chair. "You sure you want to hear?" she asks. "My story, it's not a happy one."

"Do I look like I'm interested in hearts and flowers and shit right now?"

She laughs. "No, you don't."

"So tell me something to get my mind off my own misery and make me feel horrible for wallowing in self-pity."

She sighs and takes off her glasses. "Leroy came to

work for my family as a gardener/handyman the summer of 1960. He was nineteen, and I was an extremely impressionable fifteen."

I nod. "The gardener and the girl, I got it."

"He was also African-American," she says.

"Oh."

She nods. "Georgia in the sixties was not a kind place for black men."

"No, I don't suppose it was," I agree.

"He was with us for a few years and we grew to be friends, then more. I told him I wanted to go to college, against my parents' wishes, and he told me he wanted to be a musician. All the money he earned working for us he spent on records and music, anythin' he could get his hands on to help further his talent." She shakes her head. "Boy, did he have talent."

"You guys fell in love," I assume.

She nods. "We did. Desegregation started in 1959, so we thought it would be okay. Highly controversial, but okay."

"But it wasn't."

"No. When my parents found out, they fired Leroy on the spot and forbade me to ever see him again. They arranged a marriage with one of their friends' sons, Walter Hamilton the third. I told them I would not marry Walter, that I wanted to marry Leroy and go to college. You can guess how well that went down."

"Not at all well," I say.

"My senior year they shipped me off to France for boardin' school. Leroy and I tried to keep in touch, but it was hard. Letter delivery was slow and not very reliable. Eventually they just... stopped."

"So you have no idea what happened to him?" I ask.

She shakes her head. "No. I like to think he did follow his dreams and become a musician, but I resigned myself a long time ago to never knowin' what happened to him. I still can't listen to classical music without my heart breakin' in two."

"Man, that's tragic. You loved him?" I ask.

She smiles. "With all my heart. Leroy was my other half, a true soul mate."

"Damn."

She chuckles.

"And you never married?"

"As much as my parents wanted me to, no. Every time they brought it up, I threated to run away. Back then, having a daughter run away was worse than one who wanted to go to college and refused to get married, so they let me enroll at the University of Savannah in 1962."

"Wow."

"I kept hoping that one day Leroy would come back for me, but he never has."

"Is that why you never married? You're still waiting for him?" I ask.

She sighs. "It took me a long time to realize he was never comin' back. It was hard, but eventually I learned to accept it. By then I was old, way past my prime. Nobody wanted me."

I reach out and squeeze her hand. "I don't know about that. I'd have you in a heartbeat."

"Ah, but your heart belongs to another," she points out.

"Thanks for the reminder," I grumble.

She chuckles. "You can't deny your heart. It doesn't work that way."

"Did you try? To love again?" I clarify.

"I tried. I failed. The heart wants what the heart wants."

The bell rings, and she pats my knee. "You'll be okay, Harley. Things might not be perfect right now, but I have faith everything will work out."

"How?" I ask. "After everything you've been through, how can you still believe in love?"

She gives me a smile, but it doesn't reach her eyes. "Because once love is lost, all we're left with is hope. Now go on, get to class." She literally shoos me out of the library.

Violet's words swirl in my head as I walk down the hallway. I love Cerulean. I will *always* love Cerulean.

Just like my first day, the crowd parts, and she and her sisters are huddled around their lockers. I know she's my one and I will do anything and everything necessary to get her back.

Cerulean

CHAPTER THIRTY-FOUR

MY SISTERS LET me wallow for two days. On the third they put a stop to it. Of course, that was helped by seeing that twit Trinity Barnes all over Harley every chance she got. I took heart that he never returned her affection. Annoyingly, TK was still buzzing around, thinking he got the best of me. He may have won this battle, but he won't win the war. Of course he's still supplying me with my pills, something that kills me every time I have to ask him for more, but what can I do? I need them, and right now they're the only things keeping me together.

"He may be spending time with her," Indigo whispers in my ear. "But he doesn't want her."

"You know this for a fact, huh?" I ask, turning my back on Harley and Trinity.

"Of course I do, everyone does. You're just too stupid and too stubborn to admit it, *again*."

"You know what happened, and I've told you why I can't be with him or anyone," I tell her.

"And I've told you that's bullshit," she says. "You're Cerulean Tremont, a Sovereign of Savannah.

We bow to no one, but you are bowing to TK right now!" She storms off.

Vermilion shrugs. "I agree with Ind. *But* I also get why you're taking your time. Heartbreak isn't easy to get over. It's not supposed to be."

"When did she get so wise?" I ask Magenta as Vermilion heads off.

"Probably about the same time you stopped coddling her," she replies.

"I was—"

She holds up her hands. "I know, you were protecting her, sheltering her. We all did, but somewhere along the line she decided she didn't need it anymore."

We watch Vermilion meet up with Kingsley, a wide smile on her face, and Magenta adds, "Being friends with her, as much as I dislike her sassy ass, probably helped."

"Eh," I say, not convinced.

"Then there's all the shit we've all been through. She's been there, seen and heard it all."

"Mmm." This I do agree with.

"All in all, I think it's fairly safe to say our little red is all grown up."

"Fuck me," I curse.

"You're telling me," she says. "But it's something we'll have to get used to. They don't stay the same forever." She shuts her locker and walks away.

"No, we don't," I say under my breath as Harley's head turns my way. His gaze sears into mine, and I swear my heart is about to burst.

He walks toward me, and my heart kicks into a higher gear. I turn around to grab my books out of my locker and shut it before he gets over here, but in my haste, I drop them.

"Son of a bitch," I mutter.

"Not sure my mom would appreciate you calling her that," he says, bending down to help me. His scent wraps around me, and I have to stop myself from pushing him to the ground, mounting him, and sniffing him.

"What are you doing, Harley?" I ask with a sigh.

"I'm helping my girl pick up the books she dropped."

"I told you I don't want you; I think that means I'm not your girl anymore."

"Not if you were under extreme emotional distress at the time of making said comment."

"Extreme emotional distress? What is this, an episode of *Law and Order*?"

The corner of his mouth kicks up; so does my heart.

"I'm just giving you an out, royal blue."

I close my eyes when he calls me that. "Please don't," I tell him.

"Why not?" he asks. "Because you think you're weaker with me around? Because I distract you? We both know that's bullshit. I love you, you love me; what's so bad about that?"

"Please, Harley," I plead.

"No." He grabs my wrists and shakes me. "Look at me, damn it!"

I open my eyes, his brown ones filled with so much longing, hurt, and sorrow I almost lose my breath.

He cups my cheek. "There's my girl. I know shit

hit the fan for you spectacularly the other day, but we can get through it, *together*. I know I shouldn't have provoked TK the way I did, but baby doll, he doesn't matter. *We're* what matters."

"My future is gone, Harley," I remind him. "Everything I worked for is gone."

"So we build a new future together."

I shake my head. "I can't."

He lets his hands drop. "You're letting him win."

"I'm picking my battles."

"Is that something you would've done before?"

"It's something I have to do now." I take a breath. "It's something I can't do with you."

He gets up, his strong frame towering over me. "You can push me away as far as you want, Cerulean, but no matter what you do, you won't be rid of me. That's what you do for the people you love. It's what you do when you've met your match."

I choke back a sob as he hands me the books I dropped.

"I'll be seeing you round, my royal blue," he says as he leans down and kisses the top of my head.

SOMEHOW I MAKE it through the day, but if anyone were to ask me what happened, I couldn't tell them. The pills help me focus in class, but they can't make me feel.

After school, I go straight home and to bed. A few hours later, Vermilion joins me, her passion fruit scent comforting me as she draws me into her arms.

"It'll be all right, Blue," she says.

I try to smile but I can't, so I pat her hand.

"We're Tremonts; we've been through worse than this."

"I hate feeling like this," I tell her. "Like my heart's been ripped out of my chest."

"I know. I want to tell you eventually it gets better, but I think you just learn to live with it." She pauses. "Or you know, you could stop being so stubborn and just be with the guy. He's a good one."

"I know he is, but he's also a distraction. I mean, look how long it took for me to get the.... Oh, shit." I sit up, looking at my youngest sister, one of the four things I love most on this earth. "The recommendation from Alexandrov, he never gave it to me." I told Vermilion not to worry about the application, that I would do it for her because of the awesome sister I am. Now look what's happened.

The blood drains from her face. I look at my watch. The deadline for the application is 5:00 p.m. My vintage Cartier watch reads 5:05 p.m.

"I.... Fuck."

HARLEY

"THANKS FOR MEETING WITH ME, Mr. Garrett," I say, shaking the man's hand. It's strong, I like that.

"When our number-one target for recruitment calls for a meeting, you better believe I drop everything to make it happen."

"I appreciate it," I tell him.

"So, what can we do for you?" he asks.

"Your offer, does it still stand?"

"Is there something in particular you wanted that we haven't offered you?"

"I want to know more about your international business and political science departments."

"A double major?" he asks. "On top of football? Son, I applaud your work ethic, and I know you asked about this before, but don't you think it's a little *too* much?"

"Not for me, my girlfriend. She had a spot at the Carver Institute but they rescinded their offer. This is about what you can do for *her*."

He sits back in his seat and smiles. "Our

international business and political science departments are solid; our graduates have good outcomes."

"But not great," I guess.

He shrugs. "No better or worse than most universities, I'd say."

"Any plans to change that?" I ask.

"We're always working on raising the standards of our university."

"Soon?" I ask.

"We could always accelerate our plans if, say, a highly valuable asset comes our way."

"The minute you tell me you've got a highly competitive program and a spot for my girl, then I'll give you my verbal commitment to attend your fine institution."

He chuckles. "You this determined on the field?"

"More so."

He nods. "I'll see what I can do."

"Good."

"Does your girl know what lengths you're going for her?"

I shrug.

"She's one lucky girl."

"Ha! She doesn't think so, but she will if you can pull this off."

"It'll take time," he warns.

"You show me that certain professors have agreed to terms, starting no later than the year after next, and we'll have a deal, including the terms you offered specifically for me."

"Maybe business should be on the cards for you," he says.

I laugh. "I'll leave that up to Cerulean. I just want to show her there are options out there for her."

He gets up and offers me his hand. "I'll be in touch."

"I'll be waiting," I tell him, taking his hand.

I know it's not where Cerulean had her heart set on going, but if Garrett can pull this off, then it's definitely better than nothing.

I BREEZE into school on Monday with a spring in my step. That all but disappears when Trinity appears, once again gluing herself to my side.

I suppress a groan.

"Hey," she says, playing with the top button of my shirt.

I knock her hand away. "What do you want, Trinity?" I ask.

"What I've wanted for a while now: you."

"Well, I'm taken."

"From what I saw and heard last week, I'd have to say that you're wrong about that. TK made sure of it."

"Yeah, well, TK may have won this round, but he won't win them all."

Trinity sinks into my side further, despite me trying to push her away. She snorts. "If you say so."

"I do."

She pats my chest. "Sooner or later you'll realize I'm exactly the girl you need by your side. You and me, we could do great things." Her hand moves down my chest, but I pluck it off me before she can get too far.

"The only girl I need is Cerulean Tremont. If

you're not her, I don't wanna know. There is no other girl for me. In a sea of Victoria's Secret models, it will always be her I pick, and I will do it a million times over. She is the only girl for me, now and forever."

She laughs as we come around the corner and Cerulean, not looking at all Cerulean-like, comes into view.

"That mess is what you need?" she asks. "You could do *so* much better."

I shake Trinity off and go over to the sisters. "What's going on?" I ask.

Cerulean is... frantic, harried, panicked. She's a mess. Vermilion looks off too. Her eyes are red, shoulders slumped.

Magenta sighs. I figure she's about to tell me to fuck off when she answers. "Cerulean forgot to get a recommendation from Vermilion's piano teacher so she could apply to a summer workshop put on by the National Conservatorium. Applications closed on Friday."

"Fuck," I curse.

"That about sums it up."

"Can I do anything to help?"

"Not unless you can go back in time and get the recommendation. She's been running around all weekend trying to fix everything but...."

"Is she okay?" I ask. "Is Vermilion okay?"

"Red's devastated, but she'll be okay. There'll be other workshops that she can get into. With as much talent as she has, there's no way they'd reject her. She's heartbroken right now, but she'll survive. She's survived worse."

"And Cerulean?" Her hair's a mess, eyes darting

all over the place, dark circles under them, hands unable to stay still.

Magenta sighs. "I don't know. It's been one big blow after another this past week. Losing Carver was tough, but letting down her sister?" She shakes her head. "I just don't know. We're doing our best to rally around her, but you know how seriously she takes looking after us."

"It's her life," I say.

Magenta nods. "Yup. I thought with you.... Well, I thought she might have lightened up, and she did but then...."

"Then TK happened."

She sighs again. "Yeah."

"You'll let me know if I can do anything?" I ask.

She takes her eyes off her sister and turns them to me. They're hazel as opposed to Cerulean's jade green, but still unmistakably Tremont eyes.

"I know she's your sister, but she's still my everything," I tell her.

Her eyes soften a bit. "Yeah, okay."

"Tell Vermilion it'll be all right."

"I will."

"And um, thanks for, you know, telling me what's going on."

She shrugs. "You were good for her. I want her to see her back to that."

So do I.

CHAPTER THIRTY-SIX

I SPENT all weekend tracking down anyone even remotely associated with the Conservatorium's summer workshop. Even with our name and connections it wasn't easy. When I went to Alexandrov's house on Friday evening, the fucker was only too happy to give me the recommendation. Under no circumstances could I persuade him to help me get that recommendation in front of the people who matter though.

The online portal has shut, but I will not rest until Vermilion is in that program. That's one of the good things about Ritalin: sleep is not easy to come by. Unless I'm in Harley's arms, that is, but I'm not thinking about that. Or about him. I can't. I won't. I have to fix this for Vermilion. She isn't mad at me, but I can tell she's heartbroken she won't be going to the workshop. I did that. I failed her. That knowledge kills me. *Kills* me. I'd take Carver rescinding their offer a million times over seeing the disappointment on her face when she realized what I hadn't done.

Indigo and Magenta don't blame me either, but

they should. It was *my* job, *my* responsibility. I didn't do what I said I would so everything is my fault.

My family is everything to me. The realization that I've failed them, that I wasn't able to do my job... it's heartbreaking.

I sit in class and listen to the lectures given by my teachers, but every moment I sit here is a moment I could use to try to persuade the powers that be at the Conservatorium that my sister is more than worth the risk, is worthy of bending the rules for.

I TAKE my seat in Media Studies, Harley sliding into a desk next to me.

"Hey," he says. His voice washes over me, reminding me how good it felt when he was telling me to come or professing his love for me. "Is everything okay?" he asks.

I nod. "Yup. Yes, it's fine. There's absolutely nothing wrong with my sisters or me. We're all totally fine."

"If that's the case, why is your leg bouncing like that?" He nods to the leg I didn't even realize was moving. I stop it.

"I'm just eager to get class started, I don't want to waste a minute of learning." I put on a smile that even I don't believe.

"How are you doing with, you know"—he lowers his voice—"Carver?"

I wave a hand. "That's old news. I'm totally fine about it. I'm only a junior, so I have plenty of time to figure something out."

"What about what happened with Vermilion?"

My head snaps to face him. "Who told you about that?" I hiss. My leg starts bouncing again.

"Magenta did, but it's obvious something is up. You're a mess. Your hair hasn't been brushed; you're not wearing makeup, not that you need to. You're jumpy, nervous, and anxious. It's not news that something is going on with you." He stops and takes a breath. "If there's anything I can do to help...."

I shake my head. "Nope, no way. No, it's all good. I don't need your help, I'm good, it's fi—" He grabs my arm and drags me out of the classroom.

"Hey! What are you doing?" I ask. "Class is about to start and we can't miss it. Learning is important and—"

"Get in there," he says, cutting me off once again and opening the door to the girls' bathroom.

"You can't go in there, it's a girls' bathroom, and last I checked you're definitely not a girl. Hey!" I protest as he picks me up, walks in, and sets me on the counter.

"Look at me, Cerulean," he orders as he stands between my legs.

I shake my head, looking anywhere but at him.

He grabs my chin and directs it to him, so I close my eyes. "Look. At. Me," he grits out, the pressure on my jaw increasing.

Slowly I open my eyes.

"There you are," he says, shoulders dropping slightly. "Are you okay?" he asks, his eyes searching mine.

I sigh and shrug.

"I know we're not whatever we were but I still care about you, still love you." I didn't think there was any part of my heart left to break, but the pain in my chest proves me wrong. "And with the way everything went down last week, we never had a chance to discuss what happened with TK and his... allegations."

"They're true," I tell him, my foot tapping even though it's inches above the ground.

"Oh, I know they are. Even if your behavior didn't confirm it, your pupils do."

"Okay, great chat," I say and try to get down, but he puts a hand on my thigh and stops me.

"What's with the pills?" he asks.

"I have ADHD."

"No you don't. You didn't take them all the time when we were together, so I know that's not true. I'm pretty sure it's just for classes and to study."

"Then it appears you've got it all figured out and don't need me, so I'll be going now." I try once again to get down, and once again he stops me.

"Stop trying to get away from me!"

"We're missing class, we can't miss class, class is important," I reply. I know I'm talking too fast, saying too much, but I can't help it. I need the pills to function, and if these side effects are what I have to live with, then so be it.

"Argh!" he yells, giving me a shake. "Stop it, just stop it." He looks into my eyes once more. "I know everything has gone to shit with you lately, but I'm worried about you."

"There's no need, I'm fi—"

"If you say 'fine' one more time, I'm going to lose it."

I snap my mouth shut.

"You're not fine," he says, cupping my cheek. "I'm not fine. None of this is fucking fine." His forehead rests on mine; his lips so close to my own. "Why is everything so fucked-up?" he asks.

"Because *I* fucked it up," I reply.

He pulls back. "N—"

"Yes." I cut him off. "I'm a mess. Literally and figuratively. I thought I had a handle on everything, but I got complacent, got sloppy, and look what happened." I take a breath. "The pills, they help me focus, help me get a grip on my shit."

"This isn't a grip," he tells me. "It's too much, baby doll."

I shake my head. "It's not enough. It'll never be enough, not unless I can fix what I broke."

"And does that include us?" he asks.

I press a quick kiss to his lips. "We had fun."

"And that's it?"

"What more can it be?"

"It can be everything."

"My sisters are my everything and look what I did to one of them." This time when I try to hop down, he doesn't stop me.

"That was—"

"That was me not doing my job, it was me not putting them first. I can't and I won't let it happen again," I say before walking out.

THANKFULLY HARLEY LEAVES me alone the rest of the day. When I get home, I call the last number on my list. My last hope.

"Mr. Jones?" I ask when he picks up.

"Yes, who is this?" he replies, his rich baritone voice washing over me like honey.

"Mr. Jones, my name is Cerulean Tremont. My sister Vermilion Tremont is an incredibly gifted pianist. In fact, they often associate the word prodigy with her, here in Savannah. She had her heart set on attending your summer workshop but her current teacher held her recommendation hostage until it was too late." I stop. "Actually, that's not entirely true. The truth is I, her big sister, got caught up in a boy and forgot to get the recommendation from him and complete her application before the portal closed."

"How did you get this number?" he asks.

"If I could email you her application, you'd see what an incredible talent she is and how you can't not have her in your program. I've emailed some of your colleagues, but if you, sir, could see her audition, I know your opinion would be enough to get her in. Ten years from now people will come from all over the world to hear her play. You don't want to miss out on an opportunity to shape such a star, do you?"

"Young lady, I don't know how you got this number, but this is highly inappropriate."

"I know, but Vermilion didn't do anything wrong. Her teacher is a cunt—"

"Excuse me?"

"But he's the best in the state. It's taking all I've got to keep him teaching her. My other sister is heading to UNash next year, and we suggested Vermilion go with her, find a better, nicer teacher, but she won't, she doesn't want to impose. That's just the girl my sister is, Mr. Jones. Sweet as pie, wouldn't hurt a fly. She's... she's gone through a lot in her short life, but she *loves* playing the piano, sir. Please, if you could just take a look at her application, I know you'd see what everyone else sees. You won't be disappointed, I swear."

"Miss—"

"Tremont, Cerulean Tremont, and my sister is Vermilion Tremont. They're not common names so hopefully you won't have any trouble remembering them when it comes to deciding who gains admittance to your workshop."

He sighs. "Miss Tremont, I'm afraid I cannot look at your sister's application. You put forth a very persuasive case, and I'm sure your sister has all the talent you describe, but our application process is very strict. We make it abundantly clear the time of the deadline. We have thousands of applicants and very few spots. I'm sorry, I wish I could, but it just wouldn't be fair to those who did get their applications in on time."

"But it wasn't her fault. Her teacher is evil, and I forgot about her application. It should be *me* who's punished, not Vermilion."

"How old is your sister, Miss Tremont?"

"Fifteen," I reply. "But she's been through a lot in her life. Our mom left and her best friend died in her arms. That's why we have to look out for her, it's why *I* have to."

"That might be the case, but fifteen is still old

enough to compile an application and submit it. I've seen toddlers doing extraordinary things on cell phones—cell phones, Miss Tremont. I'm sure a teenager raised in the same environment as those toddlers is more than capable of uploading files and submitting a form."

"But—"

"I wish you and your sister the very best, but unfortunately she will not be attending our summer workshop. I encourage her to keep up with her studies and apply next year. Good day to you."

With that, he ends the call.

I'M FRANTIC, calling anyone and everyone I can think of. I even try Vermilion's first piano teacher, now long retired and living in Florida. No one can help me.

For reasons even I don't understand, I get in my car and start driving.

Usually I can take in the beauty of all the squares, the antebellum homes, the river, but not today. Nobody can help me. No one. Not a single soul. My cause is lost. Vermilion won't be going to the workshop. My sister won't be going to the one thing she desperately wants to.

I pull over, my chest tight, heart pounding. Somehow, in all my mindless twists and turns, I've ended up outside Harley's house. The curtain in the living room is open. While I watch, Principal St. James walks past. It's a long shot, but what do I have to lose?

Ringing the doorbell, I ignore my shaking hands. An older woman with kind eyes opens the door.

"Hi, I'm sorry to intrude, but I was wondering if I might speak with Principal St. James for a minute?"

She invites me in. "Please wait here while I fetch him," she says.

"Thank you."

While I'm waiting, Cookie appears, winding his way through my legs. I bend down and pick him up. "Hey, Cookie," I say, scratching under his chin. "How's everything going? Haven't had any more naps interrupted by horny teenagers?" I ask.

He purrs and rubs against my hand.

"Good."

"Miss Tremont?" Principal St. James asks, coming into view. "What are you doing here and with that godforsaken cat? Harley!" he bellows.

"I, um, was wondering if you might be able to help me, well, my sister really," I say as footsteps sound overhead before coming down the stairs.

"Yes, sir?" Harley asks as he's halfway down. "Cerulean?"

Principal St. James leans over and plucks Cookie out of my arms, holding him out to Harley. "Take this mongrel and do something with it, would you?"

He nods and tucks Cookie under his arm. "What are you doing here?" he asks me.

"And just what is it you were hoping I could do for your sister, Miss Tremont?" he asks.

My head is whipping back and forth like I'm in a tennis match.

"Um, ah, my sister, Vermilion, the youngest, she wants to attend a summer workshop put on by the National Conservatorium, but I forgot to send in her application before the deadline. I know it's a long shot but—"

"If she was careless enough to miss a deadline, then it is not my place to spend whatever capital I may have on lazy and negligent students."

"But it's my fault," I say. "She did nothing wrong! She's a good person and an incredible pianist. Please, you're my last hope." I'm all but begging, but I'm desperate.

"As I said, I cannot and will not spend any capital I have on irresponsible students. How else will she learn?"

"But it wasn't her fault!" I plead. "It was mine. Punish me, not her." I grab his hand with both of mine. "Please, sir, you're my only hope. No one else can help me; no one else will help me. *Please.*"

He looks down at his hand sandwiched between mine. "Get your hands off me," he orders.

I do as he says. "Will you help me?" I ask. "I have all the phone numbers and email addresses of everyone on the Conservatorium board. I'm sure if you tell them how incredible Vermilion is, they'll accept her."

He studies me, not giving anything away.

"If it helps, tell them what a screwup I am. Tell them about my drug use, tell them how the Carver Institute rescinded their offer. Tell them I'm not fit to empty trash or clean whiteboards or whatever. Tell them whatever they need to hear in order to let Vermilion in."

"Cerulean," Harley says, walking closer to me. "You need to stop. You're not talking or thinking straight."

I look to Harley, so strong, so sure. "I can't," I tell him. "This is my last chance, Vermilion's last chance. I will do whatever I have to in order to make things right. I can't let her down." I turn back to Principal St. James. "Please, will you help me?"

He folds his arms across his chest. "No."

HARLEY

AFTER MY FATHER'S flat refusal to help her, Cerulean calmly thanked him for his time, turned, and walked out the door.

"That's your girlfriend?" he asks.

"Ex. She dumped me last week." For simplicity's sake, I go with this. Telling him we hadn't put a label on it and were fucking wouldn't help my cause.

"*She* dumped you?"

I shrug. "It happens."

He shakes his head and goes back to his study.

"Drug use?" Mrs. Stark asks, coming out from the hallway where she was obviously listening.

"Ritalin. She's not shooting heroin in her spare time."

"Still."

"I know. I tried talking to her about it today. It, ah, didn't go well."

"She's spiraling," she tells me.

"I know, but what can I do about it? She won't let me in. The only thing she cares about is her sisters."

"So go to them. Maybe they might be able to get through to her?"

I tilt my head, considering.

"You need to do something, Harley. That girl is lost; she needs someone to find her. If she won't let it be you, maybe she'll let her sisters." She pauses. "You love her, I can see it. She loves you too; she's just lost right now."

"You're right," I tell her and hand over Cookie.

She smiles, patting him on the head absentmindedly. "You're a good man, Harley St. James."

"I just hope it's enough," I reply as I grab my phone and keys.

WHEN I GET to Cerulean's house, her car isn't in its spot in the garage. If nothing else, that convinces me I'm doing the right thing. I hope with everything in me that her sisters can do something I can't.

I knock on the door, and a harried-looking Magenta, her daughter on her hip, answers the door. I've heard people mention Emily at school, but it's not something people really talk about all that much, for whatever reason.

"I thought you were Cerulean," she says in greeting.

"Why would she knock?" I ask, entering.

"She's not in the right frame of mind, who the fuck knows what she'd do."

"Should you really be swearing around a baby?" I question as I follow her into what I presume is the living room.

"She's ten months old, she'll be fine," she says as she sits down and offers the whimpering infant a bottle.

"Can I ask where the dad is in all of this? I know from some of the stuff the girls have said that he's not in the picture, how come?"

Magenta sighs and looks down at her daughter. "Beckett and I.... We met the summer before last. It was a fling. He was going off to college. We were never supposed to last. I called him when I found out I was pregnant, and he, um, didn't react well."

"He wanted you to get an abortion?" I ask.

She nods. "Yeah. I'm not against them but I wanted this baby. *My* baby. *Our* baby. I was stupid to think it could work. I ended the call when he asked me that. It was the last time we spoke."

"He doesn't know you didn't go through with it?"

"I don't know what he thinks. I ended the call without really discussing with him what I wanted to do. I think it's best that he doesn't though. His family would flip if they knew he has a daughter. It'd totally ruin their image so we stay quiet. It's better that way, it means I get this one all to myself."

"Wow."

She shrugs. "So this is nice and all, but what exactly are you doing here?"

I sit back in my seat and run a hand through my hair. "Cerulean came to my house just now. She wanted to talk to my dad about the possibility of him calling whoever to get Vermilion into this workshop. She was, um, quite worked up."

She sighs and lifts the baby to burp her.

"She's cute," I say. "Thank God you didn't call her Umber or Ecru or something similarly colorful." The words are out of my mouth before I even realize what I'm saying.

Magenta shoots me a look.

"Shit, I'm sorry." I run my hands over my face. "I don't know why I said that."

"My sister has you all kinds of worked up, huh?" She gives Emily the bottle again.

"Yeah."

She smiles. "Once everything settles, she'll figure out she's all twisted over you, too."

"*If* things settle down." I look up, her same but different eyes staring back at me. "I'm worried about her, Magenta. *Really* worried."

She nods. "I am too."

"I want to do something, help her, but she won't let me. I've got something in the works, you know, since Carver rescinded their offer, but I have no idea if she'll want it or if it'll be anywhere near enough to bring her back even a little bit."

"It'll be enough," she says. "We'll make sure of it. All of us."

CHAPTER THIRTY-EIGHT

NO ONE CAN HELP ME. No one.

HARLEY

CHAPTER THIRTY-NINE

GETTING AN HOUR OF SLEEP, if that, the night before the regional playoffs isn't ideal, but it is what it is. Around 2:00 a.m. Indigo texted to tell me Cerulean had finally made it home, but that was it. It made me feel marginally better, but my anxiety when it comes to my royal blue is still sky-high.

Things aren't any better at school. She's not as twitchy or as on edge as she was yesterday, but I'd almost take that over how she is now. Listless, uninterested, seemingly dead inside. It kills me to see her like this. When we were together, she was vibrant and full of life. She was happy. So was I. Now.... Now everything is a mess.

"How is she?" I ask Indigo during History.

She sighs. "Not good. When she came home last night, or this morning I suppose, she was almost catatonic. If we're looking for positives, she's not at the moment, so that's something."

"The pills?" I ask.

"We looked for them but couldn't find them. Vermilion googled them and read that sudden withdrawals can be really dangerous, but so can being addicted."

I nod. "If you need help, my mom's a doctor, she can tell you how to go about getting her off them."

She smiles, but it doesn't reach her eyes. "Thanks."

"Is she going to make it?" I don't even know why I say that, but I'm desperate to know the answer.

"We'll do our best to make sure she does."

THE CAFETERIA BRINGS its own set of problems. I'm still spending my lunch breaks with Violet, hearing more about her and Leroy and just her in general. She's a fascinating woman and completely underutilized in the library. But a growing boy still needs to eat. I'm line for food when Cerulean is ushered in by her sisters.

"Well, well, well," TK says in a big, booming voice. "Look what the Hued Hussies just dragged in."

"Fuck off, TK," Magenta spits.

"Ah, yes, the feisty one. Tell me, how's your kid, Magenta?"

She snarls at him, and I clench my fists. Given what Magenta told me the other night I assume that's the reason nobody talks about Emily, but if he harms a hair on that little girl's head, I won't be responsible for what I do.

"That's enough," I say, leaving my spot in line.

"Ah, there's our boy wonder QB. Tell me, Harley, how's your druggo girlfriend going?"

At this, Cerulean lifts her head.

"Leave it, TK," I tell him, clenching and unclenching my fists.

By now his act has had the desired effect. All eyes are on us, and there are whispers going round the cafeteria. "No, I don't think I will. After all, don't we as their loyal subjects deserve to know the truth about our 'Sovereigns of Savannah'?"

"Are you going to tell them our deepest, darkest secrets?" Cerulean croaks. "Because you may have destroyed my future, but I can also do the same to you, don't forget that."

Seeing this glimpse, however brief it may be, of the Cerulean I know and love gives me hope we can bring her back. TK pales but doesn't back down.

"Go on, tell them," she goads. "Why don't we start with Vermilion. Tell everyone *all* about her deepest, darkest secret."

I'll give Vermilion credit; she doesn't shrink under the attention. Instead, she hitches her chin just like her older sister would.

"Yeah, go on, TK," she says. "Spill all my secrets."

The whispers turn from intrigued to angry, matching looks thrown TK's way. Sure, the girls may not have a ton of friends, which by all accounts is their own choice, but that doesn't mean people don't care for them. Unlike TK, whose reputation is somewhat... questionable. It seems while the students of Forest Park Academy may enjoy seeing their queens brought down to their level, they *don't* enjoy seeing them exploited for entertainment. Who would've known?

"Come on, man," Jon, our punter, says to TK. "You don't want to do this."

"They need to be taken down," he insists.

"They're down," Jon tells him. "No need to pile onto that."

"No! I'm sick of their shit! Vermilion killed her best friend! Cerulean is a druggo, Indigo wrecks marriages, and Magenta's baby daddy needs to know—"

It takes me a little bit to get from where I'm standing to the football table, but I eventually get there. "You shut up," I hiss as I and a couple of other guys drag him out of the cafeteria.

"I'm sorry, man," David says to me. "I didn't think he'd say those things."

"What's done is done," I tell him as we drag TK out to the parking lot.

"Get your fucking hands off me," TK says, finally shaking out of our grip. "Y'all are finished."

I laugh. "Man, you are seriously deluded if you think you have any power over us," I tell him.

"You think you're so great," he says to me. "Coming in from fucking nowhere and being our great football hope, but you're no one and nothing. By the time I'm done with you, no one will want to touch you with a ten-foot pole. You'll go back to where you came from with nothing to show and your tail between your legs."

With that he turns, gets in his car, and drives away.

David shakes his head. "He's fuckin' crazy."

I nod. "I know."

"What he said about the girls back there? Not cool."

"Not even a little," Jon agrees.

"He's out of control," David says.

"I know."

"He has been for a long time. I don't know about you two," Jon says, "but I sure as fuck don't love the fact we're on the same team as him."

"Nope," David agrees. "We've put up with his shit for a long time, but, well, ever since you arrived, he's been getting worse. Plus, some of the things he says about you, about what he does with the girls he picks up." He shakes his head. "Some of that shit is downright wrong. I don't want to be associated with it."

"He's been saying shit about me?" I ask. This is news to me. Not that I care, but saying shit behind my back? That's so fucking weak.

Jon nods. "He's jealous, man. At first it was just a dig here and there, but slowly he's been escalating, ending with the shit he's done to Cerulean. That ain't right. Playing with him, knowing what he's done, what he's doing, it doesn't make me feel good. It doesn't make me *want* to play."

I sigh. Coach will have a shit, but I've got to do what I've got to do, and I've *got* to stand up for my girl, her sisters, and her niece. "Spread the word," I tell them. "Tonight, and every other game we play this season, we freeze him out. I don't care if this means tonight's the final game of our season, I will not pass to him."

"After what just went down just now, I don't think you'll have any arguments," David says as the front door opens and all four Tremonts walk out.

"We'll give you guys some space," Jon says, nodding to the girls as they pass.

"Are y'all okay?" I ask.

Indigo ushers Vermilion and Cerulean to the car.

"We're okay," Magenta says. "But we're going to head home, close the door on this shitshow of a day."

I nod. "I'm sorry for what he said in there, and everything else."

She squeezes my arm. "It's not your fault. We've known TK since we were kids; we know what he's like. Did we ever think he'd stoop this low? No, but I have a feeling he'll get his," she says, a slight twinkle in her eye.

"I'm going to try."

She nods. "Good luck tonight."

"Thanks. If you need anything at all, at any time, give me a call?" I ask as she walks toward the car.

She turns and walks backward. "You just focus on winning tonight."

I tilt my head. "Are you telling me you're an *actual* fan?"

She chuckles. "Knock 'em dead, QB."

PART of my routine before a game is to get to the stadium before anyone else. I like to get a feel for the field, the locker room, everything. The more familiar I am with something, the more comfortable I am.

As the guys file in, they all give me a nod. I have to admit I'm more than a bit surprised. Most of these guys have been playing with TK since peewee. I'm a kid from a very nontraditional football background, here for no other reason than to catch the eyes of scouts so I can go to college. Plus, I know there's no major love lost for the girls. They're tough, they're unflinching, and they don't take shit from anybody. At any school in Georgia, or try the whole fucking South, I'm sure the powers that be at any high school are the jocks. But the girls are the exception to that rule. The guys having their backs proves to me that it's respect, not fear, that keeps them at the top.

ALL NIGHT I've been freezing out TK, our plan going flawlessly. I can hear the frustration and confusion coming from Coach and the stands as once again I ignore the perfect route he runs, opting for a more difficult pass to Matt, but he doesn't let me down. The score is closer than it should be, sixteen to fourteen, closer than it would be if I abandoned my boycott of TK, but I hold firm. We're still in the lead. Just. Hopefully, it'll be enough.

In the last play of the game they set up for a field goal. I pace the sideline, chewing on my mouth guard. The ball is snapped, the QB catching and placing the ball for the kicker. His contact is perfect, the ball soaring through the air.

I swear the whole stadium is holding its breath. The ball is heading for the uprights, hooking a little to the left, but not horribly so. I thought I'd feel worse when our season eventually came to an end, but instead I feel... calm, resigned even. That is, until somehow the ball continues to hook left, missing the goalpost by an inch at most. The home crowd goes crazy, my teammates surrounding me, slapping my head, back, shoulders, whatever they can reach.

We go back on the field to shake the other team's hands before embracing each other, although no one goes to TK. I expect him to be mad, livid even. What I don't expect is for him to look smug, to have a smile on his face like he knows something the rest of us don't. Regardless, I don't give a shit. Tonight I won, on and off the field.

When we get to the sideline, about to run down the tunnel to the locker room, Coach pulls me aside.

"I don't know what you were playing at out there, but I hope you had your fun. I just got a text from the recruiter from Savannah. They're pulling their offer."

HARLEY

CHAPTER FORTY

"THEY'RE PULLING THEIR OFFER." The words swirl around my head. My knees go weak, but mange to hold my weight. Barely.

"Not sitting so pretty now, are we, superstar?" TK asks as he runs past.

I grab him and throw him up against the tunnel wall. He laughs as Coach and some of his assistants pull me off him.

"You really should be more careful who you associate with," he says as I'm held back. "Coach Ford was only too happy to hear about how his number-one recruitment target was spending a *lot* of time around a known prescription drug abuser, one whose own scholarship has been rescinded."

I try to grab him again but am prevented from doing so.

He laughs. "Your girl may own this school, this town, but don't forget that I've got my own connections. The right ones too."

"Get out of here, TK," one of the assistants says as they struggle to contain me. For once in his miserable life, he does as he's told.

"I know you're upset, son," Coach says. "But there are other schools, other offers. I'm not entirely sure what's going on right now. I can hazard a guess, but regardless, you need to stop this nonsense before you do even more damage to yourself and your career."

"And let him get away with all this shit?" I ask. "I don't think so." I shake out of their hold.

Coach grabs my shoulder pad and shakes me. Hard. "Listen to me. Guys like him take immense pleasure in seeing others, especially their rivals, fuck up. Don't give him that pleasure."

"You're on my side?" I ask.

"I'm both of your coach. I can't, and don't, take sides, but your teammates have and they've spoken loud and clear. Does this put our run at state in jeopardy? You bet it does, but if that's how you boys want to play it, then that's how it's played. Even if I tell you otherwise, you're still going to do what you want, aren't you?"

I nod.

"Just be careful. Don't let it get to you. There are bigger things, better things, better *people* waiting for you after this."

I sigh and run a hand through my hair. "Yeah." I nod. "Yeah, okay."

"You're okay?"

"I'm okay," I confirm.

"Good." He pats me on the shoulder before letting me go. "Having said all that, that was damn fine playing tonight, son. I'm proud of you." He gives me a shove. "Now shower, change, and go find that girl of yours. Enjoy your night and come back on

Monday ready to get back to work. We've got a title to win."

ON THE WAY to the locker room I'm stopped by several boosters, as well as a local reporter who thankfully missed all the off-field commotion with TK.

I chat to him for a few minutes, explaining I was merely hoping to share the receiving burden tonight. I may also have suggested TK was carrying an injury, and I was concerned for his well-being if he took a particularly hard hit.

By the time I make it back to the locker room, I'm expecting it to be empty, but the whole team, minus TK of course, is still there.

"I thought y'all would be long gone by now," I say.

"We wanted to wait," David explains.

"You didn't have to do that," I say as I set my helmet down and start getting undressed.

"We heard about Savannah," Jon says.

I strip my jersey off and freeze. "Oh."

"We're really sorry," Matt, my new go-to wide receiver, says. "We know it was one of your top choices."

I shrug and lift my pads off. "There'll be other offers, other schools."

"TK...," Jon starts. "I can't believe he did that."

"Why wouldn't he?" I ask. "Look what he did to Cerulean, what *we* did to him. I knew he would hit back, and he did. I'm just glad it didn't blow back on any of y'all."

"So what happens now?" Matt asks.

I sit down and untie my cleats. "Now, we let me have a shower because I stink something awful." There are a few chuckles. "We enjoy our win tonight. It really was extraordinary work, gentlemen." There are more smiles and murmurs going round the group now. "Then we come back on Monday, ready to move on to the next game."

"And TK? What does Coach say?"

"Coach says he'll back us. He said it's pretty clear where y'all's loyalties lie and he backs his team." I stop and take a breath. "On that note, I want to thank you, all of you, for having my back. I know I'm still the new guy here. You didn't have to, and I'm.... I'm grateful," I manage to get out before I make a fool of myself by crying or doing something stupid like that.

"You're our QB," Damon, a safety, says.

"And that's it?" I ask.

He shrugs. "Plus, what he was doing, what he said about the girls? That ain't right. They might be colder than Antarctica—"

"Except for Indigo," someone says to snickers.

"—but they've never done anything to us. TK is jealous. That's no reason to say nasty things about them."

I nod. "Well, I appreciate it."

They filter out after that, while I shower. By the time I'm finished, the locker room is empty. Grabbing my stuff, I head for the door.

"That was some show you two put on." Trinity is leaning against the wall outside the door.

"I don't have the energy for this right now," I tell her.

"Not even if I tell you it's all part of TK's plan?"

I stop dead in my tracks. "What?"

"I mean, it's fairly obvious what he's doing. He's not being subtle about it. But don't you want to know why?"

"I know why; he's jealous."

A small smile crosses her lips. "I heard you and Cerulean put on quite a show at his party the other week. Showing him up at his own house? Ballsy."

I run my hand through my still damp hair. "Seriously? This is all about that? We're a couple, we're allowed to publicly display our affection for one another."

"Yes, in anyone else's mind I suppose you are. But not TK's."

I blow out a breath. "So he's going after me because I'm in love with Cerulean?"

She laughs a little. "He's not just going after you."

My blood runs cold. "He's going after Cerulean?"

"He's *already* gone after Cerulean. Remember that thing with Carver?"

"Shit."

"And you two played right into his hands."

"How?"

"You're not together anymore, are you?"

Oh. Holy. Fuck. I look at Trinity. She nods. "You're getting it now, aren't you?"

"Why are you telling me all of this? What's in it for you?"

She shrugs. "Remember way back at the start of the season when I tried unsuccessfully to get in your pants?" I chuckle but nod. "TK saw what was happening between you and Cerulean. To say he didn't like it is an understatement."

"But the girls, the young ones...."

She waves a hand. "Those are to keep his ego intact, get his blood pumping while he waits for something better. Some*one* better. The ultimate prize."

"Cerulean."

She nods. "She's always been his end game."

"She'll never go for him."

"No?" she asks. "Not even with everything she loves falling apart? TK has been supplying this school with drugs since he was a freshman. Anything he wants is at his disposal. How hard do you think it would be to convince her to take something, given her current state of mind?"

Shit, she's right. "Why are you helping me?" I ask. Don't get me wrong, I'm grateful as fuck that she is, but she's never hidden her disdain for my royal blue.

She shrugs. "Maybe I'm seeing what TK's done to you, to Cerulean and I want to help fix it."

I raise an eyebrow.

"Okay, okay." She blows out a breath. "You remember the party after the first game of the season? The one in the club?"

I smile. That's really where Cerulean and I first put aside our shit and connected. "Yeah, I remember that."

"Do you remember a girl, a freshman, got her drink spiked?"

I nod.

"TK was the one who did it."

"How do you know that?"

"Because he tried to do it to me. I saw him put something in my drink but I didn't drink it, I tipped it out when he wasn't looking. As the night wore on he started bitching about how his methods weren't working, how he'd already struck out once that night."

"Why didn't you say anything?" I ask.

She shrugs. "I don't know, I didn't think people would believe me. It's not like I don't have a reputation. Why would TK even need to drug me? I'm willing enough as it is."

"Why are you telling me this now? Telling me about what else TK has planned?"

"What he's doing, it's not right. It's one thing to fuck with someone's relationships, but to fuck with their future? That's taking it too far."

"What do you suggest we do then? Do you have a plan?"

"Who do you take me for? Some amateur? Of course I do."

For the first time in this conversation, a smile tugs at my lips. "Tell me about this master plan then."

FORTY-FIVE MINUTES LATER, I finally make it home. With the effort the game took on top of what Trinity dumped in my lap, I'm more than beat.

"Harley," my father barks from his study.

I suppress a groan and prepare to face the firing squad. He's sitting in his big, imposing armchair with ornate arms and a high wingback. It weighs an absolute ton. I should know because he's made me move it several times. It kind of makes him look like a monster is sitting on his shoulders.

"What the *fuck* was that tonight?" he asks before I can say or do anything.

"It was us winning."

"*Just.* You just won. If not for the breeze getting a hold of that kick you would've been out of the play-offs because of what? Some pissing competition you're having with TK Thomas?"

"I'm not having a pissing competition with TK."

"I don't particularly care what you pussies call it, all I know is you made Forest Park look like a laughingstock tonight. I did not interrupt my life so you can throw away your shot at the foolhardy *career* you are intent on forging."

"I didn't throw away my shot," I tell him.

"Savannah told me they're pulling their offer."

"There are other schools."

"Not if you keep playing like you did tonight."

"We've got it under control."

"Not without TK you haven't." He takes a sip of whiskey. "This is all about that Tremont bitch, isn't it?"

"It's about TK thinking he can have whatever he wants."

"He's a Thomas, he can."

I cross my arms over my chest. "Not when it affects my and Cerulean's futures."

"So it *is* about the Tremont bitch." He shakes his head. "Girl must have a cunt lined in gold for all the idiots she has trailing after her. None bigger than you."

"I thought you'd be happy I'm standing up for my future," I tell him.

"But you're not!" he yells, spit flying everywhere. "One school has already pulled their offer; how long until others do the same because of your petty bullshit?"

"It's one school," I repeat. "The others won't follow."

He laughs. "Please tell me how you're so certain."

"Because Savannah is the only school where the Thomases have sway. Do you really think Daddy Thomas will write seven-figure checks to *all* the schools who have given me offers?"

"Humph," he grunts.

"Yes, losing Savannah was a kick in the guts, but I hope for their sake they have enough distance from the Thomases so they can deny the shitstorm that's about to rain down on TK."

"You're going after him."

"Am I? Or am I going to let him dig his own grave?"

My father takes another sip of his drink. "You need to leave TK Thomas alone."

"I never said I was going to do anything *to* him."

"I mean it, Harley. Leave. Him. Alone."

"How much are they paying *you* to ensure that?" I ask. "A new floor for the school in Botswana? More computers for the one in Indonesia? Or are they going to ensure the next one has everything you could ever need?"

"They are conscientious global citizens." He uses his well-practiced line.

"And I'm a fighter against injustice," I parry. "Have a good night, Dad."

Cerulean

I USED to think the monotony and frivolity of school was boring, but now, it's the only thing that's keeping me together. Well, that and the pills. They keep me awake, functioning, and focused. Their ability to do that is being tested right now, though, as Harley and Trinity walk down the hall, looking all cozy and shit.

"Seriously?" I ask no one in particular.

"I heard Savannah pulled their offer," Vermilion says.

My head snaps to her. "What?"

"TK's parents are like mega boosters," Kingsley adds. "I'm sure that, plus what went down on the field on Friday, helped them come to that decision."

"Have any other schools pulled their offers?" I ask. *Please let them say no,* I chant in my head. *Please let them say no.*

Kingsley shrugs. "I haven't heard anyone else has."

I let out a breath.

"What's it matter?" Magenta asks. "There'll be other schools, other offers."

I whirl around to face her. "He wanted Savannah. They were offering him a full ride."

"And if he brings home state, I'm sure he can go back and ask others for that as well. Not that he needs it."

I shake my head. "You don't get it."

She shuts her locker with a bang. "What I don't get is why you're all worked up over it. *You* broke whatever it is you two had off. *You*, not him. So why are you still caught up in him?"

"Because she still loves him," Kingsley answers.

"Who asked you?" I snap at her. "You're not part of our family, so why are you even in this conversation?"

"Because Vermilion's my best friend. I'm also here because y'all secretly love my sassy comments that are one hundred percent correct, even if you don't want to admit it." I arch an eyebrow. "What? You know it's true. You also know that he loves you too. That doesn't change overnight, even if you are being a total bitch."

I catch Magenta nodding. "What the fuck is going on here?" I ask.

Indigo closes her locker and threads her arm through mine. "What's going on," she says as she leads me away. "Is that we're trying to get you to focus on you. Just put your head down, don't listen to anything anyone is saying, don't take any notice of what they're doing, just do you."

IT TURNS out Indigo's advice isn't so easy to follow, even with the help of pills designed to make following tasks easier. I know I'm taking too many—a couple of times I've even had to resort to downers so I can get a hold of myself, or lose myself, whichever is preferable at that particular moment in time. And as much as it sickens me to deal with him, if I want to stave off total destruction, I need TK.

"I need more," I mutter as we stand side by side in front of his locker.

"This is the second time this week," he comments.

"What's it to you?" I ask. "You're not my counselor or my doctor, so why do you give a shit?"

He holds up his hands. "No shits given here, just stating simple facts."

"Well, how about you do less of that and more of giving me my goddamn pills?"

"Downers too?"

"Not too many. I don't like the fog they make in my head." I also like it *too* much sometimes.

"Would've thought that would be welcome right about now. Your boy and that slut Trinity seem to be nice and close."

"So she's a slut now, is she?" I ask. "If I recall correctly, it wasn't too long ago that you were trying to get in her pants. Not that it would do you much good once you got there." I go to grab his dick, but he knocks my hand away. "Still having troubles, are we?"

The bell rings, and the hallway empties quickly. He looks around to make sure we're alone before grabbing me by the neck and slamming me against the lockers. "Shut up, bitch."

I laugh. "Or what? You're going to choke me right here, right now?" I ask. "Leave my body on the cold floor for some poor sap going to the bathroom during class to find? I wonder who the suspects would be?"

He squeezes tighter before letting me go.

"You're a joke," I splutter, bending over to get some air in my lungs. "But on the bright side, looks like your little friend has popped up to say hello." I nod to his semi—or maybe he's fully hard, he just has nothing to work with.

He looks down as if he wasn't even aware he's rocking a hard-on.

"So that's what gets you going, huh?" I ask. "TK gets off on hurting women. Have to say, if I'd thought about it, I probably could've worked that out. What a cliché." I shake my head.

He slams a fist into the locker next to his.

"Now give me my pills before that deflates and you lose your one shot to get off."

He shoves the pills in my hand before storming off. For a moment I feel triumphant at once again getting the better of him before I remember what he's done to me, to Harley. Before I remember what's in my hand and what I have to do to get them. I hate myself for needing these pills, but I can't function without them. I can't get through the mess I made without them. I open the bottle and shake two out. I swallow them dry, hating myself the whole time.

BY THE TIME Friday rolls around, I'm barely hanging on. But no matter what's going on with me, I'll *always* be there for my sisters, and that means chaperoning Vermilion's piano lesson.

Ever since the Conservatorium debacle, Alexandrov has been more than accommodating, the prick. Today he's even more chirpy than usual.

"What are you smiling at?" I snap as he comes in. "You're late, by the way. I expect you to make it up."

"I don't have to do anything," he says.

"No?" I arch an eyebrow.

He shakes his head. "It seems your efforts to get Vermilion's application seen worked, only not in the way you hoped."

"And how's that?"

"They listened and were so impressed by my tutelage they offered me a position on their staff. Finally my talent is being appreciated. How impressive it will look on my resume too. I leave in two weeks."

HARLEY

CHAPTER FORTY-TWO

COACH WAS true to his word and backed our boycott of TK. The other guys on the team aren't as brilliant as he is, but I'm determined to make up that shortfall. It's putting more pressure on the guys in front of me, but they're stepping up, everyone is, and I'm so incredibly grateful. I guess only time will tell if this stand is worth it.

"You sure you're set on freezing him out?" Coach asks after our final practice before the semifinals.

"It may not be the best thing for our performance, but it's the best thing for our team environment," I reply.

He nods.

"Are you catching a lot of heat from this?" I ask.

He shrugs. "Some." The official word is that he's "injured," taking my white lie after the game on Friday and running with it. It means he can travel with the team, but will have to sit on the sidelines and watch. I can't deny that makes me feel just a bit better.

"Well, I appreciate you backing us, backing me."

He blows out a breath. "It's what teams do. I may

not know everything that's going on, but I know enough, and I don't like it, any of it. Guys like TK, they think because they have money that means they have everything. There's no doubting the boy's talented, but I couldn't in good faith and conscience let him go out into the world as a product of the Forest Park system. I've worked too damn hard and too damn long for him to ruin the good name I'm building here. What he did with Savannah? That ain't right."

"Thanks, Coach."

"I know they were one of your top choices, but I want to let you know I haven't stopped trying to get them to change their minds or to get better offers from other schools."

I chuckle and slap him on the shoulder. "You angling to be my agent, Coach?" I ask.

He chuckles as well. "Just rewarding hard work. I see how you are, on the field and in the locker room. You're one heck of a quarterback, but you're also a great leader. A cocky son of a bitch too."

That gets a full-on laugh.

"Few people can come in here with basically no experience under their belt and turn a locker room like you have. Any school would be lucky to have you."

"Thanks, Coach."

"I have faith in you. If things don't turn out how we hope, then c'est la vie."

"Hopefully it doesn't come to that."

IT'S GOING to come to that. This game couldn't

have gone worse if we'd tried. Within the first five minutes, two of my preferred running backs have gone down with injuries, and Matt, our second-string wide receiver, has got a major case of stage fright. Every time the ball comes within three feet of him, he drops it. If it weren't so frustrating, it'd be impressive.

Still, with all of this we're only six points down coming into the final two minutes. There's just the small matter of us being camped on our own ten-yard line, though.

"We've gotta march it down as far and as fast as we can," I tell my guys in our huddle. The guys all nod. "Park on three. One, two, three—"

"Park!" they all yell.

Steadily we progress down the field, my guys doing their best to run out of bounds whenever they can, stopping the clock and allowing us to get the men on the field we need for whatever play Coach calls.

We've made it to their forty when we stall. It's fourth and ten with a minute left. Coach sends on our runners, and I know I've got to go for it.

"Just give me and the receivers as much time as you can," I tell my protection.

They grunt, and I take that as acceptance. I clap my hands and the ball is snapped. The pocket forms around me but is collapsing rapidly. If I don't get out of here, I'm going down and we're done. Season over. I scramble both for room and time. Finally, I know I can't delay any longer. The defense is charging for me, my guys giving all they've got, but they can't hold forever. The receivers are all in the end zone, and I let the ball loose, hoping someone in maroon and white can bring down the ball.

It's out of my hand for a second, if that, before I'm driven into the turf, the air whooshing out of my lungs, my head crashing into the hard ground.

It seems forever before the crowd goes up, but I can't see enough to know if it's for us or for them. It's only when my teammates swarm around me, throwing off the behemoth who tackled me and slapping me on the back that I get an idea of what happened.

"Fuck, yeah, baby, that was one sa-weet throw."

"He brought it down?" I ask. I don't know who "he" is, but I don't care.

"Matt, that scrawny motherfucker. I'm gonna kiss his pretty white ass."

Matt bringing down the touchdown is good, but there's still work to be done. We're one point behind with the conversion to be added and forty-seven seconds still left on the clock.

"Go for two," Coach shouts on the sidelines. It's risky, considering Matt's made one catch all night and we're out of running backs, but c'est la vie, right?

Once again I clap my hands, the ball sailing into them. No matter who I turn to, they're covered. The crowd is screaming, and I know I've got to do something. I smack Pete, my offensive tackle's back. He inches forward slowly, more guys coming to help push me over the line.

Five yards, four yards, three yards, two. We're maybe a half a yard out when we come to a grinding halt. With everything I have, I fling my arm out, hoping it's enough for the ball to break the plane. The whistle blows, and the ref's arms go up.

The final forty-seven seconds are brutal. It's a

full-on assault for our defense, breaking up pass after pass, but they manage. Somehow. I have no idea how they do it, but they do.

"We're going to state!" David yells and is met with cheers both on the field and in the stands.

Coach comes over and gives me a look. "I know," I tell him.

He gathers me in a hug. "You've been touched by an angel, boy."

I laugh. "Or something." He releases me.

"State won't be easy."

"I know, but c'est la vie, right?"

He nods. "C'est la vie."

BECAUSE WE HAD to make the four-hour drive back from Atlanta, all the parties are being held on Saturday.

I'm at the club where the party after our first game was held, holding court with most of the team, when Trinity comes over. She's wearing a Kleenex as a top and a Band-Aid for a skirt, or so it seems.

"We have a problem," she tells me.

"You realized you're not wearing any clothes?" I ask.

"What? No! TK's having a party."

"So? It's a free country."

"I heard he invited mainly freshmen girls."

"Of course he did."

"And...." She stops, biting her lip.

"And who, Trinity?"

She blows out a breath. "Cerulean. I thought for sure that she wouldn't be there, but people are telling me she is, and she's more fucked-up than her usual, right now."

"Fuck." My feet are moving before my brain realizes what they're doing, Trinity matching me step for step. Or more accurately two steps for step, but she's with me, which is surprising.

"It's at his house?" I ask as we race to my Mustang.

She nods, panting slightly.

After everything that's gone down recently, we tried once again to get the security footage to see if TK slipping the roofie into Karlie's drink was recorded. Again, we got their standard "because of the activities taking place that night, they'd turned the cameras off" line.

I mean, it makes sense, but I'm betting if some damage had occurred? That footage would've surfaced quick smart. I know Cerulean's upset, but to go into the lion's den? He's already ruined two of our chances for our future; how far is he willing to go in order to get his revenge?

THE DRIVE to TK's house seems like it takes forever, but in reality it's only fifteen minutes or so. When we arrive, there are people everywhere. The guys, I suspect, are attracted by the presence of the girls, all of whom look *way* too young to be at such a party. There are bowls of pills scattered around the place, menu cards next to them explaining what to take for what purpose, and trays of shot glasses filled with cough syrup.

"Looks like someone raided Mommy and Daddy's factory," Trinity says.

"This is insane," I reply. "And dangerous." I gather as many of the bowls as I can while we look around, stopping to tip them down the sink in the kitchen. No one stops me, no one would dare, not their savior QB. I realize calling the cops would probably be the best option here, but does everyone here really need to get caught up in my quest to stop TK? Sure, a lot here are minors, and any charge would be expunged once they turn eighteen, but enough people have been caught up in this as it is.

"I don't see either TK or Cerulean," I say to Trinity.

She shakes her head. "Upstairs."

As I climb the stairs, I pray my royal blue isn't here, that her sisters stopped her.

I don't bother with any of the doors lining the hall, heading straight to the master bedroom.

What I find there makes me sick.

Cerulean

CHAPTER FORTY-THREE

TWENTY-FOUR HOURS EARLIER.

I've well and truly fucked everything now. Those cockheads at the National Conservatorium must truly be high if they hired Brian Alexandrov. The guy's a psychopath. He's also the only teacher in the state worthy of Vermilion. What is she going to do now?

"I'm—" I say before she cuts me off.

"Please don't," she replies. "Just for one night, I don't want to think about any of this."

I nod. "Okay."

She squares her shoulders. "I'm going to go down to the Peach Blossom, have a burger with my friends, and watch Harley totally kick ass and send us to state."

I nod again. "Okay."

She turns to me. "And you will _not_ wallow or beat yourself up about this. It wasn't your fault; you didn't do this. We'll figure something out, okay?"

I give her a small smile that I may not feel, but I am proud of her growing up and defending herself, setting her own terms. "Got it."

"I mean it, Cerulean. This isn't your fault. I know things have been... shit for you the past few weeks but they're not the end of the world. Are they real kicks in the guts? Yeah, but we've been through worse, come back from worse. This time is no different."

"I know."

She reaches over and grabs my hand. "I'm worried about you. We all are."

"Don't be, I'm fine."

"You're not, but you will be."

I squeeze her hand. As much as I want to think she's right, I know she's not.

ARRIVING HOME, the difference between my sisters and me is further on display.

Magenta is playing with Emily on the sofa, soft giggles coming from my niece.

Indigo is in the kitchen, whipping up a storm. A literal one too, if we're not careful.

Vermilion's phone rang as soon as we walked through the door, so she's catching Kingsley up on all the gossip she missed in the two hours since they saw each other last and despite the fact they'll see each other soon.

"Daddy not home?" I ask Indigo as I walk into the kitchen so I'm close if she sets anything on fire.

"Extended his trip in New York. *Again*."

"I thought he was in San Francisco?" I say.

"Wasn't he supposed to be in Dallas?" Magenta asks.

Indigo shakes her head. "Nope, he's in the Big Apple."

"Huh," I reply.

Our dad's a good man, he just isn't cut out to be a father. He especially isn't cut out to be what is effectively a single one. Sure, he was here for us after Mom left, but I guess he figured when Indigo and Magenta turned fifteen, they were old enough to take care of whatever problems would arise. He comes home often enough to check on us, make sure we haven't killed ourselves or burned down the house before leaving again. I'd think he has another family stashed away somewhere, but he didn't want the first one; I can't see him wanting another.

"How'd the lesson go?" Indigo asks as she chops some cauliflower.

"Shit. Alexandrov's leaving."

She drops the knife. "What?"

I nod. "The National Conservatorium offered him a position. Apparently they saw Vermilion's workshop audition piece after *I* begged them to and decided anyone who could handle her needed to be on their books. He leaves in two weeks."

"Fuck."

"What are we going to do?" Magenta asks, putting Emily in her high chair.

"I don't know, I'll figure something out," I tell them.

"This isn't all on you," she replies.

"Isn't it?" I ask. "*I* was the one who begged them to watch her audition tape, the tape which they used to hire Alexandrov. How is it *not* my fault? He was the best teacher in the state and look what it took to get him. What is she going to do now? First the workshop, now this? I've fucked everything up."

"First of all," Vermilion says as she breezes into the kitchen, her gossip session apparently over, "I told you I didn't want to talk about this tonight. Second of all, if the Conservatorium did see my audition and still didn't want to accept me, then obviously they have no taste or eye for talent, which is backed up by their hiring of Alexandrov. Thirdly, I told you, numerous times, that what happened wasn't your fault. I also said, which can be fourth, that we'll deal with this after Harley gets us to state." She pops a floret of cauliflower in her mouth. "Now, if you'll excuse me," she says around the vegetable, "I'm going to get ready. My Uber will be here soon."

Any other day I'd be impressed that my youngest sister put me in my place. Today I just feel numb. I leave the kitchen without a word. I know my sisters want to do something to help me, but the truth is there is nothing they can do. They can't fix this any more than I can. Sure, I know they're here if I want to talk, but I don't. I want to wallow in my pity, in my failures. They've tried several times to get me to snap out of it, but is it ever that easy? No, I don't think it is.

UPSTAIRS IN MY ROOM, I change into the loosest pair of sweats I own, as well as the rattiest hoodie. I keep the lights off, but turn on the TV, burrowing deep under the covers. I have several seasons of 90 Day Fiancé I can watch, but it doesn't hold the appeal it used to. How is it that some of those people can find and keep love but I can't? A little voice in my head says that I had it and let it go, but I don't listen to it.

I flip channels for a while, nothing taking my

interest until I hit the pregame show for the semifinals.

"Forest Park have a bona fide star on their hands with Harley St. James," one pundit says. "I have no doubt, as soon as he decides to nominate for the draft, we'll be seeing him playing on Sundays."

"What about Savannah pulling their offer?" another asks.

"Pfft," the first guy says. "You don't wanna go there, anyway. Dallas is a *far* superior school. Go Bulls!"

They all laugh.

"But what about this business with TK Thomas? Not going to him last week? St. James hinted he was injured last week, and that's confirmed by his omission this week, but why let him play if that was the case?"

"Thomas is a big loss," Dallas guy says. "But I think my man Harley can get them through."

They move on to the other team, and I stop listening. What is Harley playing at? Freezing out TK? Doesn't he realize he's jeopardizing his whole future? One school has already pulled their offer; how long until others do the same? My nerves are shot, my heart in my mouth. I can't handle it.

Cerulean: I need something, Prozac, Zoloft, anything, but I need it now.

TK: Feeling a little anxious there, sweetheart?

Cerulean: Can you get me what I need or not?

TK: Chill, I'll get you your candy.

TK: By the way, party at my house tomorrow night, all the candy you can handle.

HALF AN HOUR LATER, one of TK's little errand boys delivers my "candy," and come the final two minutes of the game, I couldn't be more grateful for them.

The ball is snapped into Harley's strong hands. The same hands that have caressed every inch of my body. The same rough fingers that have been inside me, brought me to my knees. I swear half the state of Georgia, maybe even some of South Carolina, holds its breath when he finally lets the ball fly.

I hold it again as he reaches out for the two extra points and as the final seconds tick down. But they do, and Forest Park Academy is going to the State Championships. I want to feel excited for Harley, and proud as fuck of him, but I can't. I can't do that because I gave him up. I gave *us* up, and for good reason too. Too many things went wrong because of us being together, because of my inability to be the woman my mother told me to be when she left.

My eyes start burning, the pressure that comes with tears building up. But I won't cry. I can't. I don't cry. That's not who I am. I didn't cry when my mom left. I didn't cry when Magenta had Emily—those were allergies, thank you very much. I didn't cry when Carver rescinded their offer. So no, I won't cry over Harley St. James and what we could've had.

So I do the one thing guaranteed not to make me cry.

Cerulean: I'll be there.

TK IS PRACTICALLY GLOWING when he sees me make my way into his house. My sisters tried everything to stop me from leaving tonight. While they may have been determined, I'm stubborn. If I want something, I get it. Nothing and no one can stop me. I hated the looks in their eyes when I left, but I hate the feelings inside of me more. This is the only way I know to stop feeling.

"If it's not the bluest Hued Hussy."

I pick up one of his "menus" next to a bowl filled with pills. "Which one of these will fuck me up the most?" I ask.

He plucks the card out of my hand. "You don't want that, you want this." He hands me a drink.

"What's in it?"

"Do you care?"

"Not really," I say and down it one sip. The grin on his evil face grows bigger. "I'll also need a refill on Monday," I tell him.

"No problem, they'll be in your locker, waiting." He grabs my hand, but I shake him off. He grabs it again. "Let's have some fun, shall we?"

We dance for a bit in a sea of people I don't know. Girls who look too young, guys who look too creepy before I start to feel good. *Really* good. My body feels loose and warm and kind of tingly. A giggle escapes my mouth.

"Looks like that drink is finally kicking in," TK says.

"What did you give me?" I slur. I feel so light, like I'm not here anymore. It's wonderful.

"I gave you what you asked for, so I can give you what you deserve and we can finally be together." The smile on his face is gone now, replaced by a sneer. He grabs my hand and drags me upstairs. I know I should be afraid, I know I should resist, but I just feel so free.

"I don't think I want to do this," I tell TK, some sense staying with me. I know I never should've come here, but I just wanted to not feel for a few hours. I wanted to forget it all. I thought I could handle myself, but like everything else lately, I was wrong.

"Uh-uh," he says. "We're going to have some fun. You've had more than your fair share, now it's my turn."

I try to pull my hand out of his grasp, but his hold is tight.

He pulls me to the master bedroom, closing the door behind us. He pushes me on the bed, and I know I should try to roll off, but it's so soft and fluffy and I just want to lie here all the time.

He climbs on top of me, pinning my arms to the bed. "It's my turn now."

"What are you going to do to me?" I ask.

"Whatever I want. For too long you've thought you had the better of me. Buying pills off me, using me to get your fix, rubbing my nose in your 'superiority,' then that fucked-up relationship with Captain Fantastic QB. Well, no more. You were never supposed to be with him, it was always meant to be me. *Me!*"

"You're right," I say.

"It was always supposed to be the two of us together. We fit; we're made for each other. Both of us are willing to do exactly what we need to in order to get what we want. And now you're mine."

"Okay." I know I should fight, but I just can't seem to care. I want to float away and never come back.

He kisses my jaw, holding it firmly in his grasp. "I'm going to fucking destroy you." He moves, down my neck, to my chest, my breasts. "Pity these aren't bigger, but I know those Ritalin side effects can be a pain in the ass."

"They're not so bad," I tell him.

He laughs. "See? Why can't you be this cooperative all the time? You're always such a pain in my ass. Why, huh? Why did you act like that?" he asks.

I shrug. "I don't know, but it's nice. I like this place. Do you like it?"

"Oh, I more than like it. I've got you exactly where and how I want you."

"Are you sure?" I ask him. I look to the front of his pants, where he's not even sporting a semi. "It doesn't look like you are. That makes me sad."

"Shut up," he tells me, gripping my face harder.

"Do you need me to do something? 'Cause I don't like being sad," I tell him.

"You need to shut up."

"Don't you want to be happy?"

"I'll be happy if you do as you're told."

"Okay."

He kisses me some more, but it's still not doing it for him.

"Is it working?" I ask.

"Shut up, just shut up." He rips open my top, the buttons flying everywhere. He pinches my nipples through my bra, and I cry out.

"Ow!"

"Yeah, that's it," he says. "Scream for me. Let me know how much you hate me."

"No." I shake my head. "This isn't what this place is. It's fun here; you're no fun."

"I'll show you fun." He leans down and runs his nose from my shoulder to my ear. "God, you smell good. I bet he liked that, didn't he?"

"Who's he?" I ask.

"That's right. God, I've dreamed of this for so long, having you at my mercy. All the things I can do to you.... Oh no," he says, noticing my eyes closing. "Are you leaving me? Good. Let your imagination run wild with all the things I do to you. I'm going to do them all. Every depraved thing you can think of, and even a few you've never even dreamed of. Yeah, that's it," he says. I open my eyes again, try to get away from him, but I have no strength left. He takes off his clothes, his pathetic dick small and only semi-hard. He jerks it, trying to get it hard, but it doesn't do much.

"I-I...."

Vaguely I hear the door fly open.

"What the fuck?" TK shouts, not even bothering to try and cover up.

Harley charges in, punching TK square in the face while Trinity comes over to me.

"Are you okay?" she asks.

"I like this place, it's nice."

"Let's find you some clothes." She opens a chest

of drawers and pulls out a shirt, handing it to me. "Here."

She helps me sit up and pulls the material over my head. "Are we leaving this place?" I ask. "Why? I like it. You don't like me. Why are you here?"

"Because you're a mess and it's pathetic."

"You can leave me here, it's okay, I like it. You don't like me. You like Harley."

She rolls her eyes. "As much as it confuses me, he doesn't want me. He wants you."

Harley comes over and cups my cheek. "Are you okay, royal blue?" Harley is safe. Harley is kind. I like Harley too.

"I think so," I say, my eyes closing.

"I think he gave her something," Trinity says.

"I've no doubt he gave her something," Harley replies as his arms come under my legs and behind my back. "Let's get her out of here."

I rest my head on his shoulder, breathing in his familiar scent, letting it warm me, bring life back into me. I nuzzle his neck, and he brushes his lips over my cheek. "I got you, baby doll. You're safe."

"You're so nice," I tell him. "I'm not. I don't deserve you."

"It's exactly because you think you don't that you do."

I smile.

"How are you feeling? Do we need to get you checked out?"

I yawn. "Can we go home now?"

I think he tells Trinity to grab his keys, but I'm not sure. I do know that he somehow gets into the car without having to put me down though.

"Memories," I mumble.

He chuckles. "Yeah, this car holds good memories for us."

"Oh, gross," Trinity says from the driver seat. "I hope it's been detailed since."

"Just drive, Trinity," he tells her.

"Love you" is the last thing I remember saying.

HARLEY

SEEING Cerulean on that bed at TK's mercy.... It made me sick. TK's blood is drying on my knuckles, which are cracked and swollen, but I don't care. He deserved that and more.

Cerulean mutters something before she falls asleep.

"Thanks for helping me get her out of there," I tell Trinity.

She shrugs. "That was fucked-up. Even on the scale of fucked-up things rich kids do, that was *way* fucked-up."

"Yup."

"Will she be all right?" Trinity asks. "Do we need to take her to the hospital?"

I brush the hair back from Cerulean's face. "She should be. I'll get my mom to check her out, just in case." I don't really want to take her in, have an official record of her visit. It'll only add to the rumors about her.

"You two are good together, you balance each other out."

"We're each other's match."

She nods. "Exactly."

"What happens next year? She's only a junior, she'll be stuck here."

"I have to work on the rest of this year first, but I have a plan in place."

She nods and continues the drive to Cerulean's house.

INDIGO OPENS THE DOOR. "What the fuck happened?" she asks as I step past her.

"TK happened," I tell her.

"Is she all right?"

"She should be, but I'll get my mom to come over and give her a quick check, anyway."

I carry her up the stairs and wait while Indigo opens her bedroom door and pulls back her blankets. Gently, I place her on the bed. Indigo tucks her in.

"I don't know what to do," she says, her bottom lip wobbling. "We called our mom, our dad but...."

I give her a quick hug. "I'm working on something I hope will help," I tell her. "It won't fix everything, but hopefully once she realizes there's hope for her future, the rest will fall into place."

"God, I hope so."

"She'll be okay, I'll make sure of it." And I will. If it's the last thing I do, I swear I will bring Cerulean Tremont back. It doesn't matter what the cost, or what I have to do, I'll do it. I'll bring my royal blue back to me. She might be stubborn, but I'm determined, and I will not fail. I'm Harley St. James, I don't fail at anything.

CHAPTER FORTY-FIVE

TK'S PARTY is the talk of school on Monday. I woke up yesterday with a hangover to end all hangovers, but thankful what happened didn't go any further. I guess I have Harley to thank for that.

As promised, my pills are waiting for me in my locker. I hate myself for needing them, but I can't survive without them. What's particularly hard to swallow is the fact Harley is *still* spending time with Trinity. Yes, she helped me out on Saturday but with my declaration to him in the car I thought.... Whatever, it doesn't matter. I ended things; I told him I didn't want him. Yes, he said he'd fight for me but I can't expect him to do that forever. Not that it matters. I'm Cerulean Tremont; I don't need a man, and I have other problems to fix: finding my sister a piano teacher worth their salt for one. I rub my temples. Yes, that's more than enough to keep me occupied until the stupid organ in my chest realizes we don't need Harley St. James anymore, not that we ever did. We did enjoy his company though.

· · ·

I GET through the week relatively unscathed, but not without needing a refill from TK. Once again, it's waiting for me in my locker. The level of self-hate it takes to get these pills is crushing, but what can an addict do?

I'm sitting in Media Studies, trying to listen to the lecture Ms. Victoria is giving but my focus is all over the place, which shouldn't be possible.

The bell rings and I get up, my legs just barely able to hold my weight.

"Are you all right?" Harley asks, hands out as if he's preparing to catch me if I fall.

I brush them away and stumble out the door. My vision is going in and out, the hallway looking almost impossibly long. I know my sisters will be in the cafeteria but it's too far away; I don't know if I'll make it. The library is my only other option. It'll take everything I've got, but I can make it; I *will* make it.

I zigzag down the hall, my hand keeping in contact with the wall, helping me to stay upright. Vaguely I'm aware of someone following me but I can't worry about that now.

The doors of the library come into view, and I breathe a sigh of relief. Almost there.

I push on the door and almost fall but catch myself.

"Cerulean?" my great-aunt Violet says.

"I-I...." My legs give out and blackness overcomes me.

HARLEY

I FOLLOW Cerulean as she zigzags down the hall. I'm close enough to catch her if she falls, but far enough back so she doesn't think I'm hovering. Something isn't right, that's obvious, but she's still with it enough to know she doesn't want my help. I get it. I'm still spending a lot of time with Trinity, but only because we're working on getting the tapes from the club the night of our first win party. Even though the manager was her hook up, he doesn't like the idea of his club being implicated in something as shady as this. She thinks she's almost convinced him to give them to her, but until we have the footage in our hands, we won't get carried away. I'm determined to see TK get what's owed to him.

My stubborn royal blue keeps putting one foot in front of the other.

The library comes into view, and she gets a burst of... whatever. Energy, determination—I've got no clue. Violet looks up when Cerulean pushes open the door. I think she tries to say something but collapses before she can get it out. I catch her just before she hits the ground.

"Cerulean!" Violet yells, dropping the book in her hand and running for us.

I lower us to the ground, pushing the hair back from her face. She's pale. So pale. I feel for her pulse. It's there, but it's weak.

"We need to call an ambulance," Violet says, fumbling in her pocket.

I shake my head. "I'll drive her to the hospital, call my mom on the way. She's an ER doc."

"What have you done, you silly girl?" Violet asks as she cups Cerulean's cheek.

I stand up and start running for my car. "Can you go tell her sisters what's happened?" I ask.

"I'll call them on the way."

"Wha— How?" I ask. Even though Cerulean's dead weight, she's not heavy, weighing maybe 110 pounds.

"I'm their great-aunt, boy," Violet says, having no trouble keeping up with me.

"Really?"

"My sister, Sienna, is their grandmother."

"Again with the color thing," I mutter.

She laughs.

We reach the front doors just as a very large African American man is coming through them. He has to be at least six foot five, and I'm going with 250 pounds. His hair is a mixture of dark brown and gray, his eyes brown and wide when he sees Violet.

She stops dead in her tracks. "Leroy?"

He clears his throat and shuffles his feet. "Yes, ma'am." His voice is a rich baritone that oozes over me like honey.

"It's, ah, miss," she corrects.

He cracks the slightest of smiles.

"Look," I say. "I *really* hate to break up this reunion, like *really* hate it, but I have a girl in my arms who has collapsed and who we desperately need to get to the hospital."

They both come to their senses at the same time. Leroy opens the door for us. "We can take my SUV; it's parked right at the door."

We run for the vehicle. Violet opens the back door for me before getting in the passenger seat. I get my phone out of my pocket and call my mom, telling her what's happened.

THE DRIVE to the hospital is mostly silent except for Violet's directions to Leroy and a call to Indigo, telling her what's going on.

About halfway there, Cerulean stirs.

"Shh," I soothe, kissing her on the forehead.

"Harley?" she whispers.

"Hey, baby doll."

"W-what happened?" she asks.

"You collapsed. We're on our way to my mom and the hospital to get you checked out."

"I-I d-don't f-feel w-well," she says, before passing out again.

My poor royal blue. What's it taken for her to get up every day and put on a brave face? What massive weight is she carrying on her shoulders, but insisting she's fine? That she can do it? I have no doubt she's able to shoulder any load she takes on, but only if she takes care of herself. It's clear she hasn't been doing that. I was afraid she wasn't. But how could I be sure, one way or the other, if she wouldn't let me in? Pushing her would've only shut her down tighter, but maybe me leaving her be wasn't the right move either.

I brush another kiss over her forehead as we tear up the driveway to the hospital, stopping at the doors to the ER where my mom and her team are waiting for us.

"She woke up a few minutes ago," I tell her as I place Cerulean on the gurney. "But she passed out again not long after."

"Thanks, bud," Mom says, and fires off a round of orders. "We'll take good care of her."

"I'm her aunt, can I come with her?" Violet asks.

Mom nods. "But please stay out of our way. You can stand outside her room, but everyone else will have to stay in the waiting room." They all hustle away, Cerulean looking smaller than ever on the bed. I take a seat in the waiting room, scrubbing my hands over my face. A few minutes later, Leroy joins me.

"Is she going to be all right?" he asks.

"I hope so. My mom will do everything she can."

He nods.

We sit there in silence for a while before my curiosity gets the better of me. "You're Violet's Leroy, aren't you? The one who used to work for her family?"

"Violet's Leroy, I like that," he says, the corners of his mouth ticking up slightly. "Yes, that's me."

"Where'd you go?" I ask before I can stop myself.

He blows out a breath and stretches out in his seat. "New York. I had a cousin up in Harlem who knew someone who said he could get me a gig in one of the clubs up there."

"So you *did* become a musician."

Just then Indigo, Magenta, and Vermilion come rushing through the ER doors. They sprint over to me when they spot me.

"How is she?"

"What happened?"

"Where is she?"

I stand and lower my hands to get them to calm down. "She collapsed after class. She woke up on the way but passed out again. My mom is back there," I point to the doors that say Authorized Personnel Only. "Your great-aunt is with her."

Indigo and Magenta nod and head to the information desk.

"Mr. Jones?" Vermilion asks Leroy. "What are you doing here?"

"You know him?" I ask.

"Of course I do, he's an incredible pianist and on the board at the National Conservatorium."

HARLEY

CHAPTER FORTY-SEVEN

"I AM INDEED, YOUNG LADY," Leroy says. "And you are Vermilion Tremont."

"You know who I am?" she asks.

He chuckles. "I make it my business to know all the promising students wanting to attend our institution."

"Oh, wow."

"Vermilion," Indigo calls. "They said we can go back with Aunt Violet."

"Oh!" She rushes off. "It was nice to meet you, Mr. Jones," she shouts over her shoulder.

"The National Conservatorium?" I ask.

He nods.

"That's why you didn't come back?"

"That and I didn't think there was anything for me here. I figured eventually Violet's parents would wear her down, force her to marry and start a family. I couldn't bear to see her with anyone else, so I didn't come back. I was a penniless musician—what could I offer her, a girl from one of the oldest and most respected families in Georgia? She was better off without me."

"Eh," I say, moving my head from side to side. "She never married, went against her parents and went to college. It's her story to tell but I know she never forgot you, never stopped thinking of you."

"And I never stopped thinking of her."

"It's none of my business, but did you ever marry?" I ask.

He laughs. "No. There's only one woman for me."

"Why did you come back?" I question. "Why now? Are you back for good or just to visit?"

He laughs, resting his hands, pianist's hands, with long, thin fingers, on his stomach. "I *am* back for good. I left New York for a couple of reasons, chief amongst them the fact I never stopped loving Violet. Sixty years, or thereabouts, may have passed, but I still love her. As for why now? I felt like the signs were all telling me this is where I needed to be."

"What signs?" I ask.

"Your friend Vermilion's audition tape, for one. It's not a very common name she has, and coming from Savannah? I also received a rather panicked call from her sister, Cerulean. There's only one family crazy enough to name their daughters after colors, so I watched the tape. Vermilion looks just like her aunt did all those years ago."

"Wow."

He nods. "Other members of the board received phone calls from Cerulean, and while we were mighty impressed with her sister, we couldn't bend the rules for her, no matter how much some of us wanted to."

"I get it. Vermilion—and to an extent, Cerulean—did too."

He continues. "But that wasn't the only thing that caught our eyes. The application said Brian Alexandrov is her tutor. A student as talented as Vermilion isn't easy to handle; not everyone has the talent to do it."

"She is highly talented." A few times while Cerulean and I were... whatever, I'd sat in on her lessons. She blew me away. So much talent in such an unassuming package.

"She's a savant," Leroy corrects. "Members of the board felt that if he could handle her, he should be on our faculty."

"Even though they knew what a shitty thing he did to her? He withheld her recommendation on purpose so she wouldn't get in."

"A matter I raised when we were discussing his employment. But," he sighs, "it was suggested that rumor was simply an excuse made up by a student who failed to meet our deadline."

"He did it on purpose," I reiterate.

Leroy nods. "For many years there have been rumors swirling about Brian Alexandrov. I thought it was over once he retired, but then your friend managed to get him out of retirement, and now.... If the National Conservatorium is to continue attracting talent from all over the country and the world, it needs to have capable instructors. Strictly speaking, he fits that criteria."

"And when students leave because of his methods?" I ask.

"Then the Conservatorium's reputation suffers,

and that's why I could not sit back and watch that happen."

"What will you do now?"

He smiles. "Savannah was my home once; I plan to make it that again."

I nod as my mom comes out of the doors to the ER.

"How is she?" I ask, jumping out of my seat.

"She's dehydrated, so we're addressing that first."

"Is that why she collapsed?"

"We're running tests to determine that."

"Can I see her?"

"Her family's with her right now."

"Right," I say, taking my seat once again.

"Harley, you have the state championship game tomorrow, and you have practice today," she reminds me.

I pull out my phone and text Coach. "I'm not leaving until she's better."

"That could be days. Are you going to miss the game?"

"If I have to."

"Your father—"

"Dad's an ass. I *love* that girl with all my heart. If it means I miss the game, I miss the game." I know I'm going to royally fuck my team by doing so, but Cerulean is the love of my life. She might be okay now, but until I see that for myself I'm going to stay right here.

She looks to Leroy, who shrugs. "No offence, ma'am, but you can't argue with a man in love."

She sighs. "Will you at least get some clothes and

food for the girls? I can't see them leaving anytime soon."

"Will I be able to see her if I do that?" I ask.

Her shoulders drop. "I can't make any promises, but I'll do my best."

I hop up and kiss her cheek. "That's all I ask for. Go get someone's keys and I'll see what I can do." She turns to leave. "Oh, shit!" I exclaim, stopping her. "What's happening with Emily?"

"Who's Emily?" Mom asks.

"Magenta's daughter."

"I'll ask," she says before disappearing again.

Leroy looks at me when I sit down. "What?" I ask.

"You got it bad, huh?"

"I don't know their mom or grandmom, but I know Violet and I know she has the same spunk the girls have. It's a wonder I didn't put two and two together, actually. But you know what they're like. They're... undeniable."

He nods. "Yup, that's them all right."

MOM AND VIOLET come out about ten minutes later, and it's Leroy's turn to fall all over himself.

"It's not so funny now, is it?" I mutter.

His eyes don't leave Violet, and I know that's how I look at Cerulean.

"Violet will relieve Emily's babysitter and stay at the girls' house. She has Magenta's keys. She's also got instructions from them about what they'd like brought here, including Cerulean."

"She's awake?" I ask. "How is she?"

"She's resting. If she's feeling up to it, you can visit with her later."

"Does she know I'm here?"

Mom gives me a small smile. "She knows you brought her here." I blow out a breath. "Go get their things, change, grab some food for you *and* them, and come back. Cerulean's not going anywhere, not tonight, anyway."

I nod. "Okay."

THE DRIVE back to Forest Park so I can get my car and Violet can get Magenta's is seriously charged. I can tell both Leroy and Violet are desperate to say something to each other, but either they don't know where to start or don't want to say it in front of me.

"Vermilion and Cerulean would like some books," Violet says when we pull into the school.

"Cerulean needs to worry about getting better and not about fucking school," I reply. Violet purses her lips. "You know I'm right," I tell her. "And don't think you're getting away with not telling me you're her aunt."

"How was I supposed to know she was the girl you were talkin' about?"

"Are you telling me that was the one piece of gossip in this place you didn't hear?"

Leroy chuckles. "I see some things don't change."

Violet whirls around and glares at him. It's my turn to laugh. She turns back to me. "We don't advertise our relationship."

"Why not?" I ask. "Wait. That night Karlie

Jamieson was drugged, you were Cerulean's contact, weren't you?"

She shrugs. "York women have ruled this school since its inception. My great-nieces are no different."

"But they're Tremonts," I point out.

"York blood runs through their veins just as much as Tremont or any other name."

I hold up my hands. "All right, I'm sorry."

She hands me a list. "This is what the girls are askin' for and where to find it. I'll meet you at the house after you've changed and eaten."

I take her in, arms folded, toe tapping, mouth tight. It's Cerulean's—or a York, I guess—battle stance. I nod. "Yes, ma'am."

"Good." Her shoulders drop marginally. "And you," she says to Leroy. "I don't even know where to start with you."

He smiles at her, wraps one arm around her waist, and cups her cheek with the other hand before dipping her and kissing the shit out of her.

I whistle as they break apart. "You want me to give you an extra hour or two?" I ask. "I can go to the hospital before I get the girls' stuff."

"You," Violet says, "don't be an ass. And you." She points to Leroy. "Ugh." She throws her hands up.

He smiles as she walks off.

"Good luck," I tell him.

"You too." He reaches out to shake my hand, and I give it to him before he follows Violet.

I RACE up the front steps of the school, eager to get everything done and back to my royal blue. Unfortunately, that doesn't appear possible, as my father stands in the school foyer.

"Care to explain why I got a message from the football coach informing me of the whereabouts of *my* son?" he asks.

"He was the first one on my contact list," I say, trying to get past him.

"He's not your father."

"Yet he treats me better than mine."

My eyes water and cheek stings when his hand makes contact.

"You are *my* son."

"Then treat me like it," I say. "Not like a burden or, dare I say it, an inconvenience."

"You have practice for the game tomorrow."

"Coach is letting me skip it to be with Cerulean."

"That girl is trouble."

"That girl is the love of my life."

I try to walk past him again, and he grabs my arm. "I did not give up a year of my time so you could piss it all away at the final hurdle."

"And Mom didn't raise me to be a heartless bastard," I say, extricating my arm from his grip. "Fuck knows how she ended up with you." This time I see the slap coming and block it. "Coach knows what's going on and has given me permission to be where I need to be. That's with Cerulean. I don't give a fuck what you say about her." Finally, I get past him, but I stop. "I will always be thankful you brought us back here so I could have my shot, but sometimes there are more important things than a game of football. If what I've shown all season isn't enough, then it's not enough. This doesn't reflect poorly on you. *Your* reputation will be intact, so don't worry."

I'M GRABBING the books Cerulean and Vermilion asked for when Trinity finds me.

"There you are," she says. "I've been looking everywhere for you."

"I've been at the hospital with Cerulean. What's up?"

"But you're going to practice, right?" she asks.

I shut Vermilion's locker. "Coach has given me a pass."

"Harley!" she screeches. "You're playing in state tomorrow."

"I'll see how Cerulean is. If she's okay, I'll play, if not, I won't. Ow! Ouch! Stop it!" I say, trying to defend myself from Trinity's slaps, but my arms are full so I can't.

"You're. Playing. State. Tomorrow," she says with each slap. "State, Harley, state! The thing we've been working toward all year."

"We?"

"Yes, this school, the team, hell, the whole fucking town. You can't just throw it away."

"Cerulean is sick. She collapsed and is in hospital. I'm not doing anything, going anywhere unless I know she'll be all right."

Trinity looks at the books in my arms. "Are some of those books for her?"

I nod. "She asked for them."

"If she asked for them, then that means she's awake and functioning, which means she's fine." She drags me down the hall. "Practice starts soon. I'm sure she won't mind if you don't get her stuff to her right away. I'm also sure she would want you to play tomorrow."

"Trinity, stop," I tell her. She's only dragged me half a foot, but she stops. "I know what the game tomorrow means to everyone, as well as me, but I know what Cerulean means to me, and it's more."

She huffs and crosses her arms. "You're really hard to hate when you're being sweet."

I shrug. "All part of my charm."

She growls, and I throw her a cheesy smile. "Now, what was it you wanted to tell me?"

"Oh," she says. "In all your stupidity I forgot. I've got the tapes."

"What tapes?"

She gives me a look like I'm stupid, which, let's face it, I might very well be. "The tapes from the club. We've got him."

CHAPTER FORTY-EIGHT

I WAKE to a lot of beeping, my sisters asleep on various sofas and a cot, Harley sitting in a chair beside my bed, reading. He looks up when I shift slightly.

"Hey," he says, putting down his book and standing up. "How are you feeling?"

"Like I'm dehydrated and going through Ritalin withdrawal." After doing some tests, Harley's mom concluded that's what's wrong with me. The pills I bought from TK, which I thought were Ritalin, were apparently nothing more than sugar pills. The placebo effect might be real, but when you're dependent on a medication and taking a high dose like I was, it doesn't quite work.

"Hmm," he says, brushing my hair away from my face.

"Are you angry with me?" I ask. I hate how small my voice sounds, how inscure my words are, but it's not like I'm in a position of strength right now.

"About what?"

"Anything. Everything. Take your pick. I've fucked up enough that you *should* be angry with me."

"Hmm," he says again and takes a seat on the

edge of my bed. I scoot over so he has more room. "Yes and no."

I nod. "I get it. I deserve it."

"Argh!" he exclaims, burying his face in my neck. "You really need to stop that." My neck muffles his voice; his breath rushing over my skin gives me tingles.

"Doing what?" I ask, my voice no longer small; it's now breathy.

He chuckles and pulls back so he's looking me in the eyes. "Playing the martyr. I know you've taken responsibility for your sisters since your mom left, but look at them."

I do as he says. All four of us are so similar in appearance, but different as well.

"Indigo and Magenta are eighteen, legally adults. Hell, Magenta has a child of her own. And Vermilion? She's getting stronger every day. They may have deferred to you when you were younger, but they don't need you as much anymore. *That's* what I'm pissed at you about, for taking on too much of other people's problems."

"They're not other people, they're my sisters."

"And they're more than capable of looking after their own lives. You can't shelter them from everything and...." He stops.

"And what?" I ask, rolling to my side, being careful of the drip in the back of my hand.

"And seeing as Magenta has Emily, you haven't sheltered them from everything, anyway."

"He's right, C," Magenta says from where she was obviously pretending to be asleep.

I throw my hands, as much as I can, in the air.

"What's this? Rag on Cerulean day? In case y'all haven't noticed, I'm in the fucking hospital."

"And whose fault is that?" Indigo asks, arching an eyebrow.

"Of course we noticed you're in the hospital," Vermilion chimes in. "We're the ones who have to sleep in uncomfortable positions while you get a freaking bed."

"I'm sorry my health issues are causing you an inconvenience."

"They're not causing us an inconvenience," Vermilion says, grabbing one of my hands. "They are causing us to stress the fuck out, though."

We all laugh at our youngest sister swearing.

"But Harley is right," Indigo says, getting up and perching on the end of my bed. "You *do* need to stop sheltering us from everything. We're not and never have been your responsibility. We never should have let you take control once Mom left, but I guess it was just... easier or something."

"You were the one who took it the best," Magenta adds, standing next to Vermilion. "So we looked to you, we let you guide us out of the hole she left."

"But we're grown now, or getting there," Vermilion joins in. "We can handle ourselves, handle any problems *we* find ourselves in, ourselves."

"But—"

"We know it's been your role for so long," Indigo says. "And you like it, you're good at it, but it's time for you to live your life *for* yourself."

"So you're not angry about the pills then?" I ask.

"Oh, we're angry about the pills," Magenta says. "But we know your reasoning for using them stemmed from what you thought were your responsibilities. You needed more hours in the day, Ritalin gave you that. We also know your usage increased because of your perceived 'failures.'" She makes air quotes.

"And don't worry," Harley interjects. "TK will get his, not just for switching your last lot to sugar pills."

"You still need to get off them, though," Vermilion says.

"I know, and I will." Dr. St. James has already recommended a program designed to slowly and safely wean me off Ritalin, and I've agreed.

"You won't do anything that gets the rest of your offers pulled, will you?" I ask Harley.

"Why?" he asks as he leans over me, forcing me to my back, his lips hovering inches above mine. "Are you worried about me?"

I nod. "You didn't get out of this unscathed either," I remind him, tracing his lips with my finger.

"And you *will* play in that game tomorrow," Vermilion orders from the cot. At some stage during Harley and my... whatever, they've all gone back to their original positions.

He pulls back, eyes wide. "Excuse me?"

The rest of us nod.

"Vermilion's right," I say. "It's state, you've got to play. It's what we've been working toward for years, Harley, *years*."

"Again with the we," he mutters. "I thought you didn't like football."

I press a hand to my chest. "I'm a good Southern

girl, I'll have you know, Harley St. James. Football is in my blood."

He sighs and flops back on my bed—as much as he can.

It's my turn to lean over him. "You need to play, Harley."

He looks up at me and cups my cheek. "What if I don't want to?"

"*Bullshit*," Magenta coughs.

"This is your moment," I tell him.

"*You're* my moment."

Indigo makes retching noises while Vermilion shushes her.

"Oh, babe," I say, tilting my head. "That's sweet. It's not true, but it's sweet."

His brow furrows. "What do you mean it's not true?"

"I mean I'm not your moment. I'm not your be-all and end-all."

He throws his hands up and sits up. "Again with this shit?" he asks. "What happened to 'you deserve your life too?' Or do you not believe *that* as well?"

I have to hold in my chuckle. "Are you done?"

"Are you?" he retorts. "'Cause if you're not, I can go all night and all day tomorrow."

"Oh, I *know* you can," I purr.

"For fuck's sake, Cerulean."

I put my hand over his mouth. "Are you ready to listen to me explain?" I ask.

He rolls his eyes but nods.

"Good. Now, if you'd let me explain my previous statement without flying off the handle, you would've heard me say I'm not your moment because you already have me." I take my hand off his mouth. "You've had me for a while now."

"Really?" he asks, eyes wide.

It's my turn to roll my eyes. "Yes, really."

"Oh my God," Magenta says. "It's like the blind leading the blind."

I flip her the bird.

"Play the game, Harley. *Win*. Show everyone what you're made of. Shove it to TK and prove to Savannah that they're missing out on a big fucking deal."

"I love you," he says.

I chuckle. "I love you more."

Our lips meet, and everything is... right. I feel... home.

"But I'm not leaving until my mom gives you the okay and you're settled at home," he says once we break apart.

I throw my hands up. "Seriously?"

He nods, a smug look on his face. "Seriously. Don't get me wrong, your bit about how irresistible I am and how I need to shove it to everyone was awesome, but I'm still not convinced you're not going to up and die on me, so if Mom says you're good, *then* I'll go."

"You're impossible," I mumble as I snuggle into his chest.

"So are you," he rebuts.

"I guess it's a good thing we found each other," I say, sleep already starting to take hold again.

"A *very* good thing," Magenta says. "Lord knows no one else would have either one of you."

Harley replies, but my eyes are closed and sleep takes me.

IN THE MORNING, Dr. St. James comes and checks me out and determines I'm well enough to go home.

"Remember to take it easy," she tells me. "I'm sending you home with some Ritalin, but make sure you only take it *as directed*."

I nod. "I will."

"I'll be personally checking your progress, so don't think you can get away with the dosage you were taking before."

"I won't. I'd love to be rid of them entirely, but I know I need to do it safely."

"Good," she says. "And you." She turns to Harley. "You need to get home, have some decent food and a proper rest before we leave for Atlanta."

"I'm good," he replies. "And I'm not going until Cerulean's at home."

She crosses her arms over her chest. He grins back at her.

"Don't worry, I've tried to convince him too," I tell her. "But he's being an ass."

She sighs. "I guess we better get you discharged ASAP then."

I DON'T KNOW whether it was Dr. St. James's pull that got me discharged so quick, or the threat of Harley not playing in the championship game, but either way, I'm out of there and at home in no time at all.

"You okay, royal blue?" Harley asks me as I get settled in bed.

"I'd be better if you started doing whatever it is you need to do in order to win today," I retort.

He chuckles and kisses me chastely. "I love you."

"Endearments will get you nowhere," I tell him.

He hands me the TV remote. "I'm going, but make sure you watch, okay?"

"I wouldn't miss it." I beckon him in for a kiss. "Now go win state, QB1."

HARLEY

CHAPTER FORTY-NINE

SPENDING the night before state in a hospital isn't the ideal preparation, but there's nowhere else I'd rather be. I meant every word I said to Cerulean about her being my moment. If my life overseas taught me anything, it's that family, in whatever form that takes for you, is one of the few things you can depend on. Cerulean may not be my family yet, but I have every intention she will be one day. Watching her collapse, seeing her lying in that hospital bed, so small and helpless, made me realize how deep my feelings are. And they're deep, *way* deep, like Challenger Deep, deep. I don't want to sound cocky, but I think her feelings are the same. And that's worth more than any trophy I may win today. Although the trophy would be nice too.

There's a chorus of "heys" as I walk into the locker room we've been given at Georgia State Stadium.

"Nice to see you, St. James," Coach says, slapping me on the back. "How's your girl?"

"She'll be fine," I tell him before realizing the rest of the team wants to know too. Once I say that, they all unfreeze, continuing with whatever they were doing. I smile. So does Coach.

"Good. I know your preparation hasn't been the best, but you ready to play?"

"I'm ready to *win*," I correct.

He slaps me on the back. "Go get ready."

THERE ARE some moments where everything goes right. No matter how badly you throw the ball, it winds up in your receiver's hands, or how badly your kicker connects with the ball, it still sails through the goalposts. Today, that doesn't happen.

We're playing like shit. Nothing is clicking; it almost seems like we've never played together before. Matt, fresh off his heroics last week, is once again allergic to the football.

"This blows," David says as we sit on the bench, watching what will probably be the last play before halftime.

"It's not good," I agree.

As much as I'd like to say it doesn't matter because I've got all I need in Cerulean, I know it does for other guys. Guys who are depending on a good showing here for a last-minute offer, or those who know an offer's not coming and this'll be the last time they line up on the field. So when we trudge off the field once the whistle blows, my head isn't down.

"All right, guys," I say once we're assembled in the locker room. "I think we can all agree that sucked." There are a few muted laughs. "But it's only one half. There's still another one to go, and yeah, I'll be that guy who says we can do it, because we can.

Twenty-one, seven down isn't bad. It's not great, but we can come back from it." I take a breath. "I want to thank you guys. From day one you've had my back. Yes, I've repaid that faith," I get a few chuckles. "But I've also asked a lot from you. I know this would be a lot less daunting with TK with us. The guy has talent, no one's denying that, but what he's done off the field.... Well, it's not something we should overlook, and we haven't. Matt may not be TK, but there's also no way in hell TK could ever be Matt." Hearing this, he sits up straighter. "I know for some of you, this'll be the last game you ever play. Some of you may be okay with that, others may not, and for that I'm sorry. I wish we could all get what we want, but we can't. What we can do is end this *our* way, on our terms. That's also something TK can't do. He won't be playing college ball either." He'll be lucky to stay out of prison, but I don't say that.

"Show him, show everyone that you're better than him. Show all those scouts who said 'no' to you they're wrong. Show those schools you want but who wouldn't take a second look at you what they're missing out on. But say yes when they come knocking." I get even more laughs. "Show the girls, or guys, you want just how badly they should want you." Even more laughs. "Show the manager at Chick-fil-A why you should get more than four sauce containers." They're yelling now. "Show the owner of the cinema why you should get in for free!"

"Yeah!" they all yell back.

"Show everyone we end this on our terms, because we bow to no one." Yeah, so I *may* have stolen my girl's catchphrase. She won't mind. I hand the stage over to Coach so he can give us some actual advice.

I START the second half eating turf, sacked hard and driven into the ground. I'll feel it tomorrow, but right now, the pain barely registers.

I throw pass after pass, handoff after handoff. Some work. Some don't. But my team never lets me down. They never quit.

We claw our way back to twenty-one all with seconds left to play.

I've marched the team down the field as far as I can, stopping at the opposition's twenty-yard line.

"It's all up to you," I tell Jon as Coach sends out the field goal unit. "Show 'em."

He nods, strapping on his helmet and chewing on his mouth guard.

The ball is snapped, and Jack, our backup QB, places the ball for Jon. He strikes it true before, just like in the regional playoff, the wind catches it and pushes it wide.

The whistle goes, pushing us into overtime. It's tight, it's desperate, neither team willing to do anything to risk losing. But neither does anything to win, either. For the first time in Georgia High School football history, the state championship game ends in a tie.

"It's like the best foreplay in the world without an orgasm," David laments as we sit in the locker room after the game.

I chuckle and rub at a smudge on the offensive MVP trophy I won. "It's better than losing, though."

"I suppose," he concedes.

"Besides, it'll look worse for them. They came to a grinding halt, where we gave it our all and but for a breeze, we'd be state champs."

"You're infuriatingly positive," he grumbles.

I laugh and slap his shoulder.

"We going to see you at the bonfire tomorrow?" he asks.

"I dunno, depends on how Cerulean's feeling."

It all depends on her, now and forever.

CHAPTER FIFTY

I DID INDEED WATCH the game, and while I was disappointed Harley didn't get the win, I know he'll be okay with the way things played out.

I wake, sweltering for some unknown reason. It takes a second for the heavy arm around my waist to register. I then notice the hairy leg between mine, the erection pressing at my back and— "Why is there an Offensive MVP trophy in my face?" I ask as I take it in, sitting on my nightstand.

Behind me, Harley stretches, pushing his erection harder into my back, his arm tightening around me. "Because your awesome boyfriend won it," he says sleepily.

"My boyfriend, huh?"

"Yes, your boyfriend."

"I don't know if I agreed to that."

"Maybe not, but you didn't *not* agree to it, so I made the decision for you."

"And is that going to be a recurring theme in this relationship?" I ask.

He chuckles. "Of course not. I just thought I should make the decisions while I can."

I turn to face him. His eyes are still closed, scruff thick on his jaw, hair a mess. But one overriding thought comes when I see him. *Mine.* "What do you mean?"

Finally his eyes open, showing me the deep brown I love. "Good morning," he says, kissing me on the nose.

"When did you get here?" I ask. "Why are you *here?*"

He stretches once more, bones creaking, erection rubbing against my belly, making my thighs clench. "I'm here," he says, nuzzling my neck, "because there's nowhere else I'd rather be. As for when I got here?" He sits up to see the clock next to my bed. "About four hours ago." He yawns.

"So what did you mean when you said you should get the decisions in while you can?"

He cups my cheek. "Baby doll, I'm under no illusion that I'll be the one wearing the pants in this relationship. Although, come to mind, I don't know if I've ever seen you in pants. I know you're the boss, and I'm totally fine with it. But enough about me. How are you? How are you feeling?"

"I'm okay," I tell him. "I mean, I did wake up to my totally awesome boyfriend wrapped around me, so how could I be anything but?"

He stares down at me for a while, those brown eyes burrowing deep into my soul. "You want to talk about it?" he asks.

"About what?"

"Anything. Everything. Nothing if you'd prefer but I think we should talk about some of it."

I blow out a breath and roll to my back. He sits up, head resting on his hand as he looks down at me.

"I'm not going to judge you for whatever's happened while we were broken up, I just want you to get whatever you're feeling off your chest. I think.... I think a lot of this happened because you internalize everything and try to shoulder it all yourself. It's my job to remind you that you don't have to do that anymore."

"We were broken up?" I ask, stalling. "I didn't know we were even officially dating."

He rolls over on top of me, fitting himself between my legs. I groan when his hardness grinds against my core. He chuckles and does it once more. "Yes, royal blue, whatever we were doing before was dating, even if we never put an official title on it. And don't think I don't know what you're doing."

I sigh and run my hand up his arm and over his shoulder. "It's just hard," I tell him.

"Oh, I know it is," he says, grinding against me again.

I laugh as I smack his chest. "Stop it." But I am grateful for his attempt to lighten the mood.

He nods. "I'm sorry. We're trying to be serious. Go on."

I keep running my hand up and down his arm, the movement soothing me. "I'm so used to taking care of everyone else. I figured out a long time ago what I wanted to be, where I wanted to go. That was the foundation I built everything on. Then I lost it."

"You didn't lose it," he corrects. "TK *took* it from you."

"Semantics," I argue. "Either way, it's gone, and

my foundation crumbled and suddenly I couldn't do anything right."

"You know that's not true," he says, brushing my hair back from my face.

"Isn't it?"

"Shit happens," he tells me. "There's nothing we can do about it. You only think it was all your fault because you carry the weight of the world on your shoulders."

"Maybe." I shrug.

"Well, that ends today," he declares. "Or Friday, but shit's getting real today."

I can't help it, I giggle, and his whole face lights up. "That's the most beautiful sound," he says. "Well, besides when you're screaming my name and coming on my cock."

My thighs clench but I still slap him.

"I can't help it! You're insanely beautiful and mine and I'm a horny eighteen-year-old guy who just won the state offensive MVP, by the way."

"Really? I hadn't noticed." I point to the massive trophy beside my bed.

He grins, showing me all his teeth. "But seriously, you know you're not alone anymore, right? I'm here for whatever you want or need."

I nod. "I know."

He stares into my eyes before agreeing that I'm telling the truth. He lowers his head, but I stop him. "Er, what?" he asks, my fingers against his lips.

"Morning breath."

He slumps against me. "Really?"

I nod again. "Yes, really."

"Please tell me, little-miss-dental-hygiene, that you have a spare toothbrush I can use."

I smile, even though he can't see it. "I do."

"Good," he says, jumping up and extending a hand to me. "Let's be good boys and girls and brush our teeth before we get very, *very* naughty."

Once I'm up, he wraps his arms around my waist, attacking my neck and making me squeal. "You're so annoying," I tell him as we walk to the bathroom attached to my room.

"You love it," he replies.

I turn in his arms and cup his cheek. "I really do," I say before turning his head and kissing his cheek.

We stand side by side as we brush our teeth, sending each other furtive glances like we're in junior high or something. I lean over to spit the toothpaste out, and Harley takes the opportunity to thrust his tented boxer-briefs when I'm at eye level with them. I rinse and straighten, eyebrow arched. He shrugs and gives me a toothpaste-y grin before following my actions. Only when he straightens I reach for his erection, rubbing it through the material.

"Fuck," he hisses, thrusting into my hand.

"Always so cocky," I say as I slip my hand under the waistband.

"You lo— Oh fuck," he groans as I squeeze his head. "Yeah, just like that."

I throw a towel on the tile floor and lower to my knees, taking his underwear with me as I go. I give him a few jerks before taking him in my mouth.

"Oh, God, yes," he breathes as I take him as far as I can. "Damn, baby doll, you suck me so good."

I hum around him, and he jerks, a drop of precum bursting across my tongue.

"Wha...?" I say as he pulls out of my mouth, lifting me to my feet and spinning so we're both facing the mirror. His hand travels from my hip to my panties before sliding underneath the waistband.

"So wet," he murmurs as he slips a finger, then two inside me.

"Harley," I whisper.

"I love it when you say my name," he tells me.

"I love it when you look at me," I say, my eyes meeting his in the mirror. "Like I'm the most amazing thing you've ever seen."

He presses a kiss to my collarbone. "You are." He withdraws his fingers and pulls my panties down my legs, leaving kisses in his wake. "Tell me you have a condom in here," he says.

I lean over and open the cabinet behind the mirror, grab the box, rip it open, and hand him one of the foil squares. The foil crinkles as he opens it, and then he's in me, filling me, taking my breath.

"This, right here," he says, slowly thrusting in and out, "is *way* better than any trophy."

"Even the Lombardi Trophy?" I ask.

He runs his hands up and down my thighs, his calluses scratching me but leaving tingles in their wake too. "Well, seeing as though it'll be a while until I'll get to hold it, I guess I better keep you around so I can compare when the time comes."

I laugh and lean back on his shoulder, my hands gripping his muscular thighs, nails digging in. "I like that idea."

"So do I." He sucks on my neck, and I clench

around him and close my eyes, letting the sensations overtake me. He continues his relaxed pace, leisurely thrusting in and out of me, his hands wandering all over my body. I feel... loved, cherished even. Yes, Harley and I have had sex before, but this, he's making love to me. Yes, we've done that before too, but this time it means more, it feels like more. The realization gets me even hotter, sending a rush of moisture to where we're joined.

"Shit, that's hot," he says. "Look."

I open my eyes, and it's not the sight of him entering me that sets me off, it's the unadulterated love in his gaze.

"Harley!" I scream, coming hard around him.

He slides an arm around my waist, helping to hold me up. "That's it, baby doll."

A few more strokes and he comes as well. "Fuck, Cerulean." He throws his head back, fingers digging into me, but I don't care.

He presses a kiss to my shoulder before pulling out and getting rid of the condom.

"What's that look for?" he asks when he sees my frown.

"I like the feel of you inside me." I pout.

He groans and rests his head on my shoulder. "Baby doll, if I could live there twenty-four seven, I would, but the logistics of doing so would be problematic."

I chuckle, and he lifts his head. "Good morning," he says before taking my lips in a punishing kiss. He lifts me up and sits me on the counter, standing between my legs, his hands moving to my ribs. "We've got to work on putting some meat back on your bones," he tells me, pulling the tank top I wore to bed over my head.

"You're just hoping those grow." I look down at my A cups.

He bites down on a nipple. "That would be nice, but mostly, royal blue, I want you healthy."

I reach over and grab another condom from the box, ripping it open and rolling it on him. God bless athletes and their excellent stamina.

"And I want you," I say as I guide him to my entrance. "Forever."

He slides home, and once again I feel whole.

"You got me, baby doll, now and forever."

HARLEY

EVENTUALLY CERULEAN AND I made it out of her bathroom, although moving back to her bed didn't help matters.

"I never thought I'd say this," I pant as Cerulean climbs off me and drapes herself over my side, "but I think I'm all orgasmed out." I take the condom off and throw it in the trash.

She nods and rests on my chest. "I feel ya."

I run my hand down her back and squeeze her butt. "That was some damn good lovin' though."

She laughs, and her stomach growls.

"But it looks like I'm failing in my mission to get you healthy."

She nods, her eyes closed. "So slack."

I spank her, and she moans. "Shit, that was not the reaction I was going for," I say as my cock jerks.

The little vixen laughs and rubs her pussy against my thigh.

"As much as I'd love nothing more than to stay in this bed with you all day, we should probably get up."

"Do we have to?" she whines.

"Well, we definitely need to get some food in you,

and if you're feeling up to it, there's a party or two going on today that I should probably show my face at."

She groans and burrows deeper into my side. "I can't walk, you fucked me into a noodle."

"Oh, baby doll, you're *so* much more than a noodle." I squeeze her ass for emphasis.

She lifts her head, blonde hair everywhere and a mess. "You're a royal pain in my ass, you know that?" she asks.

I circle her tight ring with my finger. "Nah, if you do it right, it doesn't hurt."

Her eyes light up.

"Oh, *really*?" I ask.

"What?"

"You want me to take your ass?"

She bites her lip. "Have you done it before?"

I shrug. "Once or twice."

"And the girls, they liked it?"

I nod. "They did." I brush the hair off her face. "You know, if you wanted to try it, if you didn't like it at any stage, I'd stop."

"I know that."

"Look, we've been at each other all day. Let's take a break, get some food in us, maybe make an appearance at the party, and we can come back to this another day."

"Are you s—"

"Whatever you want, baby doll." I press a quick kiss to her lips. "I love you."

"I love you more," she replies, smiling at me. I swear, for that smile, there's nothing I won't do.

· · ·

WE SHOWER, get dressed, and go downstairs, her sisters nowhere to be seen. I go to the fridge and pull out the makings for an omelet, plus bacon and sausage.

Once she's eaten as much as she can, we finally venture outside. We get into my car and head for the bonfire.

"Are you disappointed about the game?" she asks.

"Yes and no. Yes, for the guys on the team for whom it was their last game, but no because I know we left it all out there."

"What are you going to do about Savannah?" she asks.

"Not much I can do. They made their decision, sold their program for a new library or whatever TK's parents' money bought them."

"You'll have to move next year," she says.

I look over. Her bottom lip is out, eyes and mouth cast downward. "Hey." I pinch her chin. "It's only a year, and I'll come back as often as I can. You'll come to me as often as you can too, I hope."

"That's it?" she asks.

"What more is there to it?"

"I don't know. What about all the girls, the temptation?"

"You'll be fine," I reply. "And if you get the urge to be with another girl, make sure you record it and send it to me."

She slaps my leg while I laugh. I grab her hand and bring it to my mouth. "Baby doll, I don't want anyone else. I don't *see* anyone else. It's you, all you."

"I hate TK," she says as we pull up to the clearing where the bonfire's being held.

"He'll get his, I promise. Now let's do our rounds and we can get back to more... fun things," I say, wiggling my eyebrows. The giggle I love so much makes an appearance, and I feel like I could climb Mount Everest a million times.

THERE ARE cheers when we emerge from the car, and I reach over and grab Cerulean's hand.

I'm touched that everyone who comes over to congratulate me also checks on her. I think she is too. For so long she's kept herself distant, separate from everyone but her sisters, ruling without feeling, but knowing she was doing it for their own good. Now she's seeing the reward of that.

I spot Vermilion and Kingsley in the crowd, and they come over, the crowd parting for the youngest Tremont as they do for her older sisters.

"Hey, QB1," Kingsley says, knocking her shoulder into my arm.

"Kingsley."

"Decent game yesterday."

"*Just* decent?" I ask.

"Did you win?" she counters.

"We tied."

"Then it was just decent. If you'd won, now *that* would've been impressive."

I throw my head back and laugh. They move off toward a group of freshmen boys, and Trinity takes their place.

"You two look good together again," she says.

Cerulean growls, but I pull her so she's in front of

me, her back to my chest, my arms over her shoulders. "Thanks," I say.

Trinity shifts from foot to foot. "So, um, I looked over the footage from the club. I'm just not sure if it will be enough, you know, given his parents and everything."

"Oh."

"Yeah," she agrees.

"You're going after TK?" Cerulean asks.

"I promised he would get his, so that's what we're working to make happen." I turn back to Trinity. "My mom could testify as to what was in Karlie's bloodstream?"

"But without Karlie herself, your mom can't break patient confidentiality," Cerulean interjects.

"Fuck. What else can we do then?"

"Leave it with me," she says, escaping my arms and wading into the crowd.

Trinity laughs.

"What?" I ask.

She gestures to where Cerulean's already deep in conversation with a group of girls, sophomores probably, seeing as though I don't know who they are. "Witness the Sovereign of Savannah at work."

I can tell the girls are reluctant to talk to Cerulean and maybe a bit intimidated, but the more she talks, the more they seem to relax.

"She has a way with people," I comment.

"And Jesus just has a small following."

"She's earned their respect," I tell Trinity. "She's never exploited it."

"She's just perfect in every way, isn't she?"

I shrug. "She is for me."

"Ugh," Trinity says, and I laugh.

Watching as Cerulean does her thing, talks to her people, I'm in awe. *This* is who she is. She's caring and protective, not just of her sisters, although they do rightfully take precedent. She's strong and fierce, and she's full of so much love that I'm honored she chose me to bestow some of it on.

"Jesus," Trinity curses, her nose wrinkled.

"What?"

"The amount of pheromones coming off you while you watch her is disgusting."

I laugh and sniff my arm. "I've showered today."

"Was that before or after fucking her for hours on end?"

"During," I say, laughing again.

She shakes her head and walks off. I grab a bottle of water from a cooler and sit on a log near the fire. A few of the guys from the team migrate over, and soon we're relaxing, shooting the shit and enjoying the end of our high school football careers.

WHAT COULD BE minutes or maybe hours later, Cerulean comes over and settles in my lap.

"Well, hello there," I say, my arms going round her.

"Hello, yourself."

I nuzzle her neck, inhaling her sweet berry scent.

"You smell so good," I tell her, and she laughs.

"Parfum du Grande."

"Huh?"

"The name of the house who makes the perfume I wear."

"Oh."

She laughs, grabs my face, and kisses me.

"I thought we weren't this kind of couple," I joke as we break apart.

"What kind?" she asks.

"The kind where you sit on my lap." She goes to get off but I hold her firm. "Uh-uh, you're not going anywhere. So what did your people tell you?"

"My people?"

I wave my hand around the gathering. "Your people. You are one of the Sovereigns of Savannah, aren't you?"

She sighs and slumps against my chest. "I thought so, but maybe I shouldn't be."

"Why shouldn't you?" I ask.

She sits up, looking me in the eyes. "I'm a drug-addicted mess."

"First, you're getting treatment for your problem. You've recognized you have one and are doing something to fix it. Second, you're not a mess. Yes, things haven't been going great for you, but I doubt there's a lot of people around here who could say they're going great for them either. On top of that, people were talking to you, weren't they? They weren't ignoring you, they weren't treating you like a leper. You still have their respect, Cerulean. They know you're human; now you have to realize it."

She slumps into my chest again. "I'm being selfish, aren't I?"

I brush a kiss across her forehead. "Given what you've done for everyone else, I think we'll allow it." She sighs and snuggles into my chest. "So what did your listening tour uncover?" I ask again.

"Just what we thought: TK's a sleaze."

"Are any of them willing to say something about him?"

"They're scared."

I nod. "Would you... you know, be willing to speak up?"

She bites her lip. I reach up and gently free it from her teeth. She takes a deep breath. "Yeah, I would. I guess I can't ask these girls to share the horrific thing that happened to them and not share my own experience."

I lean forward and kiss her. "You're incredible," I tell her.

She ducks her head.

"Hey," I say, lifting her chin. "You bow to no one, remember that."

CHAPTER FIFTY-TWO

FOR SO LONG I'VE built myself up. I'm so strong, I'm fierce, nothing and no one can get to me. Preparing to blow that persona to shit? Terrifying.

Harley squeezes my hand. "Are you okay?"

I nod, my stomach churning. "I think so."

He presses a kiss to my temple. "You'll be fine, and I'll be right there beside you."

I turn and wind my arms around his waist, resting my chin on his chest. "Have I thanked you for everything you've done for me?" I ask.

He brushes my hair back from my face. "You don't need to, that's what you do for the people you love."

I nod. "Okay then, let's go."

TRINITY, Karlie, and a few other girls meet us at the police station. I feel kind of bad for all my horrible thoughts about Trinity, especially when she was spending time with Harley while we were... apart. He explained that once she realized he would never go for her and she saw what exactly TK was willing to do, she flipped the switch on him.

"Thanks for coming," I tell everyone. "I know reliving what happened to you won't be easy, but we can't let him get away with this." They all nod. "But I want you to know you're not alone, you have support, and I am so proud you're willing to do this. I know it's scary and it might be invasive and humiliating, but it's something we have to do, if only so we can say we tried to stop it from happening to anyone else." With that, they follow me up the steps.

"FUCK ME," I say, flopping back on my bed.

"That can be arranged," Harley says, lying down beside me.

I try to shove him but I'm too emotionally and physically drained. And let's face it, even if I was at full strength, like I'd be able to move him anyway.

"How are you?" he asks.

I blow out a breath. "Tired."

He twirls a piece of my hair around his finger.

Telling several detectives my sordid history with TK wasn't easy. But what he did to those girls.... It was *so* much worse. I got off lightly. I can't and I don't want to imagine what it would be like to go to a party and be enjoying yourself, thinking you'd caught the eye of one of the most popular guys in school, only to wake up the next morning with no memory of what the fuck happened. Some of the girls went to the hospital the next morning, some didn't. Of those who did, only two still had traces of Rohypnol in their system. All of them woke up naked and next to TK.

Having that evidence is useful even if the girls weren't willing to make statements or press charges at the time.

I don't know what the police will do now, but at least we can say we tried.

"What do you think they'll do?" Harley asks.

I shrug. "I don't know. Obviously they'll go to the Thomases with the accusations, this is Savannah after all and the Thomas name means something, but from there? Who knows?"

He continues to play with my hair, the other running up my side before landing on my boob, giving it a quick squeeze, then tracing my nipple.

"Mmm," I moan, arching my back, pushing my breast into his touch.

"Are you up for this?" he asks.

I open one of my eyes. "Are you?" I raise my knee and encounter the hard-on tenting his pants.

He moves out of my reach. "This isn't about me, it's about you. You've been through a lot, and I want to take care of you."

"When you put it that way," I say, a twinkle in my eye, a smile on my face. "Do your worst."

"HOLY FUCK," I pant as Harley makes his way up the bed, wiping his mouth. I never should've told him to do his worst. Or maybe I should tell him to do it more often. Actually, more often, *definitely* more often. "I don't think I can feel my toes."

I turn my head; the corners of his mouth are upturned. "I'd shove you," I tell him, "but holy fuck."

He chuckles. "I fulfilled my brief then?"

I nod. "Yeah, no doubt."

He drags me into his arms so I'm draped over his chest. "Good."

"Are you sure there's nothing I can do for you?" I ask, his erection pressing against my hip.

"Nope," he says. "I'm a big boy, I'll survive."

"Oh, I know how big you are." My hand travels down his chest to the waistband of his boxer-briefs. He stops me before I can go any further.

"Just go to sleep," he says, kissing the back of my hand. "Tomorrow's a new day."

WAKING UP TO HARLEY IS... bliss. He holds me all night, never letting me go, making me feel cherished and adored, like I'm something precious. It's something I could do every day for the rest of my life. Finding the love of my life in high school was not something I ever set out to do. In fact, I wasn't sure marriage would even be on the cards for me. But with Harley in my life now, I can't imagine life without him. Next year will be tough, and we have some decisions to make. *I* have some decisions to make, but we'll get through it and we'll overcome whatever life has to throw at us.

He stirs in his sleep, his morning wood poking me in the butt. I smile and think back to how thoroughly he took care of me yesterday. My core clenches when I remember just how hard I came.

I gently roll him to his back, one of his arms still reaching out to where I'd be if I weren't making my way down his body. As carefully as I can, I pull down his underwear, his hard-on slapping against his ripped abs.

"Mmm, Cerulean," he moans when I take him in my mouth.

I suck on his crown, my hand running up and down his length before I suck him deep.

"Holy shit, baby doll," he says, his voice rough with sleep. "That is one hell of a way to wake up."

I hum around him, continuing to bob up and down on his dick, his hands threading through my hair but not exerting any pressure.

"Fuck, you suck me so good," he tells me. "I'm gonna come any second."

I swallow around him, and he throws his head back. "Holy shit, do that again."

I do, and he jerks in my mouth, his cum spilling down my throat. I lick him clean, still semihard, and crawl up the bed.

"Good morning," I say, settling in to his side.

"It's a fucking fantastic morning," he corrects, and I giggle.

I was never a giggler before I met Harley. Just another change he's made to me, I guess. I thought having a boyfriend would mean me having to give up a part of myself, having to change in order to fit in with his ideals, but I've done none of that. Sure, I've changed a little. I think my sharp edges have dulled just a bit, and maybe I've become a little more approachable, a little less high-strung. But those aren't bad things. Harley fills in my gaps, all my shortcomings. He supports me through all my faults, of which there are many, and I'll support him through his, of which there are also many. We're a perfect match, and I couldn't be more thankful he never stopped pursuing me.

"I love hearing you giggle," he tells me.

"I never did it before you."

"That's because I'm the only one with the requisite skills to bring it out."

I roll my eyes so hard they hurt.

"How are you feeling this morning?" he asks.

I shrug. "Okay. We did all that we could do. If nothing else happens, at least there's that."

He squeezes me tight. "Well, if I know you, and I like to think I do, I know you won't let them make that decision lightly."

I shake my head.

"We bow to no one," he says, pressing a kiss to my hair.

"We bow to no one," I repeat.

USUALLY I'M the first one downstairs for breakfast. Emily wakes up early, but Magenta likes to feed her in her room where my niece isn't distracted. This morning though, I'm not the first person in the kitchen. I stop so suddenly Harley can't stop himself and runs into me.

"Mom?" I ask.

"Hi, baby." She comes around the counter, and I take in her lithe five foot five frame, perfectly coifed light blonde hair, my own jade green eyes, her skin unchanged but for a few more wrinkles around her eyes and worry lines on her forehead.

"What are you doing here?" I ask as she hugs me, her signature rose scent strong.

"Your sisters called me last week. I was tying things up when I got another call from Aunt Violet. I was... worried."

I scoff. "Worried? Really?"

She sighs. "I know I haven't been here for y'all but I'm still your mom." Hearing y'all come out of her European/American accent is weird and reminds just how long she's been away.

"We don't need you," I tell her.

"I know you don't, but I guess I just wanted to... I don't know, check on you, make sure you're okay."

"Why now? Why didn't you come back when Vermilion broke down after Dean died, or when Magenta had Emily? We've needed you before and you've never come back so I'll ask again. Why. Now?"

"I thought by leaving you I was doing the best thing for you."

Beside me Harley scoffs.

"I wanted to raise strong girls, strong *women*."

"And leaving us was the way to do that? We needed you before, we don't need you now."

"I see that." A small smile ghosts across her lips. "Still, you are my daughters."

Just then my sisters and a babbling Emily enter the kitchen, all stopping dead.

"Holy fuck," Magenta says.

"Mom?" Vermilion asks, while Indigo crosses her arms over her chest.

"My babies and grandbaby," Mom coos, sweeping over to them, arms wide.

Emily shies away from her and starts crying. Magenta bounces her, trying to soothe her. Mom stops dead in her tracks.

"What are you doing here?" Magenta asks.

Mom's shoulders drop. "Can't I come home and see my daughters and granddaughter?" she asks.

"No," Indigo says.

Vermilion's biting her lip, eyes swinging from Mom to us. Mom sighs.

"Just tell us," I say. "It can't be worse than not really being there for the past ten years."

She takes a seat at the table. "You know I think the world of you girls," she begins.

"Have a funny way of showing it," Magenta grumbles.

Mom ignores her and carries on. "I never would've left all those years ago if I didn't think y'all could handle yourselves. I left when I did because I truly believed you would be fine without me, and you are. I wanted you to become strong women, and you all are, exceedingly so."

I see Harley nod from the corner of my eye, and I grab his hand, giving it a squeeze.

"I came back to make sure you were everything I wanted you to be."

HARLEY

I'M JUST gonna say it, the girls' mom? A little nuts. All this bullshit about her leaving her daughters so they'd be stronger? May have worked, but I'm also pretty sure there were other ways she could've achieved that. Then again, I've never known a Tremont to do things half-cocked.

"And just how are you going to do that?" Magenta asks, putting Emily in her high chair and grabbing a few Cheerios to put in front of her.

"TK Thomas," Cyan says. "Aunt Violet told me all about that."

"It's fine, I've got it covered," Cerulean says.

"I know you do, and I couldn't be prouder."

"You know this is totally fucked up, right?" I ask.

Cyan turns to me. "And you are?"

Cerulean sighs. "Mom, this is my boyfriend, Harley St. James. Harley, my mom, Cyan Tremont."

"Nice to meet you," I say, but don't extend my hand.

Cyan chuckles. "You don't approve of my methods of raising my daughters, Mr. St. James?"

"No, I don't. This whole thing is batshit crazy. You left them here, for *ten years*. Why couldn't you have them with you in Switzerland, huh? Why leave them here to fend for themselves?"

"I was busy building my career, I couldn't be distracted."

"They're your daughters, not a distraction."

"I wanted them to grow into strong, independent women, they couldn't do that with me holding their hands the entire time. They were better off here, without me."

"Glad we agree on that," I say. "And now you're back to check on how well your experiment went?"

She shrugs. "You can call it that. I call it checking on my daughters, supporting them in their time of need."

"And this has been their only time of need in the past ten years?"

"My girls have done me proud," she says.

"They did you proud every other time you abandoned them too. They don't need you."

"No, but I'm here if they want me."

The girls all look at each other.

The tension in the air is broken by a knock at the door.

"I'll get it," I offer.

"Well, sugar, are you goin' to stand there or let me in?" Violet says once I open the door. Leroy is behind her and chuckles.

"Sorry, Miss Violet," I mumble as I move to the side.

They sweep in, but Violet stops in front of me and pats my cheek. "Good effort at state," she says.

"And don't worry, we won't hold the result against you for too long, only fifty or so years."

I chuckle and mime wiping my brow. "Thank God. I was worried I'd be damned for all eternity."

She pats my cheek a little harder, but moves toward the kitchen.

"I would apologize for her," Leroy says in his rich baritone. "But—"

I hold up a hand. "I'm well versed in the ways of the York women," I tell him. "It's good to see you again."

He holds out a hand and I shake it. "You too."

"Come on," I say, closing the door. "We better get in there."

"IT'S about time you got your skinny ass back here," Violet says as Leroy and I walk back into the kitchen. He shakes his head while I head to the coffee maker. I doubt anyone else will take over breakfast duties, and I'm guessing no one will go to school today, at least not on time.

"I was busy helping run a multinational corporation, Aunt Violet," Cyan rebuts.

"Meanwhile, your family is here, flounderin' without you," Violet shoots back.

"We weren't—" Cerulean starts.

"Hush, child," Violet tells her. "I'm guilt trippin' here."

I chuckle and shake my head.

"Good Lord," Leroy curses softly, coming to help me.

"These girls needed a mother," Violet says,

walking over to a still shell-shocked Vermilion and putting her arm around her shoulders.

"They've turned out fine without one," Cyan replies. "If you push a baby bird out of the nest, its only options are to fly or die."

The two women stand at opposite sides of the table, eyes narrowed, mouths pinched, arms crossed.

"Okay, okay," I say, placing cups of coffee on the table. "How about we put those issues to the side for *just* a moment, huh?" They both look at me. "Whatever's gone on in the past, whether right or wrong, won't change anytime soon. We have bigger fish to fry."

Violet looks to Cerulean. "He always like this?"

She nods. "Unfortunately."

I send her a wink.

Finally Violet takes a seat at the table. "Well, we better make sure this trip isn't wasted then."

YOU'D THINK HAVING five Tremonts and a York descending on your police station would be intimidating, but I have to hand it to Chief Israel, he stands his ground.

"Cyan," he says, hands resting on his belt, stretched around a rather rotund stomach. "Long time, no see."

"You too, Tony," she says.

"And what can I do for our lovely ladies of Savannah today?"

"Cut the bullshit, Tony," Violet says. "We're here to make sure TK Thomas gets what's comin' to him, to make sure the work my great niece and her friends did isn't swept under the rug as things have been known to do. We wanted to make sure you knew there were people watchin' you."

"Now, Violet," he replies. "The boy has made mistakes, for sure, but should that affect his whole future?"

"He raped some of those girls," Cerulean says. "He almost raped *me*."

"That was not proven," Chief Israel says.

"The other girls didn't give consent and woke up naked in bed next to him, how is that not proven?" she asks. "He would've done the same to me if Harley hadn't burst in. And what about him swapping my pills, throwing me into sudden withdrawal? Do you know how dangerous that is?"

"Ah, yes, your own illegal drug use. You know I could have you up on charges for that, too?"

I want to punch the smug smile off his face.

"Tony?" A voice comes from behind him. "What's this?" A man and a woman come down the hall, TK in tow, as well as my father.

"Dad?" I ask. "What are you doing here?"

He puffs his chest out and adjusts his jacket. It's his classic "I'm a powerful and important person" gesture. "I'm here to assure Chief Israel the heinous allegations leveled at Mr. Thomas are nothing more than the jealous ramblings of girls scorned."

"Of course you are."

"Tony?" Mr. Thomas asks again.

"These ladies have come to express their... displeasure that we are declining to investigate the allegations against young TK here."

"You've got to be kidding," I say.

"Now, son," Chief Israel says to me. "You got what you wanted and took out the player competing for attention. Just leave it be. Being a sore loser doesn't suit anybody."

I can't help it, I throw my head back and laugh. The hypocrisy of this guy. TK couldn't get those girls so he got revenge in the worst way.

"I think you're making a mistake, Tony," Cyan says, her voice quiet but with an underlying edge. "From what I've been told, you have more than enough evidence to build a solid case."

"That's a matter of opinion, Cyan, and in my opinion TK has no case to answer."

"Are you really going to be *that* guy?" Cyan asks. "The one who ignores *all* the evidence my daughter brought you?"

"That's enough," my father interjects. "The chief has made his final decision; it's up to us to respect it."

"And you are?" Cyan asks, turning on a glare her daughters have perfected.

He does his powerful and important person gesture again. "I am Cary St. James, principal of Forest Park Academy."

"Is that a slight accent I detect from you, Mr. St. James?" she asks.

"I have spent many years overseas, that is correct."

"Switzerland, perhaps?"

"Yes. We were there just last year."

"And while you were there, were you principal of the International School in Geneva?"

He nods. "I was."

She nods too. "I remember reading something not too long ago. You see, I too am based in Geneva. I believe the article mentioned donations from less than reputable sources. And was there something also about cash for grades?" she asks.

"I-I...," my dad splutters. He clears his throat. "I surely don't know what you're talking about."

She laughs. "No, of course you wouldn't. But isn't it interesting that you're here defending a boy accused of some *very* serious offenses? You add that to the donation rumors, the grades scheme, and it doesn't look all that above board for you either, does it?"

I have to hide my smile.

"I am a good principal," he says.

"Oh, I don't doubt it, but your alliances leave a little to be desired. We wouldn't want one small mistake to sully an entire career, now would we?"

My father looks from Cyan to the Thomases, to the chief, back to the Thomases. "I'm sorry," he says finally. "I have too much at stake. I can't jeopardize it on one boy." He scurries past them, stopping in front of me. "I did what I had to do," he tells me. "I *always* do what I have to do."

"No," I tell him. "You do what's best for *you*."

He nods to Cerulean. "You think this one won't cause you trouble? Look at what she's already cost you."

"She hasn't cost me anything." I jerk my chin to TK. "It was all his doing. But you know what? She's worth it."

"You're a fool."

"And you're going to end up a washed-up old schoolteacher, the only jobs available to you the ones no one wants."

With a "humph," he turns and walks out.

"So, Chief," Cyan says. "About that investigation...."

"YOU LADIES," I say, holding my glass of sweet tea in the air, "are really something."

"Here, here," Leroy seconds.

"You're all also a little scary, but as I have no intention of getting on your bad side, it won't be a problem."

There are laughs all round as we once again sit in the Tremonts' kitchen. After my father turned tail and ran, the chief succumbed to the "rainbow wall," as I'm calling it.

"We're bred with fire in our veins," Violet says.

"That may be true," Cyan says. "But—"

"If you're going to apologize," Magenta says. "Don't bother."

"What's done is done. You made your decision, we've lived with it. Are we better off for it? Worse? Who knows? Who cares?" Indigo adds.

Cyan nods. "If it's any consolation, I truly thought you'd be okay and able to handle it."

Violet shakes her head, but Leroy pats her knee, placating her.

"How long are you here for, Cyan?" I ask. She might be crazier than a cut snake, but she's still my girl's mom and I know Cerulean misses her.

She takes a sip of her drink. "As long as I'm wanted, I suppose."

"You're not," Violet snaps before anyone can reply otherwise.

"Actually," Vermilion speaks up. "I was, um, wondering if you would, um, maybe, um, help me find a new, um, piano teacher?" She twists her hands in her lap.

Cyan's eyes light up. "Of course, sweetie."

Leroy clears his throat. "Actually, meaning no disrespect to you, Mrs. Tremont, but that's also one of the reasons why I came back." He turns to Vermilion. "Young lady, I saw your audition piece and was blown away. A talent like yours.... Well, it should be allowed to thrive. If you'd have me, I'd be honored to offer my services."

Vermilion's face lights up.

"I thought you came back for *me*?" Violet asks.

Leroy pats her hand. "Yes, dear."

We all laugh.

Vermilion looks to her mom. "Go on," Cyan encourages.

"I-I'd l-love to," she stammers.

Leroy nods, his eyes shining. "Good."

"Then I guess my job here is done," Cyan says, getting up.

"You could always stay because you wanted to," Cerulean says. Vermilion nods, as does Indigo.

Magenta sighs. "You do have a granddaughter you could get to know."

Cyan looks at all of them. "Really?" She bites her lip, eyes wide.

"Sure," Indigo confirms.

She sits down again. "Okay."

"Besides, we have Alexandrov to take care of," Cerulean adds, a twinkle in her eye.

"He doesn't stand a chance," Leroy says.

CHAPTER FIFTY-FOUR

SIGNING day for colleges happens on the first Wednesday of February every year. Although some athletes sign in December, the majority of deals happen today.

So many times I've tried asking Harley what he's going to do, where he's going to go, but he's kept tight-lipped. The only thing I do know is he won't be going to Savannah.

After the police opened an investigation into TK, Savannah quickly changed their tune, offering Harley the world if he would commit to them. But it's like he said, they sold their program to the Thomases. How could he go there knowing how easily they turned on him?

My mom stayed for a little over a week, helping us deliver some questionable and highly embarrassing footage of Alexandrov to the National Conservatorium. Not long after, they started calling Leroy, begging him to come back, but he said the same thing Harley did. How could he go back, knowing what they were willing to do?

Some would call it cutting off your nose to spite your face. I call it bowing to no one.

"YOU OKAY?" Harley asks, coming up behind me, wrapping his arms around me, bringing my back to his front.

I shrug. "I'm eager to see where you're going to end up next year, but I still think all this attention over little old you is a bit ridiculous."

He throws his head back and laughs. But seriously. We're in his kitchen, and his living room is set up like a real life media conference. There are a heap of newspaper reporters and photographers, as well as a couple of TV cameras.

"Royal blue," he says, nuzzling my neck. "You know there's nothing little about me."

I know he can't see me, but I roll my eyes anyway. I do elbow him for good measure, however.

"Oof."

"Least of all your ego," I say as I spin in his arms.

"Guess it's a good thing I've got you around to deflate it then, huh?"

I reach down to where he's already semihard. "Oh, babe, *you* should know nothing about you is deflated if I'm around."

He groans and rests his forehead on my shoulder. "Shit, Cerulean, I'm about to go out in front of cameras."

I laugh. "I can help if you want." I rub my body against his.

"That is *not* helping." He stills my hips.

"Everything's ready for you," Coach says.

Harley blows out a breath and nods. "Okay."

"You good?" I ask.

"Just give me a sec," he says, closing his eyes. "All right, I'm good." He takes my hand and drags me with him to the door.

The photographers go crazy when he comes into view.

"Hi, everyone, thanks for coming," he says as he takes a seat. "I know this all seems a little over the top, and frankly, for me it's overwhelming, but I appreciate the interest." He takes a sip of his water. "Over the past season there's been a lot of interest and speculation as to which college I will attend next year. I received a lot of offers and I want to thank each and every school who extended me one. I looked over every one of them, and let me tell you, it was no easy feat deciding where I would go.

"I thought long and hard, but in the end, one school made it impossible to turn down." He takes a deep breath and looks straight into the cameras. "I am pleased to announce that next year I will be attending the University of Birmingham." He pulls out a U of B cap and puts it on.

"Excuse me, miss," a voice behind me says. I jump, not realizing there *was* someone behind me.

He walks past me and sits next to Harley. "Charlie Garrett, head of recruitment for Coach Penn at the University of Birmingham," he says. "And we are so incredibly thrilled to welcome this exciting and promising young man to our organization."

They shake hands, and once again there's a flurry of camera clicks.

"Harley," one reporter calls. "What happened with Savannah?"

"Savannah withdrew their offer," he says.

"But didn't they then offer an improved one?" he presses.

Harley blows out a breath. "They did, but they couldn't offer what Birmingham could."

"And what's that?"

He looks over to me. "My future."

My brows furrow. What on earth does he mean by that? I'm not going to Birmingham. Their international business and political science programs are solid but not earth-shattering.

I've had to do some readjustments post-Carver. Yes, where Harley would be *did* factor into that, but I also have to consider my future. I can't and won't give it up just for him.

"Hey," he says, coming over to me, grabbing me by the waist and kissing me. The announcement is apparently done.

"Hey, yourself. So, Birmingham, huh?"

He shrugs. "They offered me the best deal."

"Yes, your future, I heard."

He chuckles. "Come on, let's discuss this." He grabs my hand and drags me to his dad's office, that Garrett guy trailing behind us. "This is Charlie Garrett, by the way," he says, shutting the door.

"It's a pleasure to meet you, Miss Tremont," he says, extending a hand to me.

"Uh, you too." He has a firm handshake and warm eyes. I like that.

"A few months ago, when I realized what TK was

capable of and the lengths he'd go to, I went to Mr. Garrett with a proposition," Harley explains.

Garrett nods. "And what a proposition it was."

"I'm lost," I say.

Harley grabs my hands. "You know you're my future, right?"

"Er, yes?"

He laughs. "Well, you are. I knew that, and I knew after TK made Carver no longer an option for you, you'd be looking for alternatives."

"Miss Tremont," Garrett says. "What do you think of our international business and political science programs?"

"Um, they're okay?" I say, but it comes out sounding like a question.

He chuckles. "Yes, *just* okay. *Now*. But in a year's time it will look drastically different." He digs into the leather folio he carries and pulls out several sheets of paper, handing them to me. They're contracts, the names of several prominent professors in international business and political science written across the top. "Each of these professors has agreed to reshape and revamp our program."

I turn to Harley. "You asked them to do this?"

He shrugs. "I merely suggested that if my girlfriend, love of my life, found their program desirable, they might persuade me to attend."

I go through the contracts again. If these professors all come together, their program will rival Carver's. "This is incredible," I breathe.

"We're very glad you think so," Garrett says. He hands me one last sheet of paper. "Your early acceptance, should you choose to apply, of course."

"Holy shit."

They both laugh.

"So what do you say?" Harley asks. "I know it's a six-hour drive from here, but it's only for a year, if you want to go."

I look up into his deep brown eyes. "You did all this for me?"

He shrugs. "And for me. They're offering me a full ride, so it's not like I'm not getting anything out of the deal either."

I jump on him, my arms going around his neck, legs winding around his waist. "I can't believe you did this."

"There's nothing I *wouldn't* do for you, royal blue."

"I guess we're going to Birmingham."

Cerulean

CHAPTER FIFTY-FIVE

FOUR MONTHS LATER.

I try to keep the bundle in my arms still as I walk up the stairs to Harley's room. When Emily saw what I bought him, she went nuts, which caused Magenta to blow a gasket. But what are aunts for, if not to stir shit with their siblings' children?

When I open Harley's door, he's tying his tie. God, is there anything sexier than a guy in a suit? The bundle in my arms meows, and Harley's head whips to me.

A few days after signing day, we came up to Harley's room to find Cookie acting weird. We took him to the vet clinic where Indigo is a volunteer, only to discover he'd had a massive stroke. It was devastating and all kinds of heartbreaking, but the best thing to do was to put him down. Both Harley and Mrs. Stark said their goodbyes, and it's possible I may have a shed a tear. But today is all about new beginnings. Cookie will always be with us in spirit, but life has to go on.

"Hi," I say.

He comes over and kisses me. "Hi, yourself. Who's this?" he asks, taking her from me. I found her at a local shelter. She was the runt of the litter, but feisty and full of attitude—as all tortoiseshell cats are, I'm told.

"This is Crimson," I tell him.

He shakes his head and laughs. "*Another* color."

I shrug. "There's plenty available. Plus, I thought it was, you know, the perfect blend of the two of us."

He cocks his head to the side.

"Well, obviously her name is a color, like mine," I explain. "But it's also the color of our new school."

His eyes light up, and a huge smile breaks over his face. As carefully as he can with Crimson still in his arms, he draws me to his side, leaning down to kiss me. "You're incredible, you know that?"

"Uh-huh," I say, kissing him again.

He chuckles and lets me go. "So, she, right?"

I nod.

"So she's our first kid, huh?"

"She'll be our only if you don't play your cards right." I flop on the bed.

He chuckles again and lifts her so they're at eye level. "Don't listen to your mommy, she's just trying to be tough. It's okay though, I know the secret to get to her."

"And what would that be, exactly?" I ask.

They join me on the bed, Crimson circling round and round before settling down between us. "Me, duh."

I roll my eyes. "Of course you are."

He leans over and gives me another kiss. "I love you, and I love our little fur baby, thank you."

"You're welcome, but we better go or we'll be late."

"You be good," he tells the cat, now fast asleep, kissing her on the top of her head. "Mommy and Daddy will be back soon."

I shake my head but melt a little bit with how he's already taken to her.

We get in his Mustang and drive to the church.

"DEARLY BELOVED, we are here today to witness the union of Violet Mary York and Leroy Michael Jones."

I have to say, my soon-to-be-great-uncle Leroy works fast. Or slow, if you include the entirety of their relationship. Either way, today's a special day and I couldn't be happier for them both.

As we sit and watch them become husband and wife, I can't help but think about my future with Harley. Getting married, having kids.... It surprises me, or maybe it doesn't, I don't know, but I want those things with him.

I snuggle tighter to him, his arm around my shoulders, his other hand on my knee. I never thought I'd meet a guy who would knock down all my barriers, but he did. And I'd like to think that despite that fact, I'm still me. I'm still someone who loves fiercely and protects those people. I'm still snarky and maybe a little bit, okay a lot, bitchy. But Harley loves me anyway.

And he's cocky and has an ego the size of Texas, but I still love him. I think that's what love is, knowing the other's faults and loving them anyway.

. . .

AS I WATCH Violet and Leroy dance their first dance, I know Harley and I have what they have, a love that will last a lifetime.

HARLEY

ON MY FIRST day at Forest Park Academy, I thought it would be just another case of me being the new guy. To an extent, I was. But I was also home. I just didn't know it yet. Cerulean is my home. She's my everything, my mate, my perfect match. She's the peanut butter to my jelly, the ketchup to my fries, the milk duds to my popcorn. She is everything I need in a partner, and I like to think I'm the same for her.

She is everything I need her to be without even asking. She is my biggest supporter and my greatest critic. She lifts me up but brings me back to earth when I need it. She is my support, the foundation I can trust. She is my whole heart, my queen, forever my royal blue.

ACKNOWLEDGMENTS

This book is different to any other I've ever written. It also took a hell of a lot out of me, but I love it. I never thought I'd be one to relish in hard work, let's be honest, who does? But I busted my arse (yes, I'm back to that!) for this book and I couldn't be prouder.

When deciding what to write after *Rocking Racers*, I looked at the mature YA market. It's my favourite and where I naturally gravitate to, so it seemed like a natural fit.

The books there were filled with stories of tough guys on top. Don't get me wrong; I *love* reading those books, but what about the girls? We can kick arse, can't we? I definitely know we can be bitchy as hell, so why not show that?

For this book, this series in fact, I have a very acute sense of who these girls are. I like to think, at one point or another, I have been them.

I am so incredibly proud of these girls and this book. I hope you love it as much as I do!

Going from a traditional publisher to self-publishing was an *incredibly* daunting prospect, as well as a massive decision. There is absolutely no way I could've done it without the love and support of the following people.

My parents, whom have been nothing short of perfect. They have supported me, backed me and never once expressed to me the doubts I know they had to have had. I know I have, on more than occasion. Thank you for everything, it truly means everything to me and I couldn't have done any of this without you.

To my girls: Gen, Trysh, Mary and Ang. Thank you for listening to me, supporting me, encouraging me, giving me your opinions, and generally keeping me sane. It is such a comfort to know I can go to any of you and know that you will never steer me wrong.

To Rod and Laura, my incredible beta readers. Thank you for all your input, this book wouldn't have been the same without you.

Rod, thank you for your support, and your ears, listening to me and dealing with my highly-strung self at work. It helped *so* much.

Laura, thank you for your tireless efforts in helping get the word about this, and all of my books. I couldn't do it without you.

To Liv, editor extraordinaire. Part of my hesitation in self-publishing was finding an editor, but knowing I could still have you shape my words comforted me to no end. Thank you for all your hard work.

To Bex Harper Designs who straight off the bat knocked the cover for this book out of the park. Thank you for putting a cover to my words.

To Pretty in Ink Creations. Thank you for your formatting expertise.

To Dani and Jennifer at Wildfire Marketing Solutions. Thank you for helping get word out about this book. I know it wasn't easy, but you did brilliantly.

To my co-workers who had to deal with my highly-strung and scatterbrained self for three months, I apologise but value each and every one of you.

To all the bloggers who work *so* hard and without much reward, thank you. Us authors couldn't do this without you!

To you who has picked up this book and made it this far, you cannot imagine how grateful I am for you. Thank you for letting my girls into your life. Be bold and bow to no one! And please remember to leave a review! They do mean so much!

Finally, to all the girls who feel they have to be tough, who think they can't afford to fold. You are incredible. Stay strong, but know you deserve good things as well.

To the girls who wish they could be tougher. You have survived everything thrown at you so far. You are plenty tough. Stay strong, keep going because you *are* badarses!

Rocking Racers series:

Breaking the Cycle (permafree)

No Place to Hide

Breaking Away

Breaking Down

All I Want

Breaking Free

Breaking Out

Breaking Ground

Read today here: books2read.com/rl/rocking-racers

Sovereigns of Savannah

Royal Blue

Regal Purple (Coming 2020)

Magestic Pink (Coming 2020/2021)

Noble Red (Coming 2020/2021)

Keep an eye here: books2read.com/rl/sovereigns-of-savannah

ABOUT THE AUTHOR

Megan Lowe is a lost journalism graduate who after many painful years searching for a job in that field, decided if she couldn't write news stories, she would start listening to the characters whispering stories to her and decided to write them down. She writes primarily Mature YA/New Adult/Contemporary Romance stories with a difference. She is based on the Gold Coast but her heart belongs to New York City. When she's not writing she's either curled up with a good book, travelling or screaming at the TV willing her sporting teams to pull out the win.

STALKER LINKS!

If you'd like to stay informed about my books, love of pins, obsession with Earl Grey tea, and drool over good-looking men, here's where you can do that!

Website: www.meganloweauthor.
wixsite.com/withadifference
Reader's group: http://bit.ly/31Lv7nd
Bookbub: www.bookbub.com/authors/megan-lowe
Goodreads: www.goodreads.com/meganlowereads
Instagram: www.
instagram.com/meganloweauthor
Twitter: www.twitter.com/meganloweauthor
meganloweauthor@outlook.com

Sign up to my newsletter: https://
t.co/M31GCdcYtL